STARS ARE STARS

Kevin Sampson is the author of six novels –
Awaydays, Powder, Leisure, Outlaws, Clubland
and *Freshers* – and a non-fiction, *Extra
Time*. He lives in Liverpool.

ALSO BY KEVIN SAMPSON

Fiction

Awaydays
Powder
Leisure
Outlaws
Clubland
Freshers

Non-fiction

Extra Time

KEVIN SAMPSON

Stars Are Stars

VINTAGE BOOKS
London

Published by Vintage 2007

2 4 6 8 10 9 7 5 3

First published in Great Britain in 2006 by Jonathan Cape

Vintage
Random House, 20 Vauxhall Bridge Road,
London SW1V 2SA

www.vintage-books.co.uk

Addresses for companies within The Random House Group Limited
can be found at: www.randomhouse.co.uk/offices.htm

The Random House Group Limited Reg. No. 954009

A CIP catalogue record for this book
is available from the British Library

ISBN 9780099470250

The Random House Group Limited makes every effort to ensure
that the papers used in its books are made from trees that have been
legally sourced from well-managed and credibly certified forests.
Our paper procurement policy can be found at:
www.randomhouse.co.uk/paper.htm

Mixed Sources
Product group from well-managed
forests and other controlled sources
www.fsc.org Cert no. TT-COC-2139
© 1996 Forest Stewardship Council
FSC

Typeset in Sabon by Palimpsest Book Production Limited,
Grangemouth, Stirlingshire
Printed and bound in Great Britain by
Cox & Wyman, Reading RG1 8EX

For the DeAshas

1981

Llandudno

She knows the handwriting, of course. They used to laugh
about it, how the same hand that would paint with such fire
and beauty could drag such squalid print across the page. It's
been so long since his last letter. The recognition shocks her
right through, but that surge of excitement is instantly smothered by a more familiar, sickening dread. What is it now? What
does he want? How bad will it be, this time?

Nicole picks up the letter and she feels sick. She leans her
hips against the little sill to take the weight from her feet.
Once, even after all he'd brought upon her, she would have
swooped on a letter from Danny with a new hope, willing
to be lied to, ready to believe in him, wanting to make it all
good again. But his letters stopped coming, and with that she
was able to stop thinking of him and – eventually, inevitably
– stop hoping for him. Finally, she had come to embrace it.
Danny was gone. He is gone.

And now she can feel her heartbeat hammer as she stares
at his scrawl, strangely elegant against the orange envelope.
She turns it over and over, not taking anything in – just post-
poning the moment. Her hand is trembling as she picks and
scrapes at the flap, but she gets it done. She gets the letter
open. There's almost nothing. An orange-red sheet, no address,
and towards the top of the page a few words in his crabby
script, the sloping spidery crawl of the left-hander. She makes
the link straight away, of course. She knows the song.

'*Prospects diminish while nightmares swell.*'

He's left a space, then, continuing a lot further down:

'*Some pray for heaven while we live in hell.*'

Then underneath, each word looser and more crazily scribbled and harder to read than the one before, he's written:

'*Did you ever go clear?*'

Then in the bottom corner, tailing off, it says:

'*No.*'

and straggles away as though he's given up, or fallen asleep, or lost hope – or he wants her to see that he's hopeless.

Fear seeps through her, and still that desperate nausea drags down on her. She delves inside the envelope, she can feel there's more inside and, with frustration – and she is still quick to anger, Nicole – she squashes its mouth open and shakes it. A scrap of creased, yellowing paper flits to the floor. She knows at once, and at once she grieves. She picks up the tatty page, straightens it out with her palm. Crudely taped together down the middle – for a craftsman, again, he's made a mess of the job – the right-hand side of the verse is speckled with dried, near-brown blood. She's rocked by the memories this churns up. Where on earth did he get *this*? She'd left her half on their little table at Greenbank the day she walked out for good. She hadn't thought twice about it. She'd wanted to show him how final it was. Hopeless, romantic Danny had been unable to throw it away. Smiling sadly, she flattens the page out and reads it again:

> *April is the cruellest month, breeding*
> *Lilacs out of the dead land, mixing*
> *Memory and desire, stirring*
> *Dull roots with spring rain.*

She turns the page over:

> *Never leave me, baby. Never go away.*

And she's crying; not for the memory, or the loss, or the acute sensation of good times gone for ever – but because this is him. This helpless, feeble cry, this forlorn and beautiful plea – this was just Danny, to his core. And how she had loved him once, her thin gypsy thief. She raises the envelope. Llandudno postmark. She takes a deep swig of breath and raises her head. She knows where he is. She knows exactly where he will be. She starts to breathe more regularly and finds that she is giggling nervously. She has the Thrills, and she knows exactly what she's going to do.

1976

Arties

It's cold still but the ice has started to melt and he's decided he'll walk it. He's determined he's going to be seen this time, so he'll cut right through student land, past all the bars and the bistros where they'll be. That's what they call their cafés, the Arties, *bistros*. From Bold Street he's going to cut up past O'Connor's and weave his way up there, in and up, past the Pilgrim and right the way up to the art college. Bit of a detour, but they'd all see him. There's no way he wouldn't pass them, somewhere along the way.

Clamped in the pit of his arm is a Virgin bag, the sirens' heads marking him out as one in the know. And inside the bag is *Station to Station*, not even officially out yet but miraculously already available at the Virgin shop. The students thawing out in the bars and the bohos heading down from the art school, they'll all see him and wonder what record he's bought. The cool kid who walks this trail three, four times a week, the kid with the Bowie fringe who looks about thirteen, but with his wizened face could be older yet could easily be younger – they'll all be wondering what he's bought. And there they are! He sees a bunch of Arties up ahead – corduroy jackets, suede shoes on, even in this slush. He speeds up a little. They're headed for O'Connor's. Can't let them get there before him. The girl with blue hair is there, and he *needs* her to see him. He needs her to register.

4

Day after day for months now he's stood across the road from the art school, just leaning back against the cathedral railings and staring up at Lennon's Alma Mater. He doesn't go there just to see the girl with blue hair – not solely. She is beautiful, though. She's pale and delicate, and though the broken nose jars with the turquoise eyes and the fine-boned face, it suits her. It is *of* her, and he loves her twisted nose as he loves everything about her. He's a romancing kind, Danny May, and he falls easily and deeply in love with the girls he meets, especially those he hasn't even spoken to. He's infatuated with the girl with blue hair, but he doesn't hang around here *just* to see her. It's a miracle all over again every time he does clap eyes on her of course. It's the perfect end to his adventure, fuel for his rampant fantasies. But the truth is that Danny walks this route and marks this spot, several times a week, primarily to peek at his future. He will stand here and look up at the building and drink it all in, the place where he'll come alive. Four short years from now and he'll be there, among them, one of the Arties. He has the letters of encouragement, he has the will to bring it all to life. He has the talent. Already his paintings bring gasps of amazement from even the most hardened souls at Thomas à Becket. He's got a style and a vision and a big, big, talent and he knows he's good. With luck he could be great. Luck is all he'll need – he works like mad already and he's hungry for it, thirsty for it, all of it. It's all he wants. All he dreams about is the day when all this, their life, the Arties' existence will be his. And this will be him; not trudging home back to Lodge Lane but heading the opposite way, downhill, into the mystical sleaze of clubland, cutting through the freeze of an electric winter's evening, tasting the chill on his lips and the thrill and the promise of another long night at O'Connor's, glasses of brandy and gaunt cigarettes and brilliant disagreements over art and music and sex. This will be him heading down Hardman Street with a girl like her, the girl with blue hair.

He hurries up Leece Street, tearing at the serrated lip of the Virgin bag. He needs them to see he's come hot from the head shop, but he wants to give them a clue, too – let the Arties know he's already got the new Bowie album. He strips the paper bag down the middle. It's still obvious to anyone who knows that that's a Virgin bag, but now there's the bold red lettering of the album's title showing through, along with enough of Bowie's head for any aficionado to pick him out. He gets parallel with the art crowd, his eyes locked on to them, willing each one of them just for a moment to lower their gaze to his record bag. But they don't see him. They're full of the moment, wholly engrossed in whatever it is they're laughing about. Not one of them is aware of the kid as they pass him by and swell into the warmth of O'Connor's Tavern. Danny doesn't mind. They seldom notice him. The girl with blue hair looks radiant. Whatever she's saying, the others are all captivated, and she's smiling as she talks. She's having the time of her life. She's smiled at him too, since she's been in Liverpool. Twice. A third, or any glimmer from any of them, would only have been a bonus. He follows them as far as the swinging doors and gulps down a draught of the saloon-bar stench and the smoke and babble. He sees the girl with blue hair pass the hippie lad a pouch of tobacco and he can't stop the smile spreading out from inside of him. That's him, in there. That's going to be him.

1978

Reason for Living

A big day this, for Danny May. He was already tingling as he slurped his tea, so hot and good that although he wanted it finished, wanted to get going, he couldn't deny himself one last swig, then just one more, relishing that sharp sweet burn as it stung the back of his throat. He looked out of the small kitchen window and shivered, alive to the headrush of the day that lay in wait for him. Clothes, records, drinks, cigarettes – he'd planned this one for weeks now, plotted it hour by hour. And here it was at last, Big Saturday – a Saturday, in town, with money. He knew how good this was going to be; it couldn't be anything *but* good. For Danny, this was it. This was living. This was what the whole thing was all about. All the work, the darting about on that shitty little bicycle, the looking after Nin, the sitting around in damp-cold dives waiting and waiting and waiting for a mark with dough, the rushed sketches, dashed off before the punter changed his mind. The mad hours, the no sleep, the running round after his bone-idle sisters, the never having time to himself – it was all fucking worth it when Saturday came. He rinsed his mug, and, guilty that there was no time to dry it properly, turned it upside down to drain. He slipped his shoes on and headed out into the instant shock of the cold white morning, slamming the flimsy panelled door behind him.

He vaulted the little fence, big giddy joy inside of him,

excited about today, excited about tomorrow, feeling good about this and that, glad all over just to be him, Danny, now. Head down against the freeze he cut left on to Kingsley and off towards town. Big gust as he hit the broad sweep of Upper Parliament Street, a bin lid skimming right across the road. There was always a big gust on Parly, even in the summer – straight up from the river all the way to Liverpool 8.

Up ahead, the Tremarco boys were dug back into the corner of the bus shelter, staring out up the road with slit brown eyes from under their fringes. Danny wasn't getting the bus – he'd rather walk a mile than wait for anything. It was quicker just to weave his way through to London Road anyway, specially on a day like this when the buses would be trundling two miles an hour through the dirty slush. No two ways though, he was going to have to stop and gab with them – just for a minute, at least. It'd look like he was blanking them if he just nodded and walked on by. If he knew the family better then fine, but they'd only moved to the estate a few weeks before Christmas. His ma, Vera, reckoned they'd come from Devonshire Road, used to live in one of the big old houses just off the Avenue. Danny often fancied himself living in one of those grand old ramshackle piles himself, one day. If he did *really* well he'd get them one of those mansions down Sefton Park or Lark Lane, move his whole family in, look after them all, good style. Except they wouldn't want to move – his ma in particular. She'd had their name down for that house long before the estate was finished and, much as she loved to bang on about how different and exciting Toxteth used to be when she was growing up, she wouldn't give up her tidy new home for anything. Everyone seemed to hanker after brand new, these days – central heating, double glazing, all of that. Danny though, he couldn't get his head around it. Where was the glamour in a box house, identical to the one next door and the one next to that?

He slowed as he got nearer, willing a bus to rumble into

8

view, hoping madly this hurdle wouldn't hold him up too long. No sooner had he thought it though, than he chided himself. Brian and Nicky Tremarco were new to the Close and it was his job to be neighbourly. He'd seen them in the Unity a few times, let on to them, just small talk about clubs and bands. Other than that, he knew little. They worked at Copperas Hill. Their whole family worked at Copperas Hill. And they seemed like nice enough lads. Bodybuilder types, a bit straight and a little bit quiet for Danny, but they were all right. Normal. Danny pulled off his balaclava. He'd had his hands shoved deep in his pockets but his fingertips were still pink and numb with the cold. He blew on them, hunched himself up as he got close. The older one, Brian, took a step towards him and nodded.

'A'right.'

'A'right, boys.'

He made a point of nodding to Nicky, too.

'Where youse off? Match?'

'If we ever get to fucken Limey.'

The three boys were dressed the same, more or less. Pod shoes. Lois jeans. Fred Perry worn underneath a big, fluffy black mohair. Black mittens with the fingertips cut out. Hair cut short over one ear with the fringe left long enough to sweep across one eye and cover the other ear. The Wedge. They looked like a gang, dressed in the uniform of the Liverpool football lads, but football meant nothing to Danny these days. It was no big deal, he just couldn't feel that thrill for football any more. He found that, the more he got into music and art and clubs, the less other things mattered to him. He used to love television. He'd watch comedies with his Nin – *Morecambe and Wise* or *Dick Emery*. They'd sit there shouting: 'Ooh, you are awful – but I like you!'

Didn't bother, now. Couldn't force the feeling. Same went for football. He liked the fashion side of it, thought it was great that the lads had their own look. But the truth was that

Danny May had stumbled upon Liverpool's bohemian wild side – and the more he sampled it, the more he wanted to belong, properly. Those wondrous souls who frequented the Casablanca and Eric's and the Armadillo, they weren't into *football*. They were into Andy Warhol and Iggy Pop and Camus. That was what burned in Danny now, too – ideas, possibilities, curiosity. He wanted to be like them.

And if he was sure about anything, it was that. He *was* going to be like them. He was going to be a painter – of that, he had no doubt whatsoever. He knew he was good. He knew he had ability, but, more than that, he felt like he was on the verge of finally *doing* something with it – as though great things were just around the corner. It had no shape or image, this constant excitement of Danny's, but there came a certainty from deep within him, a sense of inevitability that he'd travel far and do great things as a result of this talent of his. One day, soon, the Tremarco boys would be boasting to any postman who'd listen: 'That Danny May? Know him, la. Know him well.'

The 86 shuddered into view at last, seeming hardly to move it was going that slow. Danny stood back for them.

'Not getting on?' said Nicky.

He shook his head; yet in spite of everything he still had to show the boys he wasn't soft.

'On me toes today, la. Good luck down there.'

He had to let them see he knew it was Chelsea away today. He knew there'd been a kind of call to arms among Liverpool's young fighting lads after what had happened to Everton, heralded by a terse slogan sprayed above the shops outside Lime Street Station: ORDINARY TO CHELSEA. Yet in showing them he knew the score, Danny instantly felt a traitor to himself, too. He didn't *need* their approval. If he was going to be true to his art, the thing to prize above all else was self-possession, a genuine belief in his own ability. Until he eventually moved on from the Close, people were going to find him odd – it was a fact, and he needed to come to see that as a compliment. Chiding himself again, he patted the younger brother on the shoulder and moved on, already checking over his shoulder for traffic as he dived across Parliament Street.

He couldn't remain at odds with himself for long, though. Today Danny May had big plans. In his pocket was eighty quid, money he'd saved up from his sketches. There was another fifty in his biscuit tin, his College Box, waiting to go in the building society on Monday. He'd been putting money away for months now; he'd have loads by the time he went to art school, more than enough. He probably wouldn't even need the grant. The quick-sketch was easy money when it came – you just had to go out and find it. Some nights would just not take off at all, but those were the same for everyone – club owners, cardsharps, hookers. Mostly though, he'd get paid. He'd hop on the Scream and set to it, do the rounds, trawl the clubs and shebeens until he found a crowd – simple as that. Some days the ships would be in, or people were just out drinking, wallets full, happy to play along. Other nights it could be dead. If he was prepared to work Saturdays, well, that might be a different story – but Saturdays were for him.

Any other night he'd be out there looking for a gig, weaving back and forth through Liverpool 8, hunched and ridiculous on the Scream, his tiny, green, kid-size bike, scouring the drinking dens and fleshpots for a paying subject. Danny was making a living through his caricatures, charcoal sketches of the drunks, the sailors, their whores – anyone who'd pay him ten bob for a few minutes' work. He did it in his own signature style and he was good. He could get any likeness down in a few strokes, but he liked to, or he *had* to, take that little bit longer, especially when he was working the sailors' clubs. If he made it look too easy the drunks just wouldn't pay. They didn't want to pay anyway, most of the soused-up bastards. They'd say it didn't look like them or they'd get bored or change their mind halfway through, but by and large he did OK. He stuck to the good-time places where they knew him – Dutch Eddie's, the Lucky Bar, the Somali, Abdul's, sometimes the Shanghai if there was nothing doing anywhere else. There'd always be women in these places and because there were lots of women there'd be lots of men, seamen mostly, here on shore leave and happy to spread some dough around. They didn't mind the idea of a young lad just walking into places like that and coming right up to them, fearless. They liked his cheek. He added something to the night. And it made them look good in front of the women when they'd pat him on the head and tell him to keep the change from a pound note. They paid him, these fellas. He was earning. So he was happy to stick to the same few good-time joints, even though they didn't start bouncing till late on. He worked his patch, and he dragged himself into school, bleary-eyed. He rode from place to place on a kid's bike that no one could be arsed stealing and, by and large, he did very well indeed.

He headed on down Parliament Street, the main artery of Toxteth's sprawling clubland. At arm's length from the gaudy discos and meat racks of the city centre, these elegant Georgian town houses had long been too grand for one family and, one by one, had begun to embrace a new future wholly steeped in the port city's traditions for party, for pleasure. The Somali Club, the Gladray, the Alahram – these were the haunts now of night owls, drunks and hookers and this was the main strip where Danny made his living. The Somali was probably not long closed. He'd been there only last night, hours ago, really. It'd been his last port of call as it turned out, even though he'd been planning on a quick try round the Casa, too. But he'd done this Welsh bloke in the Somali, staggering drunk, paralytic, *huge* big red crazy face – and when it came to paying up he'd slapped a Kwik-Save bag on the counter, full of coins. He wasn't best pleased with that, Danny, but the Welshman was not one to take issue with. And when he got down to counting it there was nearly two pounds there in change. Even spread over four pockets it weighed him right down, and Ali wouldn't change it for him. He just laughed at him.

'No offence, kagidder,' Ali smiled. 'See you laygater.'

So that was Danny for the night. He'd done more than ten pound in just over four hours, and that was superb. The way ahead was now clear and free – home, bed, then out. He hurled the Scream back along Prince's Ave, still loud and busy with all the blues and beanos. Black guys were necking white girls up against those regal terraces, and row upon row of taxis ranked up the middle of the boulevard waiting for the Rialto to spill out. He pedalled on, tired out but anxiously happy inside. Tomorrow. Today. Tomorrow. He was looking forward. His life was good.

Cutting right on to Bedford Street, feet slipping on slick glints of ice, he glanced up at the grand sash windows. From one came the tinkle of Chopin; from another, a vicious, slurred row. Danny gave the money a pat in his pocket as he neared the home run. Eighty nicker. He'd get to Mann's as they opened and snag that duffel coat for starters. Beautiful, fawn Gloverall with marbled brownhorn toggles and a padded check lining, it was pure *Man Who Fell to Earth*, pure Danny May. Down to twenty pound, and worth every penny of it. He'd had his eye on it since it made its debut in the window last September. He'd more than had his eye on it – he'd lived that duffel, dreamt it, worn it down the Casa and had girls queuing up to stroke it every night, every day since he'd first spotted it. He must have been in there fifty times, tried it on a dozen or more, obsessed over it, wanted it, coveted it more than just about any of the thousand other things he saw in the shops or on the street, and wanted. All the lads were wearing duffels, girls too – all the ones who knew the score were wearing them, anyway. Most would've got theirs from British Home Stores – nice enough gear but a bit clumsy, Danny thought, bit lacking in finesse. That Gloverall though, the one in Mann's – it was svelte, gaunt, beautiful, and it was forty-five nicker. Out of his reach, plain and simple. No matter how much he pulled down from the sketches and this and that, once he'd put money away for college and given his ma money and bought ciggies for him and the girls he was almost cleaned out. Then there were gigs and records and taking his sisters out round by theirs not to mention Saturday nights . . . Well he couldn't make it stretch for ever, that was all. He could buy a few great-looking items, his bare essentials for going out and looking the part, but things like the duffel were always just out of reach. And if he couldn't have the Gloverall then that was it, he didn't want any substitutes. No way was he walking past that art school in a cheapo chain-store effort.

And then it had come up in the clearances, the everything-must-go clear-out of whatever dregs are left after the January Sales and, with a tremble, he suddenly realised it was within his grasp. He'd found himself walking past there on Sunday night. One thing with Danny was that he could often find himself standing somewhere, usually outside a record shop or a bar, and he was almost in a trance – or never *completely* sure how he'd got there, at least. He'd be able to recall snatches, just little moments from the lead-up to finding himself there, but it often felt like he'd just snapped out of a daydream. That was the way it came about last Sunday. He'd walked Ninna down to mass. He'd done the ironing. He'd run messages down to Ahmed's for the girls and put the oven on, ready for when Mam got back from work; but he wasn't that hungry himself, didn't fancy dinner. What he really fancied was to get out of the house for a bit, just get away from them all, just an hour or so on his own. Any other time, he was there at their beck and call, all excepting his ma, of course. She was out first thing every morning, walked to the factory no matter what the weather. She was like Danny. Wouldn't waste time on a bus when she could walk it just as easy, though with her it was more the money. She hated wasting money, even though she made sure they never went short, ever. He knew there were families round here who were properly hard up, but Vera May was determined that the lack of a father wasn't going to do her children down. She worked every hour, Vera. Weekends she'd take the cleaning work when it was there — anything to bring money into the household.

Danny chipped in, too. Since his dad died, he was man about the house — unquestioningly. If he was making money, he was happy handing it over. He loved his ma, loved them all, but Danny needed his solitude, needed time and peace to paint — not easy, in a house as full as theirs. Vera could have been forgiven for assuming a couple of the girls would have left home by now. Maybe, deep down, she'd hoped the move from Vandyke might have given them a nudge. The old house was bigger in every sense, even the toilet seat was bigger — but with Ninna not so good these days he could see the sense of the short move across Lodge Lane. But they'd been there a year now, and it was still a full house. That it was a house full of women came to his rescue. Circumstances deemed he needed his own bedroom, which, painted in vivid, vicious shades of purple and decked out with posters and sketches of his idols, became his sanctuary. Even then, he *had* to get away from them and the house, and often, too — especially of a Sunday. Stay there on a Sunday and he made himself a sitting duck. No matter how many times he'd run out for their loosies and their Pot Noodles and whatever else they'd suddenly need, there and then, his sisters just would not let Danny be. Give us a ciggy, then. Have you got money, Daniel? Where was you till four o'clock this morning? They hated him just for having his own bedroom and they made him pay for it every day, every time he strayed across their bows.

He'd set out last Sunday with just the vaguest plan of walking right down Parly, all the way down to the pier head for a little rest, watch the boats — then make his way back up through town, see if there was any bands on at Oscar's, something like that. Even the Moonstone was starting to get away from the Sweaty stuff and put some good bands on. If there was nothing doing then he'd walk back up through Hardman Street, pop his head in at Kirklands or Streets, see what was happening. As ever, though, none of that had happened. Somehow, deep in another daydream, he'd drifted off-course and ended up in London Road, staring at the stills outside the Odeon. He came to, twigged where he was and didn't even waste time wondering how he'd got there. London Road. That meant just one thing to Danny – Mann's! He ambled over for a mosey in the window – and that's how he came to see it, his prized Gloverall duffel coat. There it was, the beauty, marked down to twenty and there for the taking all of a sudden. It was his. If it'd only just stay there till Saturday, that duffel was going right on Danny May's back.

Past the Carousel, weaving down and on through the university backstreets and he couldn't help himself, he was starting to get the Thrills. This was a condition Danny thought unique to himself and one he'd never, ever confess to, but it happened all the time. Whenever he was getting close to the object of his exercise – finishing a portrait, or next to get served in the long line outside the Empire for Bebop Deluxe tickets – he'd start to feel stirrings of a sensation inside like giggling, a quickening and gladdening of the heart he called the Thrills. He was getting it now, a huge inner grin as he cut through the Bullring, London Road dead ahead of him now. The moment Mann's doors opened he'd be in there, twenty pounds sterling at the ready. They could keep their plazzy bag. That coat was going straight on, as though he'd had it since September. From Mann's he'd head back up to the Jew shop and pick up a pair of them corduroy shoes, the ones with the ribbed rubber soles. Fiver. They were *giving* them away, but you had to know where to look. Places like the Jew shop and 81a, it was mainly still the students and Arties that went there. Not that many lads from town seemed to bother – they'd rather pay twelve nicker at Timpson's or somewhere, and the shoes they came out with were nothing like, either – feeble laces, brown soles. These ones at the Jew shop were the real thing. Beautiful, they were – fat blue cord, chunky rope laces, rubberised sole. Work of art.

Duffel coat, new shoes then into the Armadillo for a bowl of soup and a proper read of the papers. The good thing about the Armadillo's tables was you could spread the paper right out and you still wouldn't be bothering anyone. Some of the Saturday papers were starting to give good coverage to the New Wave. That's what they were calling the latest crop of indie rockers: anything experimental, anything that wasn't pure punk, anything in narrow jeans and a skinny tie was suddenly part of the New Wave. It made him laugh: ballsy pub rockers like Eddie and the Hot Rods were reinventing themselves as the Rods, grimly hanging on to the charcoal-grey shirt-tails of Cabaret Voltaire and Magazine. Graham Parker and the Rumour were New fucking Wave! But it was good to have a different, less devotional take on the scene than the *NME* or *Sounds* might give. Just before Christmas *The Times* had splashed a big write-up on the New York Scene: pictures of Tom Verlaine and Deborah Harry and David Byrne hanging out at Hurrah and Max's Kansas City. There were great photos of Iggy and the Ramones. He was devoted to his painting, but he *loved* photography like that. He couldn't put his finger on it. Somehow, it had a timeless quality to it. The Armadillo usually left the *Guardian* and *The Times* out on the tables with all the old *Punch* and *Blues & Soul* magazines, even odd tatty copies of things like *Actuel* and *Paris Match* that people had left behind. He could spend hours sifting through the mags and papers, and even though Danny hardly knew anyone in there, there was always an interesting crowd throwing their hands around wildly and spattering the tables with leek and potato soup as they argued about arcane Krautrock bands he'd never even heard of – Goethe, Proust and Nietzsche. He felt at home there.

After the Armadillo, a good hour or so in Probe just doing the one true thing that Saturdays were meant for – browsing through the racks, stack after stack of imports, rarities, coloured vinyl twelve-inchers and brand new releases. Scritti Politti, Pere Ubu, Wire, Devo and Talking Heads all had new releases he'd been after, but more than any other thing he *needed* to track down this reggae track he'd been hearing in Eric's. He'd be bound to hear it in Probe if he just hung around in there long enough, he knew he would. And this time, if he heard it, he'd just have to get on with it. Straight over to the counter, deep breath, not too pushy but no pushover neither, then out with it: What's this, please? Have you got it? Well, of course you've got it but, like – have you *got* it? Yes please. I heard it in Eric's. I go there. Go there all the time, like.

Eric's. The place had turned his world upside down since he'd stumbled in there just a few months ago. Nothing more than a damp-smelling cellar bar in Mathew Street, thirty souls stood as far from the stage as possible as a local art-rock band ran through a set of speedy Velvet riffs, but Danny had loved it, loved it, loved it. He loved the girl who took the money upstairs. Loved the way they left that little box of free pin-badges on the counter, even if the bands – the Damned, the Stranglers, Buzzcocks – were that bit too punk for him. What he loved, really loved more than anything about Eric's was the way it had become, out of nothing, really, the centre of the universe. Everything new that was happening in town had its roots in Eric's. The punks still came, sure – but punk had been and gone as far as Danny was concerned. The Pistols and the Clash, amazing highs, brilliant bits and pieces. And the Jam seemed to hint at it, seemed to want to kick out from that tinny power-punk sound they'd got themselves into and grow into something bigger. But none of them had really done it for him, nothing punk had thrown up came close to the clinical joy he got from Kraftwerk or the nervy and caustic elation of the new industrial bands: the Normal, the Human

League, Clock DVA. And none of it yet matched up to the majestic grey symphonies of the Thin White Duke, who just blew him away with each new phase. The Berlin stuff, the heroin hymns, the weird and twisted electronica of *Low* and *Heroes*. For Danny, there was no case to answer: *Sound and Vision* or *New Rose*? *Moss Garden* or *Bodies*? No contest. The New Wave was here, but Bowie was still God.

But that night when he'd paid his pound and walked down those mouldy steps and barged through the swing doors with as much vim and swagger as he could muster – well, it had taken his breath away. It was like walking into a different time zone and it took him over, body and soul. He peered into the little side room by the stairs, a few Arties draped around the jukebox, staring him out till he moved away from the door. And what a jukebox! Mad blues and folk and weird, echo-heavy reggae. He hardly knew a single track. He loved each and every one of them, and he wanted to go out, right there and then, and buy them all, have all those records for himself. He'd pondered over what drink to have, knew instinctively that beer wasn't right for this place, settled on a rum and black and leaned back against the bar. He was conscious he stood out – too young, too straight – and compensated by trying to look, if not exactly bored then distracted, detached from it all, like he was thinking these immense metaphysical thoughts that were taking him off to a different place. But he couldn't keep that up for long. He couldn't help staring, lapping it up, drinking it all in. And that smell! The room stank with a chemical sweat and it knocked him sideways. Damp and sweat and amphetamine and big crazy plans and boasts and promises – that was a smell of wonderment to Danny. It was the smell of teenage dreams and he gulped it down, took it right inside of him and held it deep down, and he was intoxicated. It was magical, all that was going on around him. The sparse crowd, twos and threes who knew each other, all had something about them. They were people who wanted to be different. People who wanted to do things, new things. People like him. And that jukebox, man – a jukie like he'd never seen or heard before. He was smitten. Eric's hadn't so much turned his world around – it had become his reason for living.

Probe had not played the reggae track and he hadn't had the nerve to even try and describe it to the gaunt vamps at the till. That left Danny with but one way ahead. Eric's itself. It was early afternoon, but this presented him with perhaps his best chance. Hesitantly, he creaked open heaven's gates, the huge iron doors above the subterranean nightclub. He had the duffel on, the cord shoes too – his battered Pod stowed now in a plastic bag under one of the huge industrial bins round the back of Central Station, behind Lewis's. If anyone was going to lead Danny to this magical mystery tune, it had to be Norman himself. He was almost bound to be there of a Saturday afternoon. They opened up the club between twelve and two most days, so's they could sell tickets, memberships, T-shirts, deal with enquiries, all of that – but it'd be a rare Saturday that Norman wasn't down there checking out the sound system, testing out his latest tunes at full volume. Every time Danny passed by there'd be some other-worldly noise belching out from down below, and every now and then you'd catch the band themselves running through an early sound-check. A cluster of kids would gather in awe around what passed for a stage door, the bolder ones inching inside, straining to catch a stab of Jah Wobble's bass or Andy Gill's mutant guitar.

It gave him the biggest kick, that – hearing the muffled, speeded-up sound of the band he'd be going to see later on. It filled him up, that sound. Always faster than the records, always harsh and speedy – but it ripped right through him every time, spun him round and took him to another place. And it wasn't just the bands. There was something about hearing any music out of time, out of context, that'd set him thrilling. It was like he shouldn't be hearing it at all – it was not quite ready, not how they wanted it to sound – but what could he do? He was there. He could hear it.

And he could hear it now, *feel* it as well as hear it, the thrum of the music trembling through the soles of his feet, this fuggy, monstrous bass line rising up from underground. That had to be Norman, and Danny *had* to nab him now, while he could, and get the message from him: what the *fuck* is that reggae track! He'd tried everywhere else – Peel, the music papers, *Roots*. He'd asked all the lads from Granby who were supposed to know their sounds, but they'd only tried to cover up their ignorance, slapping him off with the usual put-downs: 'Reggae? Why you trying to be a black man, Daniel? *Reggae!* Why you don't stick to your Bowie and your homo sounds?'

Homo sounds! These boys were into fucking Heatwave! He'd seen them queuing up at the Rialto for Edwin Starr. They were into *disco* for fuck's sake – homo sounds! He thought about trying the girls but, truly, it wouldn't have been worth the come-back. Each of them was going out with, or had recently finished with or been binned themselves by black lads. None of these were kids, either. He'd got to know a few lads since they moved there, and he still let on to the boys he knew from Lodge Lane. But his sisters knocked about with their big brothers or their dads and uncles, grown-up fellas who went to blues and drank those yard-long tubes of Red Stripe and smoked ganja. These boys'd know the track like *that* – if he could only risk asking his sisters. He might just about have been able to trust Marie with it, but it really truly wasn't worth the hassle. They could be ruthless, those girls. They'd use any little bit of information – musical taste, book of matches found, ticket stubs left out – to piece together the pattern of his life. They were obsessed with him; they wanted to know every little thing about him. This would be bad enough in any event, but what they were really after knowing was what things cost, where he got the money from and, crucially, whether he'd got any left. They wouldn't rest till they were certain they'd had him off for every last cigarette, every penny in his pocket. It wasn't worth goading them. Best say fuck all, keep your head down, get on with your life small-small. With a final gust of resolve he pushed the iron door wide open and called down the stairwell in a voice that was never meant to be heard.

'Hello?'

Somehow, hearing his own voice made him feel less unsure, less of an intruder. He went again, louder.

'Anyone in?'

This time a shuffling sound, like someone tripping, then a big, deep voice shouted up. 'Yiss? What d'you want?'

It was a hard, no-messing sort of voice but not unkind, either. Encouraged now, Danny tried to sound at ease. 'Erm – that you, Norman?'

No answer. Fuck. He backed towards the door, content now to just leave it, but footsteps, heavy footsteps, came at him out of nowhere. Far from running, as all his instincts were begging him, Danny stood his ground. He wanted that record.

'Is Norman there?'

'No. He's not here.'

Danny's heart sagged. Norman was there all right. That was him he'd just heard – he was sure of it. He just didn't want to be bothered by some pushy kid he didn't know from Adam. Then suddenly the voice came again, much closer now.

'Who wants him?'

There was a fella stood at the bottom of the steps. He could see him now his eyes were starting to get used to the light – a big, big man with a thick, priapic moustache. Danny cleared his throat.

'Oh, no, he don't know me or nothing. I . . . like – I just heard this track, that's all.'

The man came up to the bottom step. 'Yeah?'

'Heard it in here a few times, like. I just wanted to, you know. I wanted to find out what it's called . . .'

'How's it go?'

He'd have sworn there was a smile in the fella's voice.

'Well, I don't . . .'

And fuck, how does he put that into *words*? The infectious throb of the bass and the shards and stabs of reverberating guitar and the ever-building tingle in his spine, the pulsating joy that shoots up through his nape and shreds his tiny mind as that lilting melodica soaks through his soul and soars his giddy heart. How does he describe *that*?

'I'm not asking you to *sing* it, but if I don't know what you're on about I can't help you, can I?'

Danny thought about this, gulping down the Eric's stench, still fuggy and smoky from the night before. The man climbed a couple more stairs. Now he was looking right at him. He blinked and lolled back against the stair rail and this time there was a flicker of acknowledgement, a sudden ease came over his worn and lined face.

'Ah, it's you. The Sketchman. It *is* you, isn't it? Dutch Eddie's?'

Danny just stood there. The guy held out his hand. Danny stepped forward, cowed, and shook the giant hand feebly.

'Er. Danny. A'right.'

'Danny. I'm Eagle. I sort of – well, I own the place.'

'Easy on me hand, Mr Eagle. I need it.'

He chuckled, a deep, smoker's chuckle, and looked Danny up and down.

'So. Help us out. I might know this track if you give us a clue. Might even have it down there . . .'

Danny's heart was beating fast, now. This was just . . . *unbelievable*. This man, the fella that owns the club that rules his life was giving him – *him* – the time of day. He was *talking* to him – not going through the motions like would sometimes happen with a band that he'd collared outside. And he *knew* Danny – he'd seen him around, clocked his face. Could that be right? Could Danny really be *known* round there? He'd never thought about it too much, but he always liked to think of himself as a secret agent. His sketching was night work, undercover work. He was invisible, an enigma, ducking out and in. And everyone was always so *drunk*, as well. Wherever he went, they'd be falling off their stools, brushing each other down, having the time of their lives right there and then. And Danny was a mere player, a bit-part in their rollicking world. The last thing he'd think is that anyone would take *notice* of him, least of all give him a fucking *nick*name! Fuck. He was known around town. He was a legend. Meet Danny May – The Sketchman!

'Well, like, it's this reggae track right, and it –'

'You're into reggae? Excellent. Here y'are, don't just stand there catching a cold. Come on down here and give us a hand with these boxes. Make yourself useful . . .'

Danny emerged, swooning. He couldn't even guess how long he'd been down there. He had no inkling what time it was, now. He felt drained. He wanted to shout out loud – it was all coming true for him, and he was euphoric – impossibly, unbelievably high. Danny had discovered dub reggae. Not just that though – he'd been given a tantalising glimpse into a whole new world of music he always sensed might be out there, but which had until that very day been closed off to him. But what an introduction! What a deep-end dive into the mysterious depths of underground music! He'd heard sampler tracks – 'demos' Eagle called them – from so many different bands, bands from around the country and around the world who wanted to come and play at the famous Eric's Club in Liverpool. He, Danny May, had been solicited for his opinion. Oh yes indeed – he'd been asked whether he himself felt any of these bands deserved an audience, there at Eric's. Rockin' Dopsie and his Cajun Twisters? Yes please! Prince

Far-I – oh yes, yes, yes! Yes to everything, really – the Cramps, the Heat, Culture, the Easy Cure, Kleenex, Crass, the Pop Group, the Residents, National Health, Ultravox, Split Enz, Matumbi, Modern Eon, Penetration, Dalek I Love You . . . they'd all be coming, if his vote had anything to do with it. Well, maybe not Split Enz, to be truthful . . .

He'd had his head turned right round, down there. Stuff he'd never dream of even *trying* to like, he'd become devoted to. Leonard Cohen. He'd always thought Leonard Cohen was just another dull folkie – drippy, twee hippie music for trogs. And he already knew Leonard Cohen by the way, he'd heard him on the Eric's jukie dozens of times, without ever knowing it was him. That gorgeous ballad about the girl by the river – *that* was Leonard Cohen! And the other one they always put on, 'Famous Blue Raincoat'. He would never, never, never have found that for himself. He wouldn't have *let* himself find it. Leonard *Cohen*! Who? Sounds like a boring old fart, thank you very much – I'll stick with Magazine if it's all the same to you. Now, though, he felt spiritual. He felt like he'd come out into the daylight and been born all over again. He was soaring, way, way high.

And clamped tight under his armpit was the Track. He staggered out into the low silver light and squatted on one of the concrete blocks in the asphalt car park opposite, and he stared at it. He sat there and he stared at the record. It was the most exotic, alien and yet wondrous item he'd ever held in his hand. It was a Greensleeves pre-release twelve-inch sound-system mix by Dr Alimantado called 'Born for a Purpose'. Just the artwork on the sleeve, Jamaican colours and a crudely drawn scene of a faraway record shack, gave him shivers of wild anticipation. He'd stood down there, awed yet minutely disappointed when Eagle had played him the track. It seemed familiar lyrically, yet it wasn't the majestic sonic invasion he recalled, and which he'd been craving for weeks. But then he'd played the flipside, a mellifluous, reverberating cut-up of the track called 'Reason for Living' and it sliced him to bits on impact. It was the most intense slab of reggae, of *music*, Danny had ever heard. This sonic quake he now knew as dub and this smouldering, pulsating example in his hand was his to own. His, that is, at the cost of a charcoal sketch, to be sat for by Señor Eagle at some point in the future. No cost at all, in other words, because Danny had, as a result of his boldness, as a direct product of his journey into the unknown, found something big. He'd come of age. And what was more, he'd be getting into Eric's for free that very evening. He was right in there, a part of the Liverpool music underground, a known persona who would be there to see the artful Wire as a *guest* no less and he just couldn't take it all in. Who said fortune favours the brave? Well, they were bang on, whoever it was. Couple of hours ago he'd been hovering by those big heavy doors, not sure whether he had it in him to make the move and go on down there. Now he was mates with the owner of Eric's. He walked on, starstruck.

Voices carried close on a bitter jag of wind jolted him. Once again, time had passed him by. He was up by Gerrard Gardens and the voices came from a little crew of lads sat on a low wall by one of the vast arched entrances into the tenements. The gang were eyeing up his duffel and, no doubt, the clutched-tight record in his hand – but he felt calm, perfectly at ease with the situation ahead. He was alive to the threat, but he could not have been less anxious, this time. They could try if they wanted, but this was him. The duffel, the shoes, Dr Alimantado – it was all him. He'd die before he gave any of that up. They were pretty close by, now. He was going to have to walk right past them or turn back, and Danny was not for turning back. No way.

'Time, lad?'

They must have thought he was Formby or Wirral or something, some kind of puff who'd got himself lost on the outskirts of town. Danny brushed right past them, cocooned in the certainty that he'd take the lot of them if it came to it. And he'd been there before in stand-offs like this. He knew the score well enough. Lads like this, they were looking for a rollover. You'd get lads who're into the whole thing, specially the younger ones – psychos who just love it, get a buzz off the aggro, the knuckle. But these lads were not like that – they were looking to earn. They were after a gimme – and they had no chance. He got right up to them, sure that now they could suss him close up they'd see that he was no easy score and just let it go. He got six, ten paces past them. Just as he was thinking that that might be that, two of them hopped down from the wall and started to follow him. The smaller of them, dressed like a match lad apart from his tight skinhead, went into a little jog until he got up parallel with him.

'Where you from, lad?'

Hang on – what was the time? Probably nowhere near kick-off. Who were Everton playing today? Coventry? No way – these lads couldn't think he was from *Coventry*? No, this little mob weren't Park End. Just another ragarse crew from the Gardens or Soho Street looking for stragglers.

'Talking to you, knobhead! Lend's ten pence!'

Danny turned to let the lad see he wasn't arsed. He looked right into the lad's eyes, slowed down for a second, looked at him hard, said nothing then walked right on. The little skin ran after him, got right up next to him, his face bitter and nasty. Still Danny could sense no real or imminent threat. He stood back from him and took it all in. The little lad was wearing Puma, a pair of too-long Jesus jeans and a snorkel. He looked like a little slyarse – eyes slit narrow, nut-hard head – but he was busking it with Danny now. He knew it. The lad was bluffing, playing to his crowd on the wall and he'd gone too far to turn back now.

'Giz yer odds.'

Danny was not a fighting lad. He'd had fights, he *could* fight, but that wasn't him, now. He hadn't run the streets for a long, long time, yet he knew the dance, more than knew his way around and what he knew for sure was that this little skin was already plea-bargaining. What he was saying was, we can all keep face here. You give us a bit of slummy. Even if you've got money on you, just lash us a bit of slummy so's I don't look like a divvy in front of the lads. You give us your odds, I'll let you go and we all live happily ever after. Danny read it large in the lad's pinched face and stopped still now, waiting for it all to happen. This time the lad jabbed him in the shoulder, looking round to make sure his mate was not too far behind. He was ambling towards them, no particular hurry. The little fella stood right up to Danny, pushed his face right into him, trying to make him back off.

'Deaf, lad? I said giz yer fucken odds!'

This was going to be a hard one for Danny, but he knew what he had to do – and quickly. The back-up was starting to arrive. So what he did was, he turned to the kid, and in one movement he swept his fringe out of his eyes and butted him full on.

'Fuck off!'

That's what he said as he did it. He sat at the little table in the Grapes and tried to banish the episode from his thoughts. Now it was all over and his shakes were easing off enough for him to grip his pint glass properly, he could almost appreciate the absurdity of those moments, the way he'd seemed to justify hurting the lad as he was doing it. Everyone did it – everyone *said something* as they hit you.

'Fuck off!'

The lad had gone down holding his face and that had pretty well been that. Danny walked away slowly enough but the other lad never did quite pick up the pace enough to catch him. He'd bent over his mate, made a big thing of making sure he was all right while Danny disappeared out of sight.

He was starting to regret it now. Had he really needed to

butt the lad? Couldn't he just have run? Doing what he'd done — well, he was no different to any other twat, was he? He might have given in to dejection if it weren't for the girl. Trying not to look across at her again, he took a swig of his pint and rummaged for a cigarette. The packet was empty. How the fuck was he supposed to look cool without a cigarette?

He pulled up the record, flipped it over, read the credits — again — and slumped right down in his seat, staring up at the ceiling. He was dimly aware that the girl over by the window had been watching him, on and off, and he'd tried to snatch a few glances back at her. To him, she was beautiful. She was quirky, odd-looking with her big eyes and big lips, and already he was getting the feeling again. This was Danny, all over. If he was going in, it'd have to be head first and blind. He hadn't even spoken to the girl but, snatching another quick look, he suddenly felt that surge in his guts. He was falling, all right.

She'd smiled across at him once or twice, but Danny had been unable to return her serve. And this was no game with him — he didn't go in for all that macho pretence, and besides, he didn't know *how* to play games with girls. It was something that the street had failed to teach him — plainly and simply he *couldn't* smile back. He couldn't make his mouth smile. And it was not as though he was unhappy or melancholy by nature, quite the other — he was almost heroically upbeat, Danny, all the time. But in situations like this, he froze. He could not get his mouth to smile.

So, hugely though he hoped he wasn't putting her off by looking away every time she tried to catch his eye, he really couldn't beam back at her, and it wasn't an act. There are people who can cultivate an air of mystique simply by looking glum and saying very little. Not Danny. He liked to talk. More than just about anything, Danny *loved* to chatter. Give him a drink, give him a spark and get him started and he'd talk and talk all night. He wished he could send the girl some sign, offer her some encouragement, but all he could manage was a vague stab at ennui, leaning right back in his seat and throwing his head back and staring straight up at the ceiling. This way Danny hoped he might at least come across as interesting, if not exactly approachable. He was wondering how he might transmit the knowledge to her that he was on the guest list at Eric's when, to his simultaneous horror and rampant joy, the girl came over to him.

'Got a light?'

She was nice. He could tell straight away from the way she smiled with her eyes that she was a nice girl. But she was cheeky with it, impish and naughty, and he fancied her, madly. She had bright, very dyed, very orange hair and bright, brilliantine blue eyes, but more than anything he fell utterly in love with her mouth. Her full lips were painted deep red, parted and teasing him with the most beautiful, generous, curving smile. With that smile she managed to radiate fun, intelligence, sexual promise – but it was the generosity of her that got him. It was her *niceness*. It was alien to Danny, such simple and straightforward goodness. He'd met a lot of girls, he'd always been popular with girls – but he found them hard. Always, always there was a sting in the tail. The moment he'd betray any softness, any feelings at all, they'd vulture him. It would always turn into a game, a match, a fight – and one that they were looking to win. The bout would never last more than six weeks in his experience, start to finish – and the moment you said something stupid like 'I like you', you were dead. He had never met, like this, at close quarters, about to dive right in, fall in love, chance his arm – he'd never even *spoken* to a girl as nice as this one. She just stood there, stood right over him, smiling and teasing him, telling him right out loud with her eyes and her red, red lips that this was about to happen. He sat up straight, eyes locked on to hers, trying to do everything in a slow, exaggerated style – trying to be cool. He eyed her very carefully. Just like his own, her jagged fringe covered one eye.

And in spite of everything and above all in spite of himself, Danny found himself smiling back at her.

'Well?'

'What?'

She made the sparking gesture with thumb and forefinger – still grinning at him. He blew his fringe out of his eyes.

'Got a ciggy?'

He thought he was holding his own, but his heart was pounding, pounding, crashing in and out. He didn't quite know what was happening here, but his soul was swelling and he wanted to jump up and hold this girl, hold her tight, look into her sparkling blue eyes and kiss her, hard and deep. Something was happening between them, something big. And it wasn't just his heart either, it was his balls, too – his balls were churning. He was burning up. She brushed her fringe away, tucked it behind her tiny ear and looked down at him, still teasing him with her eyes.

'A cigarette? Why, I don't even know your name, sir!'

He grinned. He couldn't help himself. He sat there, beaming back at the loveliest girl he'd ever met. And he knew right there and then that this was the girl he was going to be with for the rest of his life. He knew this absolutely, but he had to slow right down and start to breathe again. He shifted his weight, forced himself to his feet and held out his hand. For the second time in a few hours he was introducing himself.

'A'right. I'm Danny.'

She took his hand daintily and, still smiling beautifully, curtsied.

'Pleased to meet you, Danny. I like your smile-dimples.'

'Eye dimples?'

She gave him a tiny, artful poke right on his cheekbone with the tip of her little finger.

'Right there. When you smile.'

And again he found himself, in spite of himself, smiling into her eyes. They stared deep into each other, trying to be playful but unable to mask themselves very well at all. She seemed to snap out of it first and, managing a coy mysterious look, eyed him very carefully, very closely.

'So Danny Dimples – two things. Don't you want to know *my* name? And will you please, please give me a fucking light?!'

Though he laughed merrily, he immediately felt a snag of dread inside. He couldn't help himself – he felt chided, told off. It already felt like he'd done something wrong. She was going to change her mind any second, turn and walk away. He nodded down towards the table.

'Here y'are, get yourself in there . . .'

Overeager, he struggled with the heavy table, its ornate, cast-iron legs making it hard to shift. Danny tugged and grappled, but as slender as she was, she still had to go right up on her tiptoes to squeeze through the meagre gap he'd fashioned for her. She plonked herself down and laughed her girlish laugh.

'Thanking you, Mr Danny. Shall we start again, then?'

'Yeah. Let's.'

He gazed into her face with as much intensity as he dared. He had to look away.

'What's your name, then?'

'Nicole.'

'Nicole?'

'*Sí.*'

'Very French. OK, Nicole. Here we go . . .'

He took her cigarette hand, steadied her slim wrist and lit her fag for her. She inhaled deeply, closing her eyes a second. He watched her blow the smoke out in a cool blue plume.

'Well?'

'Well what?'

'You know?'

He nodded his head at her cigarette packet. She smiled back at him, turning the empty packet upside down.

'Sorry.' She crushed the packet. 'Last one.'

32

He laughed out loud. 'You . . . *monster*! You sly . . .'

She took another drag, then leaned forward. 'Here . . .'

And before he could twig what was happening, she darted her hand behind his head, cradling his nape and pulling his lips to her mouth. This is it, he thought. She was going to kiss him. He parted his lips and she covered his mouth with hers, breathing sweet noxious plumes into his throat. They stayed like that. They hardly exhaled. The blowback turned into a kiss.

'Is this where you live?'

'Shhh!'

She stood back, taking it all in.

'Wow! This is just so . . . *amazing*!'

She ran her eyes over the little house. Two miles away in Mossley Hill, hundreds of students like herself would be slumbering and smoking and bickering, safe and sound in staid Carnatic Hall. She'd passed this way when she first arrived in the city, getting lost, jumping on the wrong bus. She must have passed right by the back of this house, fantasising about the lives behind these very doors. To Nicole, this was magical. It was a dream, and she wanted it to go on, and on, and on. She had had the time of her life, just now. It was everything she'd ever wanted, and more. She and Danny were de Beauvoir and Sartre, two waifs blown together by fate. They'd drunk vodka and brandy in after-hours dives and they'd danced and smoked and sunk pints of beer. *Pints!* He wouldn't hear of her drinking halves, let alone the lager and black she asked for. Danny had her hooked on Golden already – one half bitter, one half lager – and she could still taste it on her tongue, on her lips. The tastes, the sounds, the sights of Danny's Liverpool – she had fallen in love with it all. The clubs, the people, the smells – she was intoxicated with it, all of it. She loved the smell of his new cord shoes. Danny giggled shrilly as she went down on her knees in the Casablanca and sucked in the cloying odour of rubber and now-damp corduroy. She loved these shoes. She loved Danny in them.

'Attention. Listen, you. I have something to say.' She cleared her throat, eyes squiffy with drink, trying not to giggle. 'These . . .' she pointed at the cord shoes '. . . are the most . . . *poetic* shoes I have ever smelt.'

He liked the idea of his shoes being poetic. It had been his intention to take the old Pod back home, brush his teeth, make sure they all had money for the bingo. Many a Saturday evening Ninna would doze off in her chair after *The Generation Game*. Danny would anxiously scan the rise and fall of her chest, and if it faltered even for a moment he'd be out of his seat, prodding her, turning the TV up loud to startle her, anything to make sure she hadn't passed away in her slumbers. Not tonight, though. Since that first sweet, smoky kiss, time had stopped quite still for Danny, while everything outside just slipped away. It was all him and Nicole, deep into one another, deeper and deeper. They stumbled outside the Grapes and broke from another kiss and she stared into his eyes and said: 'You are like a hurricane.'

They went to Eric's, went to see Wire. Eagle had left Danny's name at the counter, but the girl on the till made him pay for Nicole. He used to fancy the girl on the counter at Eric's, but not any more. Next to Nicole, she was nobody. Wire sounded amazing – jagged, but urgent. Everyone seemed to get right into them, right away, but for Danny and Nicole it was all in the background, a dislocated snag of guitar, malevolent vocal, people cheering. They drifted right through the whole thing, kissing. They necked and necked, all night.

After, he wanted to walk down to the pier head and get a cup of tea and smoke and watch the river, but she'd already been bitten by Danny's clubland. She was entranced, giddy with his tales of an after-hours high life in lowlife bars. She'd scarcely even met a black man, and here was Danny with his mystical bazaar of friends and associates: Abdul from the

Alahram Club; Dutch Eddie at the Tudor; Jimmy the Dig from the Lucky Bar. Best of all she liked the sound of the Shadow, the gaunt Trinidadian who sold ornate dolls from his suitcase, working the same clubs as Danny. This guy had been a prize-winning designer of carnival floats back home, a true folk hero – but here, he was forced to sell door to door, pub to pub, for whatever he could get. She was determined to be nice to the Shadow when she met him. She'd buy his dolls. She'd buy them all.

Nicole drank in Danny's tales, loving the romance of his life. They tottered up towards the university, into the Casa. Of course she'd heard of the legendary speakeasy. Her fellow students spoke of it in reverent tones, but none had ever been. She loved it from first sighting; the way the guy on the door peered at them through the creaky shutter and broke into a big grin when he saw it was Danny; the way the Formica-topped table wobbled when they put their drinks down; the way there wasn't a bar, as such, just someone selling drinks and ciggies. She loved it that Danny knew everybody in there, and wanted to introduce her, show her off. A tough-looking Chinese guy came in. Danny's face lit up.

'Mickey! 'Kinell, man – haven't seen you in yonks!'

The guy was pleased to see him.

'Danny! Fuck, la – I'd a thought you'd be off to Paris by now!'

He laughed and turned to Nicole.

'Nic, this is me aul' amigo Mickey Mo. Mickey runs the Unity, little youth club –'

'Used to . . .'

'Ah, sorry 'bout that, man. I didn't –'

'Nah-nah. I'm still doing all a that. Just moved on to the Meth, is all . . .'

Danny winked at her.

'Mickey's a bit of a do-gooder and that. Walks the streets of Tocky saving lost souls . . .'

35

Mickey laughed and punched him on the shoulder, offered them a drink and kissed her hand when Danny declined. She loved it in there. She loved the jukebox. They drank vodka and smoked and put Marvin Gaye on the jukebox, shuffling close, not dancing so much as holding each other up, dead drunk.

They staggered out, down Gambier Terrace, past the great swooning hulk of the cathedral, and turned on to Upper Parliament Street. This was Danny's homeland, miles from her student cocoon, but she would happily walk on with Danny, anywhere, just to keep the night alive, to keep on going.

'You want to go skating?'

'What?'

But she was buying time. Did she want to go skating? She could have fainted. Nicole had spent just about every day of her grown-up girlhood pleading and dreaming there could be boys out there, somewhere, boys with poetry in their souls who'd steal her away and teach her to smoke opium under a desert sky. All she had encountered to date were sozzled dentistry students offering to 'pork' her. Did she want to go skating!

'Yes! Fuck. *Yes.*'

She steadied herself on his shoulder as her foot shot from beneath her.

'Shit!'

'I know. Lethal, isn't it? We'd be better walking in the street . . .'

But the cobbles of Falkner Square were just as slick. They turned into Princes Avenue, 'Prinny' as he called it. Everything had a nickname with Danny, everything had to be shortened – Parly, Lodgey, Prinny, the Casa. He kept up a running commentary for her, pointing out the landmarks and highlights.

'That's the Rialto, used to be a famous dance hall, Beatles used to go there – *everyone* used to go the Rialto . . . bit of a dive nowadays, like. Still. All's it'd take is someone with a bit of nous and it could easy be a happening place again. Look at it. Look at that big, beautiful dome. Gorgeous. Fucking beautiful, man.'

He said things like that, Danny – gorgeous, heavenly, beautiful. And he was right – the sad, majestic Rialto, a hunched cathedral with its noble gold dome, was nothing if not gorgeous. With Danny, even the park benches were beautiful. He tapped his knuckle on an ornate green specimen as they cut across the broad boulevard of Princes Avenue.

'Look at that! Just ... superb that, isn't it? Beautiful. Surprised it hasn't been zapped. Look at the work that's gone into that. Look dreamy in someone's backyard, that. Little sundial next to it, glass of Martini, loads of ice. Oh yiss!'

He led her on, pointing to a tipsy, smiling couple across the street.

'See them two? I call them the Lovelies. That's not their real name, like –'

'Never!'

He acknowledged his gaffe, but held his hand up to shush her.

'Peter and Gloria Luala. Aren't they just the most ... fucking ... *gorgeous* couple you ever seen?'

And they were. Both of them tall, slim and possessed of a lithe, luxuriant elegance, they strolled along the Avenue, hand in hand, seeming to hover just above the ground as they walked.

'God Squad, like.'

She slapped his wrist playfully. 'Daniel!'

'Nah, didn't mean that. They do go to church, mind you. Fuck me, does Peter Lovely go to church! He'd be there now, if it was fucking open. Oh yiss, milady! You want to hear him sing though, la – fuckinell, can that lad sing ... sings "Silent Night" in Swahili or something. Fucking gorgeous!'

They were now walking parallel with them. Nicole had never been so close up to black people. Gloria was, it was

37

true, an immensely beautiful lady. She was so tall, with such extravagant, high-cut cheekbones, she seemed regal. It was easy to imagine her as a princess in fine silk. And Peter – she found it difficult to digest that a man could be so *happy* just walking home on a Saturday night. Danny shouted over.

'Hey! Pedro! Glo! Where youse been? Need I ask!'

Peter just threw his head back and laughed. 'You on it, man! No wonder you a painter, kid!'

Peter made two circles with his thumbs and forefingers, held them up to his eyes as spectacles. They both laughed with slightly forced bonhomie and waved each other adieu. Danny blew Gloria a kiss.

'They'll have been the Ibo. Not really their scene, like – all the boozing and what have you. But Glo and Peter, know what I mean? They love to dance.'

He nodded at a shabby terraced town house.

'That's it, there. The Ibo. Not the worst dive in town by any stretch. Get a late drink in there, if you want . . .'

Wild highlife guitar squalled out from the jammed shebeen – laughter, shouting and the mesmeric throb of the bass notes.

'Whatever *you* want!' she laughed. She couldn't take it in. She was in heaven. He grinned and kissed her softly on the nose.

'OK. Let's skate, kidder.'

They crossed the little roundabout and squeezed through a child-sized kink in the park railings, down a gently curving path, and glinting beneath them was a silver, melting moon, flickering back at them from the frozen lake. There was nothing she could do to stop herself – she gasped, immediately clamping her hand across her mouth.

'My God! It's . . .'

'Dreamy, hey? Too much . . .'

She turned to look into his face. For a second, she was speechless – stunned by the feelings surging though her. She bit down on her lip.

'Is it . . . I mean . . .'

'Is it safe?'

'Yeah. Well . . . I don't mean *safe* safe!'

'I know what you mean.'

He ducked to his right and came back up with a fist-sized rock.

'Let's see shall we, honeygirl?'

Honeygirl. Sickly sentimental in the wrong hands but from this boy, it was just the most poetic thing she'd ever heard. She was head over heels. She lost sight of the missile as he hurled it upwards and outwards into the bright black night, then – *plock!* It landed with a crunch, skidded a moment then came to rest on the lake's surface. She could just about make it out, picked out by a moonbeam.

'Sounds safe enough to me.'

He took her hand.

'Shall we?'

'But of course.'

With him, she had no fear that the ice would break. This was his park, his garden, and with him she was safe there. They took one slippery step, then another, legs splaying out from under them like newborn foals. Ahead, a dull, cavernous creak and the splintering rip of cracking ice. She gripped his forearm.

'Danny?'

'Yiss-yiss-yiss, my ladychild!'

She smiled to herself. 'Nothing.'

She could feel the seep of water, even through her sturdy Kicker boots. She was frightened, yet by his side she was absolutely sure that no wrong would come to her. Another step. This time the water seeped right over their shoes, soaking their feet. He jerked his face to her, the moonlight picking out his fear before he had chance to quell it.

'Uh-oh Chongo! OK. Whatever you do, don't run. Yeah? Just walk, OK. *Slide* . . .'

Slowly, stiltedly, they manoeuvred their bodies round and away from the hole in the ice and back towards the grass bank. It was no more than six paces away, but any sudden movement, anything at all, could plunge them straight down into the frozen water. Both of them knew it, though neither would say so for months. They could die here.

Danny slid his right foot out. Stopped. Pulled Nicole's left leg gently forward. Stopped. A creak and groan from the ice sheet, but it was holding, and they were getting closer to the bank. Nicole's breath billowed round Danny's head. She trusted him. She put her trust in him. Another step. Stop. And in this way, painstakingly, they shuffled back ashore.

'My God! Fuck! I won't forget *that* in a hurry!' she said, throwing back her head and laughing in elation and relief. Suddenly he lay down, on his back. He reached out for her hand and pulled her down alongside him. She laid her head on his chest, listening to the thump of his heart. For a long time neither said a word, then Danny sat up.

'Hey!'

Nicole pulled herself up.

He bent his arm around her, pulling her close and lying her down again.

'Now this . . .'

He wiggled his arm under and behind her head, so he was now whispering into her ear. He dropped his voice, calm but excited.

'. . . this one you can only see from this exact point. Here. Lie flat out, right out flat on your back. Yeah? Now stare straight up. Look right up into the whole fucking big black universe. Do you see?'

She snuggled into him. The bare grass was stone cold, stone hard under the bright winter's night – but how she loved him. How she loved all this – this world, this magic going on in his head!

'See it?'

40

She stared straight up at an endless ink-blue vault, spiked with tiny stars. And straight away, she knew what he wanted her to see. One of the stars glinted harder than all the others in the cold, clear sky above.

'I see it. My God!'

'You're on it, babe. That's the Tocky Star, that is –'

'The what?'

'Star of Toxteth. You can only see it from here.'

And that was it, for her. She was gone. Her soul went soaring out from within her and for a moment she felt herself suspended above the scene, looking down on the two of them. She grasped Danny's hand and held on tight. Never, never had she felt a love like this before. She lay there, gasping for breath, and stared at the star. When she turned at last to look at Danny, his lovely face was wet with tears.

He put his key in, unlocked the flimsy white panelled door. When he'd left that morning he was in possession of his life, loving it, living it to the full. Now, he'd clicked on to another track altogether. It felt unreal – he was taking this girl back home with him, and they loved each other. They were stone in love. He could barely believe it, but there she was next to him, just too good to be true. He opened the door and went to step inside, but she pulled him back to her. Her eyes were huge and moist, devouring him, taking in every little bit of him like he was about to run away, for ever.

'God, little man,' she said. 'I *love* you.'

Winter of Discontent

He was doing the dishes while she sat watching *Grange Hill* with Ninna. With her wild blue lamps and her flaxen hair, as fine-spun and as silvery white as Merlin's, Ninna was as bright and mischievous as she was fearsome. But she was smitten from the start, Nicole, and Ninna was sold on her, too. You could see it from the way her gaze lingered on the girl's pale features. She thought this Nicole was a real catch for Danny, maybe that little bit *too* good for him. But they were all hoping the two of them would stick it out anyway, stick together and make a go of it.

'She'll go far, that girl. She'll be a professional.'

Truly, there was nothing he'd change about his bolshy old grandmother, but her reverence for academia, for medicine, for professional life cut Danny to the quick at times. Times like that when, teeth out and sloppy gums flailing to accentuate the significance of her words, she'd fix that admonitory look on Danny and say to him: 'She'll be a *professional*, that one!'

If a doctor told her to amputate her index finger 'for research', she'd have done it. 'Finest profession!' she'd purr, her eyeballs deranged with admiration. 'The finest profession in the world, medicine! Finest thing a man can do.' So as soon as she discovered Nicole was studying Politics, Philosophy and Economics she was instantly accorded higher-being status. Not that Nin had any inkling of the intricacies of PPE – but boy did it sound serious! Serious, academic and professional

– these were the qualities Theresa Doreen May revered, and she hoped against hope her flighty, daydreaming golden boy recognised a good thing when he saw it, too. She loved the way Nicole spoke; her voice was soft yet always happy, upbeat – not posh but *nice*. More than anything, she sounded confident, Nicole did. She was bright and happy and buoyant when she spoke and that made Ninna go along with whatever she was saying. She kept pulling Danny up and going: '*That's* the way to talk proper, son. You want to go to that college, you're going to have to mind your p's and q's.'

He'd never say a bad word against his Nin, but she couldn't half vex him sometimes. The *last* thing you'd need at art school was manners. This obsession of hers about education and whether he was going to make the grade, it was all born out of the olden days. The idea that you had to be polite and talk nice and keep your head down and graft hard – that wasn't far short of a slave mentality. Then again, she'd been in service all her working life, Ninna had. She'd been a nanny for well-to-do families in Newsham Park and she'd been a scullery maid for the merchants and captains. It was no surprise she was in thrall to Authority, even all these years on. Still, he was pleased she'd taken to his girlfriend. Ninna had found out more about Nicole and her folks in a night than Danny had even thought of asking in a month. She was from Darwen, in Lancashire – not thirty miles away, yet to Danny that was *miles* away. Her parents ran a small chain of bakers' shops around west Lancashire, including a busy one in Ormskirk. Ninna had lived in as a maid at a big house in Ormskirk as a girl. She told Nicole all about her days 'downstairs' and she lapped it up. They were firm friends, right from the off.

All the family had taken to Nicole, in truth – although it was more a matter of she'd taken to them. She loved the whole set-up, his home life, his family, his mixed-race neighbourhood, loved being a part of it. She was always round there, cooking or helping wash up or just doing what she was doing now –

sitting with auld Nin, watching the telly, chattering about this and that and nothing at all. She wouldn't hear a bad word about any of them. If ever he had a go at his sisters, even just getting it off his chest — say if Marie had zapped his last cigarette or something — Nicole would instantly come back at him with all sorts of good things about her. She didn't seem to see things for what they were, Nicole — she didn't *want* to see things for what they were. But he loved her for it, all the same.

A few days before, their Margi was sat in with her boyfriend Joey — Joey Amin, black lad. Joey Meanie, everyone round there called him. Danny had come through the door with Nicole and she was almost speechless with excitement. She'd sat down with Danny, quite oblivious to Ninna's questions about where they'd been, and she was almost staring at poor Joey Meanie to the point that Margi was starting to give her daggers. She didn't notice, of course. She tried chatting to them, didn't really get anywhere with it, but it didn't seem to bother her one way or the other. Margi was ignorant at the best of times anyway, and Joey — it'd be hard to remember one single thing he'd said, other than a plain yes or no. Nice enough lad, Joey Meanie — always said please and thanks — but if Nicole thought she'd get anything out of him, she was wasting her time. She could chip away with her questions and smiles and her innocence but she'd never get through to a lad like Joey in a hundred years. She didn't seem to mind, though, or didn't seem to notice, and Danny didn't see the point in bursting her bubble. He liked it that she loved coming round, chatting to his Ninna, making the tea. He wasn't so pleased about how quickly the girls had got her skivvying for them, washing their teacups and running messages to the shops and so on. It wasn't just that Nicole was so willing, so eager to be liked by them — it was Granby itself. It was all right for them, they were brought up round Liverpool 8, they knew the score. But he didn't want Nicole running round there on her own, in the dark. She wasn't used to it.

Danny continued scouring the soup pan, half listening to Nicole and Ninna but mainly concentrating on removing the charred and stubborn skin of burnt oxtail soup. That'd been Nicole, too busy chattering when she should've been stirring the pan, and on a *gentle* heat, as well. She was useless in the kitchen. To Danny, this stuff was simple – ironing, washing, helping around the house – he'd always done it. His ma had more than enough on, and besides, it kept him out of his sisters' range. If there was work to be done, they'd be some-where else, for sure. There was something soothing about doing the dishes, anyway. He always ran the water until it was piping hot and his hands could barely stand the sting. He'd take ages over each plate, each pan, making sure there was no trace of dirt or grease. But dishes or no, there was no way he'd be watching *Grange Hill* with her today. Probably never watch it with her again after the way she'd reacted last time, accusing him of being into Trisha Yates. State of her – Trisha Yates! He clamped the corner of the Brillo pad in his fingers, exposing just the tiniest tip, and chipped away at the stub-born remnants in the pan. No offence, Trisha Yates might well grow up into a fine young lady, but she was just a schoolie for fuck's sake! There was no *way* he was into her. All he'd done wrong was to make an innocent observation that Trisha's skirt was way shorter than all the other girls' and Nicole had clipped him – hard, too – right on the back of his head.

'You sexist pig! That's such a macho perspective! Trisha's just *taller* than the others, that's all!'

Cheeks stung pink, she went for the kill.

'And how do you know what her family's circumstances are, hey? How can you simply sit back and assume that they can *afford* a new school uniform every year? . . .'

She wasn't joking, either. Those big blue eyes went steely cold on him. She was angry. More than that, she was hurt, bitterly disappointed with the man in her life. He tried explain-ing, but it was getting him nowhere. She was into one, telling him that supposedly innocent observations from 'men' (he'd never really seen himself as a man) were just a poor excuse for lecherousness. He'd got up and put the kettle on and set about the dishes.

He rinsed the gleaming pan under cold water, blasting away any lingering grit or soap suds. She was mad, Nicole. It was all or nothing with her. He was either a saint or a sinner, a hero or a villain, a poet or a punk – even though to Danny himself he just stayed the same. He was just being himself. He couldn't make her out sometimes, but he was cracked on her, madly, madly into her. For one thing, he'd never known a girl who liked sex the way she did. She was always reaching for him, always looking to start it up. If they'd ever get to the house and there was no one in, she'd pull him on to the sofa, her long fingers tugging at his zip. Last week, right there in that same front room where she was sat wooing Ninna right now, she got him to screw her from behind. It was all her. He'd gone to push her down on the sofa, do it normal, but she slowed him up, put a finger over his lips, stood up and peeled her jeans off in front of him. She didn't say a word. She just looked right into his eyes and almost solemnly, knelt down on the floor in front of him, still looking at him over her shoulder. He'd gone to pull the curtains closed first but she just did that shrill, girly laugh and got up again and kissed him full on, full heat, working his cock free with one skilful hand, driving him mad. He'd never known a girl show her love like that. He'd never known a girl like her at all, tactile, demonstrative. Loving. Even when they were all just sat there watching the telly, she'd have her arm round him, stroke his neck, run her fingers through his hair. He felt daft sometimes. He couldn't very well tell her not to, but he knew the girls were clocking it all, storing it all up. He liked it, anyway. He liked her. She was an all or nothing sort of girl. By the time he'd taken their cuppas through, Trisha Yates was gone and forgotten.

'Need some help there, gorgeous?'

God, that smile. He could chew her lips, they were so lovely and curving and generous. Nicole's lips were *her*. He turned to peck her on the head, besotted.

'I'm groovy. You go on up and start getting ready. Be up in a sec.'

He checked the time on the carriage clock. Ten to seven. They were off to see a play at the Everyman. *Richard III*. He'd never even given a thought to the theatre, but he was right into the idea now, made up to be going, with her. This was one of the things that just got him wild about her, she was so cool, so arty, so open to everything. 'Bohemian', she called it, and he was bang into it, bang into her. She wasn't one of those who'd go 'I'm a punk' or 'I'm into disco' and that's them, that's it, that's all there is to say. She was into all kinds. Photography, art, classical music, books, philosophy, theatre. She'd been going on about the Everyman, how it was just a walk away, right on his doorstep, really – and how the little cave bar downstairs was full of radicals and intellectuals. She'd told him straight – if he was going to the art school he'd be needing to hang out in places like this – and he was into it. It'd be something new, something completely different to him. He folded the tea towel, draped it neatly over the tap and bounded on upstairs.

She lay on his bed, holding out her arms to him as he appeared in the doorway. He grinned at her, holding up one finger.

'Momento.'

He made as though to search for a record, but he knew exactly where it'd be, exactly where he'd left it that very morning, jutting out ever so slightly from the other albums. He knew exactly which track he was going to play for her. He'd planned it all. His finger strummed along the ranks of records, stopping on the spine of the bootleg he'd planted there. He pulled it out. Plain white sleeve, with Danny's own crabby scrawl on the front. *Bowie: Live in Santa Monica*. He turned it on its side, slid the two discs out.

Even though it was two records, white labels, no information – and he'd left it that way, other than to nick *1,2,3* and *4* in pencil – he knew just the song he was after, knew exactly where to start it from the tiny scratch about thirty seconds in. He guided the arm over the bitumen sheen of the vinyl and deftly set it down on the track he needed. 'My Death Waits There'. This was going to knock her sideways. He'd chosen the song to impress her, yes – he'd picked it out as a perfect advert for himself, his depth, his soul. But it was so much more than that, too. He wanted her to *feel* this song, to love it the way he loved it, and had always loved it, right from the very first time. This song, somehow, was for them, about them. For a while now he'd been thinking of a song to give her, something eternal that could always mean as much to her as it did to him. He needed Nicole to fall stone in love with this heartbroken melody and for it to be something they'd carry with them through their life together, something that would stand them still whenever they heard it. He'd been rooting for a song that had the power to make them stop and gasp and feel big, big things for one another all over again, every time. He wanted to give this song to her, give to her this piece of himself. But she just lay there on her side, unmoved, looking up at him, head cupped quizzically in her hand, like she thought he was joking.

'Gorgeous, hey?' he smiled.

'Beautiful.'

He looked right into her eyes. 'Don't know no one who says it the way he can.'

She nodded. He closed his eyes, trying to find a way to say what he meant.

'Simple . . .'

He could feel himself getting carried away. He'd never tried to express himself like this before. He'd never let himself go in such a way, never tried to put into words what was truly in his heart. People would just think he was soft. Even before he spoke he felt the quiver in his voice. He swallowed, squeezed his eyes tight to shut back the tears. He opened his eyes and smiled at her and said what he'd wanted to say.

'It's simple, and it's *weak*. D'you know what I mean?'

She nodded kindly, huge eyes stuck on him. He held her stare and swallowed and gave in to the florid sentiments he'd thought but could not say.

'It's like him, isn't it? It's thin, but it's so, so beautiful.'

He stood over her, ready to take her in his arms as soon as the tears started. Or if not tears, there'd be some tacit and gentle embrace between them, some admission of the heightened sensitivity they carried in their souls, too keenly felt for others to comprehend. He stood there, eyes moist, waiting for her face to crumble – then she'd tug him down to the bed and hold him close and just *be* with him while this tragic, wondrous song played out.

She buried her face in the pillow, stifling a sob. Danny bent to comfort her. If he could have seen her tear-streaked face close-up he would have been destroyed. Nicole was stifling fits of laughter. As it was, she kept her face hidden until she was able to breathe freely again. She composed herself. She sat up, her back against the bedroom wall, slightly alarmed now. Her eyes were darting round Danny's face, searching for signs he was joshing, but other than that she remained still and calm. She looked at him closely, she thought about it – and then she said it.

'It's a gorgeous version.'

'*Version?* How d'you mean?'

She looked down into her drained teacup feeling badly now, suddenly unsure whether to say or not.

'I mean – he sings it beautifully. It's so . . . *maudlin*, yet lovely, too. Totally different feel to the original.'

'What you on about? This *is* the original. It's a fuckin''

bootleg. It's taken live. How much more original d'you want, girl?!'

She sighed and met his gaze full on. She'd started, and she was going to have to finish.

'It's a cover of the Brel, isn't it? Jacques Brel?'

Stung, he found himself mimicking her.

'Dzhark Brelle.'

She got up, went to him, tried to put her arms around him. He turned away quickly, went to the window. If *she* could see *his* face now, she'd see bitter tears in his eyes. But he wiped them quickly, bit down on his lip. She softened her voice now, tried to soothe her wounded man.

'I *love* Bowie's take on it. It's –'

He turned, dragged the arm viciously across the vinyl, silenced the stereo.

'So you know it, anyway? That's what you're saying to me. Nice try, Danny lad, already on it, though. Not that sold on it, being honest with you. Not as good as the *original*!'

He stood before her, stung, eyes glinting. She looked into his injured face, and she loved him so strongly it was almost painful. She stepped towards him. He wasn't having it.

'What?'

She reached for him. He slapped her hand away, face still a storm. They stood in silence, staring at each other. He looked so hurt, so betrayed, she started laughing.

'Don't laugh.'

But she found the laughter helped her, helped ease the anguish of this hopeless stand-off, and once she'd started she couldn't stop. She was looking right into him, laughing hard and willing him to laugh, too.

'Don't laugh at me. Please.'

He gripped her wrists as she went to hold him, turned his face away from her as she went to kiss him, turned it this way and that, refusing her, refusing to be friends. But then he caught a glimpse of her anxious, big blue eyes and something inside him caved in and all he wanted, more than anything, was to be on her side again. And he started giggling. The pair of them lay on his bed, entwined, giggling endlessly.

Outside the Phil later she drew him in close and whispered: '*Angel or devil, I don't care . . .*'

Then she kissed him, really full, really deep. She kissed him like it was the last kiss on earth and pulled away, serious, and looked into his eyes.

'I love you, big dummy.'

And Danny could feel himself going under for good, flailing but not frightened.

Town and Country

Those first few months they were feeding off each other, incapable of being apart. If he had to leave her alone to study, he felt the pain of her absence acutely, in his heart and in his delusions. He conjured lurid scenarios in which subtly wooing lecturers would bend her to their will, pleasuring her with a skill and intelligence way beyond him. It was with a merciful relief that they'd be reunited back at his house or in her tiny room, sucking more and more story, more confession, more wild romance out of each other, absorbing and assimilating their histories and personalities, ingesting the vague gist and the very detail of their short lives and perspectives so much so that they were, already, living in each other's skin.

That day he cycled like a madman through the park, barely slowing to check this way and that for traffic, pedalling furiously until he got to Carnatic. Even though he could hear her music playing, even though they'd planned it only the previous night, he tapped anxiously at her door and pressed his ear up close, fearing the worst, but desperate for signs she was in and alone. She threw the door open, unable to suppress the thrill welling up from deep inside.

'Baby!'

'You!'

She dragged him down on to the bed and held his face, gazing into his eyes. He nodded to the corner of the room.

'Leonard, huh? Thought you'd be sneaking your Kate Bush on without Il Daniele here to guide you.'

'I fall at your feet in humble gratitude. Master! You have shown me the way!'

'Oh yes indeedy!'

He took such joy from those rare occasions he was able to influence her that he had to draw attention to it, remind her of his key role in the union.

'Isn't he just the King though, Leonardo de Cohen? Just *listen* to this, man. Here y'are, Nic – put this one back to the start and turn it up. This is just fucking poetry!'

She hopped up from the bed, turned the track up and dived down beside him, pulling him close and looking into his eyes.

'What do you reckon, then? Is Jane just an incredibly light sleeper?'

He was mildly irked that they weren't able just to lie back and soak in the winsome beauty of 'Famous Blue Raincoat' together. He was doubly niggled that she seemed to have taken meanings from the song that had eluded him, and he braced himself for another bout of enlightenment.

'How so, beautiful?'

'. . . or is Leonard a *really* slow writer?'

He stroked her hair out of her eyes, and tuned into the fun puckering under the surface, relieved.

'Hmmm. What do you think?'

'Well. He starts off, doesn't he, saying it's four in the morn-ing?'

'He does, ma'am. That is a fact.'

'And he's writing a letter. But then a couple of verses on

and he's saying – oh, I see Jane's awake, now. She sends her regards. So, what? Has it taken him three fucking hours to write three verses?'

'Maybe he's got a dead loud typewriter?'

'Maybe it invades her dreams, hey? That he's writing to their old *bête noire*. Writing about her?'

'Maybe it's just dead, dead cold!'

They fell back on to the mattress, giggling, tickling each other and prodding their soft spots. Danny held her down, sought her red lips for a kiss. They fell into one long, exploratory embrace, but she became distracted. She pushed him away, sat up.

'Hey. It's my sister's birthday on Saturday. Mum's doing a big Sunday roast kind of party effort. Shall we go?'

Danny was staggered. He knew everything about Nicole yet she'd never mentioned a sister. But this sudden invitation stood for so much more. It meant she'd been holding back. It meant that everything they'd been through so far had been at worst a rehearsal or at best a dream. 'Famous Blue Raincoat' played out. Whatever this stage had been, this part of their love for each other – it was over. It had never occurred to Danny that Nicole should want to go back to her home life – she seemed to despise every single thing about her prim upbringing in comparison with his own wild life – let alone take him with her, as her partner. He couldn't quite define it, but he felt the significance of it and, reflexively, he mourned whatever was coming to pass. Nicole was moving them on.

He watched her, her back to him, pulling the kilt up over her thick woollen leggings, belting it tight then crouching to lace her Kickers. His eyes lingered over her clever head, her flop of vermilion hair splayed either side of her graceful neck as she bowed to the task, and he was overcome once more by that crushing sense of grief.

But the further the train swayed and clattered out of the

city, the more his misgivings receded. Outside the misted window, malevolent crows presided over rutted, frostbitten fields, waiting for something to give itself up. The handful of frozen passengers shrank down inside their coats and mufflers, but to Danny this was magical.

He turned to Nicole, eyes alight.

'Is this where you live?!'

'Not quite. Nearly.'

'Ah, this is sound! Can we go and explore?'

'Well . . . yeah. I mean, if you want. There's not much to see . . .'

'You what? There's *this*!'

He pointed out another dull hillock, its small cluster of trees huddled around a slick green pond.

'Look!'

She put her arm around him, looked, saw nothing but kissed him on the nose, pleased at his pleasure.

'Tell you what. We can get off a stop early and cut through the fields. How's that sound!'

'Wow! Yeah-yeah-yeah! That's how that sounds – yeah-yeah-yeah-yeah-yeah!'

She shook her head and kissed him again.

Hand in hand they crunched through crusty fields. Running ahead, Danny picked up a clay boulder and heaved it at a tree stump, squealing triumphantly as it thudded into the base and split in two.

'Come 'ead!'

'What?'

'Stonking! It's your stonk, girl.'

'Oh, I can't . . .'

Eagerly he ducked down, picking out two more clods.

'Yiiisss! What the fuck's this?' He scuffed his foot at the lip of a perfectly hardened green-brown skein. 'What is it, Nic?'

She stooped over it.

'That, City Boy, is popularly known hereabouts as a cow turd.'

He peered closer.

'Yiiisss! It's . . .' He crouched down. 'It's fucken gorgeous, isn't it?'

'If you like.'

'If you *like*! What you on about? *Look* at it!'

He picked up a twig and, hovering over the cowpat for a second, drove the stick deep into its tender heart, bringing it out and stabbing it again and again, revealing the mess of seeping cud within. Something about the cut and thrust of the tool slicing through the coarse membrane of the hardened turd fascinated him, and he gouged at it until very little remained. He thrust his stick in one last time, leaving it buried in the green hash.

'Tell me that's not beautiful!'

'It's beautiful, baby.'

'Isn't it, though? Isn't that something else . . .'

She wrapped her arms around him and heaved him back up, leaning into him as they walked.

'Want to know something about that stinking pile you've made?'

'Go 'ead, then!'

'OK. You asked for it. Where d'you reckon we get our wonderful English verb *to fart*?'

'Fart? I dunno. It just *sounds* like that, doesn't it? A nice, wet, zippy fart!'

'Well – take a last loving look at your green pudding, baby. Green's the big word here, mind you. See, unbeknown to us there's really no such thing as English, yeah? It's a crazy mishmash of so many cultures and influences – Roman, Saxon, Celt, you name it. But the one influence that continually gets overlooked in our lingo-pud is the dear old Froggies . . .'

His eyes gleamed at the opportunity she'd plonked in his lap. She was forever pulling him up for saying things like that.

'Racialist!'

But she just ignored him, and carried on.

'I'm perfectly serious. The French word for green is *vert*. And in medieval times when the sight of a cow taking a dump in the village high street was common as –'

'Muck!'

'Seriously – that's where it comes from. The cow shits green. You can only imagine the noise its trumping makes. So there we have it . . . We vert. We fart.'

He stopped and took her head in his hands.

'You.'

'What?'

'You're so fucking –'

'*What?!*'

He shook his head, awestruck.

'I fucking love you.'

She looked right back, straight into his eyes.

'Fuck me then.'

'Here?'

'Here.'

He glanced around nervously but her fingers were already working his waist button.

'You're fucking mad, you . . .'

Enraged with desire, he pulled her down, snapping the buttons of her Fred Perry as he mauled her breasts and tried to free them. His hands were everywhere, frantic, trying to pull her kilt up, work his fingers underneath the tight elastic of her leggings, drag her bra down and get her clothes off and see her, feel her, naked, now.

Mrs Watson understood everything she needed to know about Danny the second they walked through the front door. He was a good boy. Nicole was utterly head over heels in love with him. And it would end in tears. For now, her job was to help the meal go as pleasantly as possible. Longer

term, she couldn't say. She knew her husband would dis-
approve of Danny on sight – that hairdo! He'd be polite, of
course – but this was *not* what he wanted for his beautiful,
brilliant daughter. He'd be gruff and remote and civil, and
he'd retreat with his pipe at the earliest opportunity. It all
passed off well enough. Mr Watson serviced the occasion
with two or three dislocated questions, barely listened to the
answers and carefully chewed his way through the meal
before retiring, as foreseen, to smoke. Yet the drift of Erimore
only soothed the occasion, marking her father's relative
absence rather than his nearby presence. Harriet, Nicole's
younger baby-blonde sister, flirted with Danny non-stop, but
he was oblivious, or immune.

'Why d'you have a girl's hairstyle?' she purred, leaning
forward to show that, at fourteen, her breasts were bigger and
rounder than her slender big sister's.

'Never really thought about it, honeygirl –'

'Ooh! I *love* your accent! Call me *hunny* again!'

Nicole's head dropped reflexively, hearing their special term
of endearment used on another, but no sooner had she fallen
than she recovered, remembering this was her kid sister.
Harriet pouted and flirted with her beau, but Nicole seemed
unwilling to take offence, or incapable of taking the joust
seriously. Mrs Watson asked lots of questions about Liverpool,
tried to sustain a thread of chatter about Charles Rennie
Mackintosh's contribution to the grand merchants' houses of
Sefton Park and generally displayed a proud indulgence of
her daughter's independence.

'I suppose you're with her lot, are you, Danny? The Lefties?'

'I don't really bother much with politics.'

'Well, you should. You might be able to talk some sense
into her. I'm telling you, little lady, the Tories are coming, and
we carry a big, big stick.'

Nicole flashed a secret glance at Danny and began clearing up the dishes. Danny jumped up to help.

'Sit down, dear! You don't have to do that!' said Mrs Watson.

'No, honest, it's nothing. I always do the dishes –'

'Well, you shouldn't! For goodness' sake . . .'

She stood and put an arm around Nicole and with a sigh and a shake of her head she said it all: she told out loud her absolute love and pride in her clever, feisty, *bolshy* daughter; she marvelled at her difference, her wilful and contrary otherness; and with that patient and loving shake of the head, she said she knew Nicole would grow out of it, whatever it was. Seeing them out down the gravel path she gave Danny a chaste handshake and as warm a smile as she could muster.

'Well. Look after each other. Don't do anything I wouldn't do.'

'I'll be voting SWP, Mummy, soon as possible.'

'Go on with you! Get along before it gets too dark!'

They trudged to the end of the path. An upstairs window opened, dissecting the path with yellow light.

'Bye, Danny Boy!' trilled a girlish voice.

Nicole turned to Danny, giggling. 'I do declare I have a rival!'

'Yeah, you do – these fields and hills and brooks. Listen!'

'What?'

'Exactly. Nothing. You can't hear a fucking thing, can you?'

'I've never really thought about it.'

'It's just . . . I *love* it!'

'You wouldn't love it if you had to live here, mate.'

'I would. I know I would.'

'Nah. Give it a week, you'd miss the noise and the excitement.'

He dropped his shoulders slightly as they walked.

'I wouldn't know. I've never been away that long.'

'Seriously?'

'Seriously.'

'You've never had a holiday?'

Had dusk not changed so quickly into dark she might have seen the slight prick of defiance in his eyes.

'We've had *loads* of holidays!'

'I didn't mean . . . shit! What I mean is . . .'

He stopped and put his arms around her.

'I know. It's just . . . I really like it out here. I can't explain it. It makes me mad if people don't see all the beautiful things. Are you with me?'

'Yeah. Yes, baby. I think so.'

'What about you?'

'What about me?'

'Like – where's the best place you've been? Where's . . . where's your paradise?'

'Mmmmmm. I dunno. I don't think I've found it yet.' She flicked a kiss at his earlobe. 'You are. *You're* my paradise.'

He dragged his toes along the lane, making a drum roll with the rubber against the pitted surface.

'OK then. Where would you go? If you and me could just get off, anywhere, now – where would you go?'

'Paris.'

'Paris?'

'Definitely. Oh, honey, it'd be so amazing. You and me on the Left Bank, strolling by the Seine, getting drunk on pastis in all those little jazz cellars . . . We could just sit, day after day at our favourite pavement café reading . . . All those big, big ideas, coming to life in front of us in the city they were born . . . Camus, Sartre, Rimbaud, Jean Genet –'

'Jean Genie?'

'You may well scoff, but that's where it comes from. I'll lend it you . . .'

She squeezed his hand. In the near distance, they heard the sluggish rattle of the Sunday-slow train.

'What about you? Where would you go? Where would *we* go?'

'Dunno. I haven't really . . .'

He faltered for a moment, eyes clouding over.

'Like, one time we all went away – this was me ma's club

organised this, right, Holy Name, two fucking coachloads of rascals . . .'

He paused, thrust his hands in his pockets, unsure whether to continue. She nodded, coaxing him on.

'It was just a shitty day trip to Llandudno –'

'Llandudno!?'

'Ah, I tell you, Nic . . . I was just blown away. D'you know what I mean? I was gone. Never known nothing like it. Like, all's the others was interested in was the amusements and the fair and that, going on the rob. But I seen this big hill, the Great Orme, and man – it was just swoonsome. Honest to God, I lost my heart. I couldn't breathe. There's this big, huge, black rock jutting out into the blue, blue sea and all's I could think about was . . . I just wanted to run to the very top, just get to the top of the highest point and scream my lungs out . . . I've never been so excited in my life. I can't explain it. I was just full of . . . full of *love* . . .'

Without understanding him, unable even to imagine or fathom what spirit or calling drove him on she knew all over again that this boy, this Danny, was the most wondrous and special thing she had ever encountered. Eyes moist, she pulled him close.

'You know what that is?'

'Some big word we get from French?'

'That's your genius. I mean it. Having that within you, the faculty to respond to your surroundings in such a visceral way . . .'

'It's just how I feel . . .'

'I know, baby. You should celebrate it. That you really do *feel* it . . .'

Suddenly, she sucked her breath in.

'Hey! *We* should go!'

'Llandudno?'

'Most definitely! We should club our money together and find a cute little B&B and you can take your paints and easel

60

and we'll climb to the top of that Great Awe and you can put it all down on canvas, what you see, how you feel . . .'

'No messing?'

'I mean it!'

'Promise me?'

She slipped her hand on to the nape of his neck, stroking him with her thumb.

'I solemnly swear that you and I shall, at our earliest opportunity, abscond to luscious Llandudno for a wild weekend.'

'Ah – I knew you'd take the piss.'

'Danny, I'm not teasing you, darling. I mean it. I'd fucking *love* to!'

Pink Flamingos

'She's not serious about it, is she! It's not like it's for real –'

'That makes it worse, if anything –'

'That's . . . *stupid*!'

'I'm sorry. I'm not doing it. I can't stand there and watch some daft bint prat about in a swastika armband and pretend that it's art!'

'I'm not *saying* it's art! It's just . . . *her*. She's always done that. Siouxsie, Jordan, the lot of them . . . it's just them being . . .'

'Being what, Danny? Being *shocking*?'

Most of the time they were so close, so together on everything, they were more like brother and sister than lovers. He felt it bitterly when they bickered. She could just carry on as though it was nothing, but for Danny every little disagreement hurt. It took him a lot longer than Nicole to take the hit and move on.

'She probably won't even *wear* that armband thing!'

She looked at him with all the patient indulgence in the world.

'But she might, Danny. She *might*!'

He could feel himself losing another little scrap. She was older than him, she'd been around a bit, she was confident. To Danny, she was never uncertain about anything. But more than anything, she was so fucking good at arguing. He'd start off from a rock-solid point of view, something he'd never shift from, and she'd have him backed into a corner, eating out of her hand, *apologising* within minutes. Always, but always, he'd end up seeing her point of view. He'd be able to take it better if she was less angry maybe, less *affronted* whenever he'd challenge her. And when she wasn't being affronted, she'd be aghast or amazed at something or other, instead. He'd only known her a minute when she was insisting he tried curry. Not *recommending* it, no – she was nothing less than staggered that he hadn't yet sampled the joy of curry. There were undertones there.

'Excuse me? You live in Toxteth and you've never eaten *curry*?'

There were definitely undertones. It wasn't that she was accusing him of being *anti*-curry for whatever reason – more of a gentle insinuation that he was safe, unworldly, unadventurous, whatever. It was all black and white with her. She saw everything very, very clearly. All he was asking her to do was come to the Siouxsie gig with him, and now he was a fucking fascist! She drew breath and went at him again.

'OK, baby, look . . . let's ignore the miniskirts, the make-up, the pandering to male wank fantasises, right?'

'The *what*?'

'If Siouxsie Sioux is being so fucking subversive, right? If what you're saying is, look, she's turning that imagery on its head. She's using fascist symbolism to *fight* fascism. She's neutering the symbolic power of the swastika, right? . . .'

Danny started laughing. 'Hey, hold it, hold it, hold on . . . Where d'you get all that from, like? I'm not saying she's cutting Goebbels' goebbels off . . .'

There was not a flicker of amusement from Nicole, only

vexation. Her eyes were wide open with admonition and there was the hint of a finger about to be raised.

'Don't trivialise what I'm saying here, Danny. You simply cannot play about with this stuff –'

'I'm not saying –'

'It's about one thing, and one thing only: whose side are you on. Are you with us or against us. Right?'

He nodded, meekly.

'If Siouxsie and the Banshees are with us then how come they're not playing Victoria Park? Hey? How come they haven't embraced Rock Against Racism? Even Sham fucking 69 are backing the ANL!'

He shook his head, lost for answers. This was another argument he was never going to win. Eric's was going to have to witness Siouxsie and the Banshees' Liverpool debut that night without the support of these two staunch regulars, while Danny was going to have to get by without his fix of gossip and intrigue from the in-crowd. He sighed hard, suddenly relieved now the spat had been concluded, and put his arm around her as they crossed Abercrombie Square, whose grand old trees were just coming into bud again.

'Look, I'm not that arsed about seeing them, like. They're a bit punk for me, if you want to know the truth.' He grinned at her and pecked her cold pink cheek. 'But I don't think they're fascists . . .'

'Baby, who knows, hey? For me . . . I just can't stand there and watch her prance about in that armband.' She paused and gave it due consideration. 'I'd probably have to bottle the bitch.'

Danny laughed generously. 'Fair dos.'

He kissed her again, this time getting a squirmy shrug of resistance from her, but a smile as well. As they emerged from the square, a leaky pale sun bled weak light across a still-low spring sky. He drew her close to him, intoxicated by her anger, her vim, her Nicole-ness.

'All of which leads me to ask of you, my dear – what the fuck we gonna do tonight then?'

'Well . . .'

'Could go Kirklands? Reggae night upstairs now on a Saturday –'

'I was thinking more –'

'You *love* reggae! Don't you?'

'I do! I *do* love reggae. But . . .' She stopped and scrutinised him closely, as though she were silently asking: is he ready for this? 'How'd you like to go see some film?'

Something inside him jarred at the way she said it: *some* film. She said it not in a dismissive way, as in 'any old film'. Rather the opposite, in that same way she could ritualise a simple trip to the chippy with a bright, exclamatory 'Let's go and eat some fish!'

This was just the same. She was testing the water, trying him out.

'Wouldn't mind seeing that *Dawn of the Dead*, like –'

'Daniel! I'm talking *real* film, right? None of your Hollywood trash. Experimental. *Really* risky stuff –'

'What? Blueys?'

'Hah! You don't know how close you are . . .'

She tugged him along by the arm, happy to be his girl again now she'd got her own way.

'You heard of a guy called John Waters?'

'Pink Floyd fella?'

'Hmm? No. Don't think so. He's this really amazing film-maker from the States. *Pink Flamingos*? I mean – we're talking *extreme*, right? Tear up the rule book.'

'Sounds ace.'

'Oh, baby, ace isn't in it. Only . . . they're having a Waters Night at Studio 3.'

'Studio *3*! *Told* you it was blueys . . .'

She ignored him.

'It's going to be amazing. All three Divine films, question-

and-answer session, and you can bring your own wine too –'

'Wow! That sounds *very* groovy.'

Danny thought it sounded not very groovy at all. He thought it sounded absolutely shit; he thought reggae night at Kirklands would be about a million times more fun. But he knew that when Nicole thought she was educating him, sex would undoubtedly follow. Sex with Nicole was something else. This was a girl who wanted to *do* things – and expected to have them done, too. None of the coaxing and wheedling for a sloppy wank or a half-spat blow job. She was willing and, when she wanted to, she'd do anything. Often, she most wanted to when she'd most bent Danny to her will. He was warming to this art-film thing.

'OK. So, what . . . will we have a pint in the Beehive first?'

She ruffled his hair, stared into his eyes and kissed him.

'Know what, Danny May? You are a very special little man.'

No matter that her eyes were shining and she hugged him with all her heart, Danny felt the put-down. He was used to it by now. She really couldn't help it. She linked her arm with his, put her head on his shoulder and walked him down Mount Pleasant. She had him – and that was just fine with Danny.

The Picnic

Good Friday brought sunshine, real shirtsleeve sunshine, and Danny was ebullient at how much she loved his suggestion. They lay back on the fragrant grass outside the ghostly quiet Carnatic, stroking each other's hair, planning the days ahead.

'A picnic? Baby, that's a *glorious* idea! How sweet of you. You're such a . . . *poet!*'

She rolled on to her side and gazed at him, surprised at him, and kissed him long and hard. Pulling away, she sat up and clapped her hands.

'A picnic – yes! Where should we go? The park? Which

park though? Sevvy's gorgeous at the moment with all the daffodils . . .'

Danny hung his head slightly. It was an impulsive, totally involuntary action with him. He hated to disappoint anyone but more than anything he hated even the prospect of going against Nicole's will. Eyes averted slightly, he tried a humble grimace.

'I thought we could have a bike ride. Go down the river, like. Spike Island or something.'

She flung herself back down next to him, and wrapped her arms around his neck.

'Oh, Danny, Danny! Yes! Let's do it! Let's have a bike ride!'

He was almost eating himself with pleasure. Warming to the subject, or warming to how much *she'd* taken to the idea, he disentangled himself and took hold of her hands.

'We'll both bring a scran along. Surprise each other, like. I dunno. Maybe you can bring the pies or something. We'll both bring little surprise treats, but we can't tell each other till we get there.'

'Oh, baby, yes! Yes yes yes! I *love* it! Ahhh, this is going to be *such* fun! I can't wait. I want it to be tomorrow right now!'

A thud of soil on her window and there he was outside, smiling and waving and looking so fine, first thing Easter Saturday. The sun was already high as they wheeled their bikes down past the Sudley gallery and on to Aigburth Road. He grinned and blew a kiss at her and she was eaten up with love for him. She would have stopped right there by the cricket ground and sucked his heart out she adored him so much. She pedalled on behind him, loving the arch of his back, the ripple of his spine as the sweat marked it out against his T-shirt. A right at the dislocated dockyard church, and on they sailed, under Garston Mud, right across the cracked and brambly old airfield and past Speke Hall to the riverfront path. There wasn't a breath of wind, only the whirr of the bike wheels' breeze as they sped away from Liverpool, towards the squat and silent chimneys of Fiddlers Ferry.

'Wow! What's this? Where are we?' shrieked Nicole as they rounded the brow at Dungeon Point, revealing the shimmering mirage of Runcorn Bridge, miles upriver, a distant land.

'That's Hale Lighthouse,' smiled Danny, glad to tell her something she didn't know.

'Wow! There's a lighthouse here? Right up the river?'

'Sure is. Dunno if it's still in use, like . . .'

She pulled over, skidding her front wheel to one side.

'Can we stop here? Just for a bit?'

'Course we can. Getting a bit too much for you, is it?'

'*No!*'

She flashed him a smile, cheeks flushed, full of promise. She set her bike down, wheels still spinning, and reclined in the sandhills. She squinted up at him, shielding her eyes from the sun, her tone playful.

'How about we have our first course here?'

He knelt down beside her.

'And what might our first course be, exactly?'

Without her eyes ever leaving his she delved inside her rucksack and produced a brown bottle, still moist with droplets.

'*Wine?*'

'Indeed, good sir. And a corkscrew.'

'Shit. I mean . . .'

He picked up a bleached old driftwood stick, sat down and flicked at the sand with it, staring out across the river.

'I haven't brought nothing like that.'

She moved over and straddled his legs with hers.

'So? You've brought the most important thing, haven't you?'

'What's that?'

She looked right into his eyes. God, she was beautiful.

'You.'

She let the bottle slip from her hand and kissed him. The kiss went on, tongue flicking tongue, both of them aroused.

Nicole pulled away, rolled on to her side and began to unzip her jeans.

'Here. Now.'

She arched her back to help tug them down and over her ankles, then her knickers. She reached her arms up to pull off the mustard-coloured sweatshirt, but Danny leaned over to stop her.

'Stay like that.'

She smiled, understanding, and lay back for him, naked from the waist down. It turned him on to see her like that. He slid one hand under her top, closed his eyes and gasped at the smooth tension of her breast. He dragged his hand between her legs, felt her shudder and tugged at his flies, wriggling his jeans down below his knees but no further, eager to drive into her. Even engorged with lust, a part of him held out for a contingency plan for their quick getaway, if disturbed.

'Now *that*' – he smacked his lips and held his paper cup up to the sunlight – 'is fucking delicious.'

Both were dressed again, and regardless of the glorious fuck in the glorious sunshine with the girl he worshipped, Danny was relieved to have got away with it and happy to get back to the script. He took another deep and conspicuously satisfied glug. She hunched her head down into her shoulders and giggled.

'Glad you like it. We'll make a bohemian out of you yet!' She reached into her purse. 'And for sir's further post-coital delight . . .' She pulled out a wonky, ready-rolled spliff.

'What's this then? You started doing drugs?' No matter his attempt at levity, he couldn't keep the approbation out of his voice.

'It's only grass.'

He shifted right round until his knees touched hers.

'How come? I mean . . . how long?' He laughed at himself,

dipped his head instinctively then jerked it back, getting his defence in first. 'I mean, I don't mind, like. There's no problem.'

'Good. I should hope not.'

She sparked it and lay back. He watched in silence as she inhaled, held it down, clamped her mouth shut then blasted it back out in a sudden explosion. She coughed slightly and sat up, embarrassed. She passed it to Danny.

'Here we go, then. Your turn.'

He waved a hand at it. 'No ta. You finish it.'

She looked hurt. 'I got it for both of us. It was one of my surprises.'

He leaned over and pecked her on the brow. 'It's a lovely thought. Honest. But I've got revising to do tonight.'

'Revising? It's a foundation course, for fuck's sake!'

'I know! But I've got to get on it, man. They won't let you into art school if you ain't done your foundation — simple as that, you know. I *really* need to get these grades, honeygirl . . .'

'Fucking hell! It's the holidays! Talk about Mr Clean . . .'

He pulled away from her.

'Don't talk to us like that, Nicole.'

'Well . . .'

'Well nothing. I said no to the pot, all right?'

'Stop fucking calling it fucking *pot*! It's not fucking pot. It's grass!'

'Whatever it is — stick it up your arse!'

She hadn't seen anger like this in him before. She'd hurt him plenty enough times, just through being herself and saying what she thought. But she'd have to admit she'd goaded him once or twice too, just to get a rise from him. He could be *too* placid, Danny, and it irked her at times. She'd never known him to lash out like this though. His ire was so basic, so childish, right down to his puerile retort, that she suffered all the more with him, instantly. She reached for his hand.

'I'm sorry, babe. Please?'

He let her stroke the back of his hand.

'That was wrong of me. I know how much it means to you.'

He turned to look downriver, back towards the city. She leaned into him, coaxing him.

'You'll do it, baby! I know you will.'

His eyes glistened. He seemed not to believe it.

'You'll breeze into that place, Danny May. I'm telling you. You'll do it with your eyes closed and your paintbrush tied behind your back. Just . . . go easy on yourself, hey? It doesn't have to be such hard work.'

'Maybe not for you.'

She took her breath down deep and held it, held it, steadied herself hard. If there was one single thing she despised in him it was the way he could imply with a word or a gesture that things came easy to her and that not only was her future gift-wrapped but that he would have to fight like a ferret for his, or any hope of one. She could break his skull with a rock when he got like that. A quick and vicious anger would take her over and she could kill him, she could stab him through the heart for saying that. But he was hurting and she wanted him better again.

'Not for you either, honey. You're a genius. Even geniuses can let up every now and then . . .'

Through the distant haze he could make out the cathedrals, the Liver Building, St John's Beacon. What a place! What a tiny, tiny part of it he was.

'Friends?'

He forced a smile and nodded, not wanting to overdo it. He'd made his point. She looped her slim arms around his neck and, standing on one foot, kissed him on the tip of his nose.

'Come on then. Let's see what treats *you've* brought us!'

He grinned wildly at her and sprung towards the plastic bag he'd fixed to the back of his bike.

'Prepare yourself, girl!'

With one hand he tore open the packaging; the other

prised out the flattened sandwiches. He came back to her, proud and somewhat expectant.

'Close your eyes . . .'

But it was too late. She'd seen enough of the clammy butties, squashed and warped inside their weeping cellophane, to know what lay in store. Still, she did her best, screwing her eyes tight shut as an antidote to the horror she now awaited, and gingerly opened her mouth. She took a tiny bite and chewed without relish.

'Mmmm! What *is* it?! Can I open my eyes yet?'

'Go 'ead then!'

The first thing she saw was Danny standing over her, grinning broadly and with huge and evident self-esteem. In his hand was a small, mottled jar.

'Prince's,' he announced. 'None of your Kwikies shite. Prince's prime salmon sandwich paste. Only the very best for my girl!'

'Ah, baby!' she shrieked, throwing her arms around him but already bilious beyond remedy. She knew what was going to happen. There was a grim inevitability to it, the only variable now being how long the process would take. Reared in a household where fat was trimmed from bacon and eggs had to be new-laid, Nicole's metabolism had developed a taste for the fouler things in life – and repelled them at source. Try as she would to gird her psyche to the puckering whirlpools of the river or the recent raptures of outdoor sex, she just could not crush the notion that, right there and then, Prince's paste was making steady, if sticky, progress through her oesophagus. That, coupled with an unusual amount of sunshine and an unusually strenuous day's exercise, caused her to welcome the privacy of the sandhills for the second time in an hour.

'Told you, girl,' said Danny, staying close enough to show concern but sufficiently far away to keep the sick from his week-old Nastase tennis shoes. 'Pot.'

Victoria Park

His heart sank as they got closer to the coaches outside the Mountford Hall. It was just as he'd feared – a loose assembly of students, politicos in slogan T-shirts, one or two punks and some men with beards milling around by the coaches, keeping to their groups but trying to nod and smile to one another nonetheless. Drongos, Danny called them – that queer assortment of idealists, radicals and hippies who'd be guaranteed to turn out whatever the weather, whatever the righteous cause. He and Nicole had tiffed for weeks over the rights and wrongs of Rock Against Racism, but what it boiled down to was this: he didn't like any of the bands. If he was going to spend six hours each way on a coach full of drongos, he wanted more of an incentive than Sham 69 and the Tom Robinson Band.

'Nicole – there's not much I wouldn't do for you, babe, but I'm *not* gonna watch the TRB. Sorry.'

'So, what? What you saying to me? You're a homophobe?'

'No. I'm a shit bandophobe! Get your head together, will you? It's pub rock! It's shite! Look at him, will you? What's going on, for fuck's sake! Your geography teacher sticks on a pair of drainies and a school tie, and suddenly he's a fucking punk messiah? Fuck that! Listen to the music, girl. It's cack!'

Even when she knew he was right, Nicole could always beat Danny back with something or other.

'That's just you all over, isn't it?'

'What is?'

'"Listen to the music"!' Is that all this is? Getting your money's worth?'

'No . . .'

'I think it is, Danny. I think you're a mealy little Tory shit! "Listen to the music".'

She drew herself up for the kill.

'There are times, little man, when the message is more important than the music. Try it one day, Danny. Fuck the music – listen to the fucking *message*!'

'What?' he wanted to say to her. '"2-4-6-8 Motorway"?' But she was way gone. Her cheeks were crimson and her eyes were wild and angry. He knew the form by now. It was down to him to apologise. Until he did, there could be no future.

It was still dark, but violent yellow streaks cut the dawn sky. There was definitely an atmosphere, a feeling that this was momentous and they were a part of something big as they shuffled on board. Danny couldn't help himself, though. This whole thing was going to be one big drag. Not even the thought of the Clash headlining could buoy him. For him, the time of the Clash had been and gone. It was punk. If anything, the Clash should be embraced in a sweaty dirt box in front of a few dozen rebels. The Clash was meant for the Vortex and Eric's – not for a hundred thousand partygoers in a London park! There was Steel Pulse, but he didn't really buy them either. Next to Dillinger or Culture they were just going through the motions, far as he was concerned. They climbed aboard and, while Nicole gladly accepted leaflets and fanzines from excitable young men, Danny feigned sleep. By the time they reached the M6 his method had overridden his madness and he was snoozing gently, head cranked at right angles to the window.

Waking suddenly, he was alarmed to find her seat empty. He screwed his knuckles into his eyes, then saw her up towards the front of the coach, leaning over one of the seats, deep in conversation with somebody. From her narrowed eyes and earnestly nodding head he could see this was serious stuff – and he was shot through with jealousy. She felt him staring at her, gave him a smile and made her way back to their seats.

'I didn't want to wake you. You were well away!'

'Fuck. How long have I been asleep?'

Nicole nodded out of the window. Painfully, he swivelled back round to see. The coach was inching its way along a busy main road.

'Where's this?'

'Dalston.'

He was still stung at her betrayal. The Nicole he'd caught deep in debate up front there was someone she kept from him. She was involved, up there. She was engaged. He thrust his bottom lip out and shrugged.

'We're in London, dummy!'

He looked back out at the jostling mob thronging the shops and stalls.

'Wow. Busy for a Sunday, hey?'

'Welcome to the metropolis.'

He took another look. 'Worse than by ours, isn't it?'

'How d'you mean?'

He glanced at her serious face and felt the purest anger. He knew what'd happen but, eyes sparkling, he *had* to say it.

'All the coons.'

Nicole felt the bite of anguished eyes burning into her. She slapped Danny hard across the face.

'You fucking pig!'

'What?'

She lowered her voice. 'Fuck off, Danny!'

She stood, gathered up her literature and stomped back up to the front of the coach. Danny watched her go, aware of the attention he'd brought upon himself and hating them all for *wanting* to be so appalled. For him, they'd had that look in their eyes since they'd set off. A load of sweats and drongos just waiting to take offence.

As soon as the coach pulled up, Nicole was off, without a backward glance at Danny. He was troubled, he regretted his moment of fun but he knew it'd be fruitless going after her. He sat back while the coach emptied, wondering once again how he'd come to be there at all. It was going to be a long, long day.

With no money to speak of, and no alternative, he dragged himself up and off the bus. Victoria Park was a walk away from where they'd parked, on the fringes of a big, mid-rise estate. It looked rough, the flats' balconies garishly painted in turquoise and yellow and rampant aqua blue, the walls stained with graffiti. He followed the crowd and the distant throb of bass tones, and the dismal council blocks gave way to posh town houses, set back from the road and sheltered by trees. Up ahead, the tail of the rally marched on towards the main park gates. A guy in a PLO scarf chanted into his megaphone: 'The National Front is a NAZI front!'

Then the answering call came back from the marchers: 'Smash the National Front!'

They were good folk, evidently – they were all nice, good people with the best of ideals and the strongest principles, and Danny felt wholly alien in their midst. In their doughty presence he felt trivial, angry, bitter, estranged and terribly, terribly *wronged*. Like the protestors, he felt tuned and ready to take offence – at them. Even their voices, their accents, filled him with a passionate loathing. For the most part, they vented their chants and slogans with a safe and modulated Home Counties ease, soothing their vowels so that even the word *Nazi* – pronounced *Nart-zee* – was castrated of its venom. It sounded like they were berating the skinheads and fascists for being *nasty*.

'The National Front is a *nasty* front! Smash the National Front!'

He quickened his step and got ahead of them. As he neared the entrance, volunteers shook buckets for donations while

75

magazine sellers and pamphleteers sought out the likely marks from the crowd.

'Magazine, mate?'

He'd seen him by the coaches before they left; beady eyes and scruffed-up hair, he seemed to have modelled his look on Mork from Ork, right down to the rainbow braces. Danny glanced down at the proffered magazine, *Temporary Hoarding*. It was more of a fanzine, in truth, and a slight one at that – home-made, stapled, rough and ready. In the bottom right-hand corner was a Rock Against Racism symbol, and to the left their slogan: LOVE MUSIC, HATE RACISM. Danny met his eager stare full on.

'No thanks, mate.'

'You don't want one?'

The guy had a nasal southern accent that only enhanced the hint of disapproval in his voice. Immediately, intuitively, Danny disliked him, yet he dissembled.

'Haven't got the dough.'

Deliberately, he stopped short of calling him 'mate' a second time. Mork looked appalled.

'You haven't got twenty pence?'

Danny shrugged. The vendor looked him up and down swiftly assessing his case.

'Here. Take one.' He passed him the mag and, as Danny went to depart, gripped his shoulder in solidarity. 'Have a good one, brother.'

Danny nodded awkward thanks and shuffled on inside. People, thousands of them, seemed to be beaming at each other, hardly daring to believe that they were there, that this was about to happen. There was a growing sense of some great, definitive moment about to happen and that they, the throng who'd flocked together from far and wide, setting off in the dark, thousands of them, for their historic show of strength, were as significant a part of the day, of the statement, as anything or anybody on the stage. A powerful and infectious spirit was spreading through the stoked-up crowd, yet it could not affect Danny at all. He sat at the very back of the multitude, hearing but not enjoying Patrik Fitzgerald. Safety pin stuck in my heart? What did *that* have to do with anything? He flicked through *Temporary Hoarding*. Again, his reaction was instant and instinctive. He didn't disagree with a single thing the magazine said – but something about the way it was said made him burn with indignation. Why the lectures? Why the ever-present sense of being told off? He read the statement of intent:

> We want rebel music, street music, music that breaks down people's fear of one another. Crisis music. Now music. Music that knows who the real enemy is.

He lay back, hands behind his head, and let his thoughts drift back to his exams. If he could scrape the grades – and for Danny it was work, it was going to be a fight all the way to the finish for him to pull off those results – he was guaranteed a place on the foundation course. No matter how good a painter or how unique his gift, he could only go on to art school once he'd completed the foundation; and for that, you needed results. He sighed hard and felt purged, if only slightly. There was no use him pining for a day's lost revision. He'd come here to be with his beautiful girlfriend, and where was she? All alone, was where. Abandoned by him. Great boyfriend! He jumped up and set about the simple task of finding one small girl in a crowd of a hundred thousand.

When finally he spotted her, he was shattered – angry enough that, although he'd scanned that front-of-stage area several times, he'd still failed to pick her out but, more than anything, floored by what he saw. Far from moping on the fringes of the festival in tragic isolation, Nicole was clearly making the best of things. With Steel Pulse thumping out their blend of reggae and sound system and the crowd eddying this way and that, Nicole rose above them, exultant. How had he missed her? Her face lit up that glowering sky. Eyes closed, lost in the moment, she writhed sinuously on the broad shoulders of a giant Rastafarian. All around her, joyous punks and dissidents swayed en masse, rising up in celebration of their cause, their music, their message of love and anger. Danny, mute and excluded, looked on from the sidelines. If this was her revenge, she'd got him good.

By the time the multitude was hurling its awesome mass to 'White Riot', Danny was back at the main gates, stewing, despising himself. Whatever had happened back there, he'd brought it on himself. The only chance he'd left himself now was to wait directly opposite the exit and accost her as soon as she came out, throw himself at her mercy and apologise with all his heart. Even that was going to be a tall order. Gurning, grinning, happy people were starting to pour out and it was almost impossible to pick out an individual for more than a flashing moment. He'd manage to fix on a face or a jacket or a haircut for just that fraction of a second before they were carried away, swallowed up by the throng. He felt a sudden gnawing dread. What if there were other exits? What if she'd been swept along in a completely different direction? She'd be completely lost in the backstreets of Hackney by now, prey to any stray chancer.

He began to panic, fearing for his innocent waif. She was sharp, and she'd become more streetwise in the time she'd known him, but really – she was so *little*! London could eat her up. Where would he start looking? Who would he ask? He told himself he'd wait for the crowd to start thinning out and if there was no joy then, he'd make his way back to the coaches and start his search from there. They might have him marked down as a scally, but the others on the coach would surely help find one of their own.

Twenty minutes later and he was down to a trickle of ecstatic Clash fans, hugging each other and trying to stay on their feet as they stumbled out into the night, high on the celebration they'd just taken part in. They tried to keep the magic alive as they babbled all over each other's recollections, but the Clash at Victoria Park was already nostalgia, already a part of their history. What mattered to Danny now was finding his girlfriend. He'd known her a matter of four intense months and he couldn't tell himself for sure that she'd never go off with a stranger. She'd done it with him, hadn't she? But in his heart he feared that Nicole, not he, had been hurt.

The thought occurred that, of all their cargo, the coach party might not wait for *him*, and he started to jog back in the direction of the estate. As the tree-lined avenues receded and the squat blocks loomed nearer, he was conscious of the crowds evaporating, peeling off into side streets and cars and minibuses. The silhouette of the coaches was up ahead now, and he relaxed his stride. There were still twos and threes in front and behind him, chattering gaily about the gig. And then it happened. The shouts came first.

'Nigger lovers!'

'Commie scum!'

'Fucking coon-loving lesbo bitch!'

This last was delivered by a chubby skinhead who'd stepped out of an alleyway, arms spread wide and face contorted.

'Come on, you fucking commie slags!'

He didn't wait for the girl to speak, or cry. He kicked her in the groin and punched her smack in the face. Danny could hear the snap of her nose-burst from twenty feet away. A few more skins came into view, jumping up and down in front of the rabble of students, punks and hippies.

'Who wants it? Come on, you fucking filth!'

There was a crack and a horrible thud as a tall, studious-looking lad took a bony fist to the side of the head. As he fell, the skinheads circled him, kicking him in the stomach, the head, the backside. Trying to shield his face, he could barely wail, 'No! Please . . .'

Those already ahead of him came running back down the

road, panicked, faces wild with terror. Danny threw himself in front of them.

'Stand! Don't fucken run!'

They poured past him. Danny turned, screaming at his comrades.

'There's only a few of them! They're fucken shithouses!'

No one stopped. Yards away, the skins were still kicking fuck out of the student. One, two, three, four of them. Four boneheads, and they'd scattered nearly a hundred festival-goers! Danny ran in, fists and feet flying.

'Fuck off!'

He got the fat lad right in the balls, doubling him over. His mates backed off for a second. One of them could have been no more than thirteen. Danny stood back and smashed his foot into the leader's mouth, kicking him again as he went down.

'Come 'ead! Get into them! They're fuck all!'

He ran in again, catching the nearest skin with a glancing blow. It was hard enough to sting his own knuckle. More in shock than fear, the skins backed away, tried to encircle him but without real belief. Danny crouched down and went to spring again, and this time the youngest skin ran.

'Scouse cunt!' he squeaked.

The others helped the fat one to his feet, eyes flashing.

'We'll be seeing you, you cunt!'

'You're fucking marked, Scouse!'

Danny was panting now, and starting to shake with spent adrenalin.

'Come 'ead then if I'm marked! I'm fucken here, aren't I?'

They grappled their bulky leader off the road and across to the pavement. The skinny lad ran a finger across his throat.

'Next time, Scouse! You're a fucking dead man!'

'Ah fuck off, you quilt!'

He ran at them, and this time they were off. Dropping their mate on the floor, they fled to the pub on the periphery of the estate and slumped against a car for breath. As Danny went to check on the groaning student, the three skins *Sieg Heiled* and chanted at him: 'National Front! National Front!'

From out of nowhere came a vaguely familiar, nasal voice. 'This the best the master race can come up with?'

Mork stood over the still-groggy skinhead.

'You OK?'

The fat skinhead nodded painfully.

'Well, have some of that, you Nazi bastard!' He slammed his fist into the bonehead's nose.

Danny pulled him back. 'Come 'ead! He's had enough!'

The vendor turned his gleaming eyes on Danny. 'No, mate. The fash have never had enough until they're crushed.'

Danny shook his head and went to board the coach. She was there, waiting, face giving nothing away, yet he knew immediately there was trouble. She'd parked her rucksack on his seat and, now they'd made eye contact, she looked away, fixing her gaze outside the window. Meekly, he removed her rucksack.

'Can I sit here?'

She said nothing, just carried on looking out of the window. There was an ambulance outside, blue light strobing the student lad, laid out on a stretcher now. Danny sat down. He tried to take hold of her hand. She pulled it away. He sighed.

'Look. I'm sorry.'

She turned on him. 'What are you sorry for?'

He hung his head. 'I'm just sorry for letting you down.'

He beseeched her with his eyes. She turned to face him now, eyes flashing.

'Right. And how did you let me down, Danny? Hey? Was it by being a racist or by being a thug?'

He could hear how it'd sound before he even said the words, but say it he must.

'I was having a laugh with you. I'm sorry.'

He took her hand. She pulled it away. He hung his head.

'I'm sorry for not being the person you want me to be . . .'

Help came from an unlikely and thoroughly unwelcome source.

'Hey, guys!' smiled Mork, palms held up flat in mediation, eyes screwed tight in wisdom. 'Tell me to butt out if this is none of my business –'

'It's none of your business,' said Danny.

'Whoa! Mate! I come in peace!'

He grinned and held out a hand to shake. Danny stared at his purple and yellow braces. Mork turned to Nicole.

'I'm Gordon. And your chap here is no racist!'

She forced a smile. 'Really? I was under the impression that use of racist insults was proof of prejudice.'

'Yeah, yeah, I'm not saying I hold with that . . .'

Uninvited, he barged Danny along and perched himself on a seat that was already too small for two.

'But if you'd seen miladdo here chase the fash off just now –'

'Oh, I saw him all right.' She turned back to the window. 'I don't know which was more sickening. That, or his verbal attack.'

Gordon shook his head knowingly, infuriating her.

'No, no, no. You've got it all wrong! What you saw just now was an object lesson in direct action. You may not like violence – who does? – but what your man . . .'

He paused for Danny to prompt him. He did so, sullenly.

'Danny.'

'What Danny's just shown is that all the peaceful protest in the world makes less impression on these bastards than a boot to the balls. I'm perfectly serious. And I don't think Danny would have been driven to violence if he didn't believe strongly in the cause.' He got up and pointed a finger at her. 'Think about it.'

She shook her head and scowled at Danny. Gordon dug into his combat trousers and pulled out a leaflet.

'And you, Danny Dynamite, should have a look at this.'

It was a Socialist Workers Party flyer, calling volunteers to an anti-NF rally on May Day. Gordon winked and placed his hands together in a praying gesture.

'I hope you'll give us a call. We need men like you. And women.'

As he made his way down the aisle, handing out pamphlets, Danny watched him go.

'What a fucking whopper!'

And in spite of herself, Nicole couldn't help giggling. Danny was almost crying with relief.

'Friends?' he said.

'I need you to make me a promise.'

'I promise.'

'This is serious, Danny Boy. Yeah?'

'OK.'

'OK. I never want to see you do something like that again.'

'I won't.'

'You know what I'm talking about?'

'It's just that –'

'Shh! There's *no* justifying violence.'

'OK – but I never started it –'

'Just don't do it. Promise.'

He didn't feel as though he'd done any wrong. He wasn't a thug. He didn't look for fights. Sometimes things happened that were plain wrong, and what else could you do? Why could Nicole not see that? He gazed right into those clever, sparkling eyes and, for the first time, it hit home deep that he could not be without this girl. He was lost to her, for ever. He was hers for the taking.

'I promise you I will never use violence again.'

She nodded, and they kissed deeply from Swiss Cottage to Toddington Services.

Our Lady of the Flowers

From the dizzying swell of absolute happiness to this miserable, debilitating low in just a few hours. He sat with his back to their boulder and tugged forlornly at a weed, turning it all over in his mind. Perhaps he should just go back down and apologise, but no, she'd said what she'd said and, worse, she'd laughed in his face. How could she take that back? There was nothing she could say to make that right again.

They'd only just got back to the Ormecliffe Guest House and filled the feeble little kettle from the bath's spluttering tap. His heart was thumping. He didn't care what they did next – tea, sex, splay out on the bed smoking, anything – he was still recovering from the shocking spiritual high of being out there in that wild wind, up on the cliffs with the seagulls. Nicole had bounced on to the bed next to him, those azure eyes of hers on fire, shining with love for him and them and their bad, mad love. She put a finger over his mouth and held up her tatty copy of *The Waste Land*. She looked right at him, seemed unsure for a split second, then started reading:

> *'April is the cruellest month, breeding*
> *Lilacs out of the dead land, mixing*
> *Memory and desire, stirring*
> *Dull roots with spring rain . . .'*

She faltered, choking over the words. She looked up at him again. She tore the page from the book and flung herself upon him, kissing him and pulling at his jeans. They fucked quickly, holding each other's faces, tears in their eyes. When they'd recovered, she ripped the page from the book, tore it down the middle and gave him half.

'Never leave me, baby. Never go away.'

He crumpled up the page in his hand. It seemed like another girl in a different time. He shuffled the base of his spine right down against the rock, pulled the sleeves of his windcheater over his hands and hugged his knees, huddled against the blast and suck of the wind. This is where they had sat. This is where they had planned their lives. Had they not just done that, perhaps the Thatcher spat would have been less bitter. But they'd opened up their hearts, and both Danny and Nicole had been dreaming the same dream. Danny pointed to a squat black island, no more than a rocky crop jutting abruptly from the sea, miles out.

'I'd go there.'

'You couldn't live *there*!'

'Why not?'

'What would you eat?'

'Dunno. Anything. I'd fish.'

'Oh yeah! I can just see you sat patiently on a rock, waiting for the fish to bite . . .'

'I *would*. It wouldn't matter, anyway. I'd have you and my paintbrushes and no one else for miles around. We'd never see anyone else. Ah, yiss! It'd be paradise . . .'

She ruffled his hair. 'Oh, sweet nutter! You'll do for me!'

She heaved herself up, threw her head back and held her arms out wide and let the wind drive through her. Danny jumped up, wings out wide, too.

'Hey!'

'What?'

'Do this, right? Are you ready? Right. Just scream!'

'Scream?'

'Wooooooooh!'

She flashed him a smile, happy to play along.

'Yeah!'

'Nah, come on. Really let yourself go! Aaaaaaaaargh!'

'Aaaah!'

He came up behind her, cupped her breasts through the nylon of her cagoule and whispered in her ear: 'You'll have to do better than that if you want to live on Danny's desert island.'

They stumbled down the rocky path back towards the guest house, hand in hand, excited for the moment but eager for the next bit, scalding hot tea and afternoon bed.

As Danny stood under the miserable dribble of the shower, still panting from the fury of their sex, Nicole switched on the tiny TV, bracketed to the wall at such an angle that you had to lie down to watch its juddering picture.

'Fuck. Look who it is!'

He came to the bathroom door, leaned through and picked up the kettle.

'Tea or coffee?'

'Don't mind. Look, Danny – it's the Wicked Witch of the West!'

Over and over, Nicole would drill their meandering lovers' chat with rude political incursions. If Danny would so much as crave a chocolate biscuit at bedtime he was decadent, and he'd long since become used to her wild comparisons between him, and some obtuse philosopher or supposed revolutionary. She pulled him towards the bed.

'Look at her eyes. She's fucking insane!'

More than for any other public figure lately, Nicole's most sincere disdain had been reserved for the leader of the Conservative Party, Margaret Thatcher. Danny hadn't been too aware of her, by and large, but with Nicole by his side he had little choice but to sit still and listen.

'My God! She's . . . *evil*! Look at that hair! That *voice*! It's distilled arsenic!'

Thatcher was live from some conference, addressing an approving, adoring throng of blue-rinsed fogeys. And Nicole was horribly correct about Thatcher's voice. Pitched at some Elysian ideal of propriety, decency and strident English authority – somewhere between *Listen with Mother* and Fanny Craddock – Thatcher seemed to exude menace through the very timbre of her voice. Above her lacquered, immovable head, a slapdash banner read: BRITAIN WOULD BE BETTER OFF WITH THE CONSERVATIVES.

Below the slogan was a Union Jack, reinforcing the message of power through traditional values. Thatcher herself was the very model of a chaste Low Church worshipper, a modest spinster from the Women's Guild in her plain grey-and-white frock, adorned with a single grey bow. With glassy, unsympathetic eyes she cast her admonitory look around the rapt audience and continued.

'There is little point in crrrree-yayting prozzzz-byayree-tee if, having done it, we fear we might be attacked in the street or assaulted at home. And I believe that above all else . . .'

Her voice rose to a harsh, near-hysterical snap.

'. . . the people of this country wish to be protected against violence, theft and intimidation!'

It was too much for sections of the starchy crowd. They began to rise from their seats, applauding their saviour.

'Look at her!' hissed Nicole. 'She's fucking loving it! They think she's the Messiah!'

'She's just a aul' biddy!'

'But, Danny, look – she's evil! She's dangerous –'

'How can –'

But Nicole silenced him with a hand as Thatcher hit her stride.

'A grrrrreat dyiterrrrent to crrrrime is the prrrrob-ab-yilllity of being caught. But over the past four years that probability has receded. We don't give enough priority to getting the police force up to strength . . .'

The audience were on their feet again, applauding wildly. Nicole turned to Danny.

'Better get out the sandbags. She's coming, and she means us harm —'

'Behave! What's a crone like that going to do? Tell us off for using bad grammar?'

'Danny my love, I don't know if you've noticed but the country's changing. There's a whole mass of people out there who hate. They *hate*! They're looking for revenge. They hate all the wogs and Pakis. They hate all the punks and losers on the dole, hanging around outside the off-licence. They hate all the strikes and the shortages and the unions and Thatcher knows them all, intimately. They have one common credo and it starts with In My Day . . .'

'How's that affect you and me, though? We'll still have tea bags and paintbrushes, won't we — whatever happens . . .'

She turned her back on him. Without having to roll over and look, he could feel the heave of her breath, rising and falling in righteous anger.

'Danny,' she flashed back at him, 'I don't know if we're on the same side sometimes!'

'How do you mean, on the same *side*? There *are* no sides!'

She drove her eyes deep into him. 'Do you mean that?'

'Fucken right I do! *Sides*! All there is is . . . *things*. What happens happens and once it's done it's history. It's what went on. That's all.'

He held her baffled, angry stare until she spat it out.

'My God,' she whispered. 'You're an imbecile.'

Cut to the quick, he turned away, but she followed, pulled him back to face her again.

'Look at me, you prick! Do you *mean* that? Do you really mean what you just said?'

He didn't know if he meant it. It was what he'd felt at the time and it seemed about right.

'Yes.'

She held his look a moment then laughed in his face.

'You fucking halfwit!'

She barged into the little bathroom and slammed the door shut. It was fifteen minutes since she'd pledged her life to him.

Hurt beyond anything he'd ever known, Danny got up quietly and let himself out of the room. Eyes stinging and head down against the cut of the wind he hauled himself back up the rough path to the precipice. Below him was the wild black sea, tossing white spume and ragged seaweed against the rocks. He walked to the edge, looked right down at the daunting breakers, miles and miles of that depthless, turbulent abyss. Above, ebullient gulls soared up and up then dropped like stones, ten, twenty, thirty feet before flicking out their wings and coasting the rolling thermals. He stepped back from the ledge, retreated to their rock and sat down, numb with cold and sorrow. Even from there he could see and hear the relentless tide smashing against the pier, pummelling the anchored dinghies, again and again and again. He should go back to her. Ask her to explain. These things that meant so much to her – he should try to understand. That's what he'd do. He'd go back to the guest house. He couldn't. He pulled out the poem again, trying to make sense of it, torn diagonally from the top but almost whole at the bottom of the page:

> *What are the roots that clutch, what branches grow*
> *Out of this stony rubbish?*

He screwed it up again, gripped it tight in his fist but still couldn't bring himself to fling it out into the tempest. A timid voice whispered from behind.

'Danny. Baby.'

He turned and there she was, eyes red and sore from crying.

'I'm sorry.'

She ran to him and covered his face and neck with salty tears and kisses.

'I'm so, so sorry . . .'

'Me too, honeygirl . . .'

'No. No! Shhhh! It's me. It's all me. I just . . . I love you so much. I'd never, ever hurt you, Danny. I hate myself. Look . . .'

She held up her wrist and peeled away the torn poem she had clamped to it. As soon as she took her hand away, a tiny nick leaked a trickle of blood. She looked solemnly into his eyes.

'I hate myself. I did this . . .'

He pulled her pale wrist to his face then ducked and licked the wound clean. Nicole took his head in her hands and hugged it.

'Oh, baby,' she stuttered, still shuddering from sobs and barely able to get the words out. 'Where will it end?'

The Age of Reason

'You didn't honestly think that was *good*, did you? Tell the truth, Danny!'

'Look. Forget about it. We won't go. We'll just go and see Dylan if that's what you want.'

Revolver was on the TV and they were sprawled in the Watsons' front room. Mother, father and sister Harriet were away in Brittany and, at Danny's urgent behest, they'd moved in to mind the property and play house. With all but one of his O levels finished, these were wondrous times for Danny. For three days it had been bliss, walks in the hills, staying in, drinking wine – he was really starting to love red wine, especially the burgundies she made him sip, ever so slowly, kissing the droplets from his lips. He loved being with her, endless days spent alone, cooking meals for each other, doing nothing.

But the Bowie question would not go away.

'No, no – a deal's a deal. I said I'd come and see your fucking hero with you . . .'

'Come on, Nic. That was genius!'

'Genius?'

She sat up.

'That was just second-rate Kraftwerk, that was!'

'Ahhh – you're just being weird with me. You liked Human League, didn't you? Who were the other ones, the electronic band we seen the other week? Dalek I Love You! What about them?'

'They were completely different. They had ideas of their own –'

'Bowie's still Bowie.'

'Yeah. Ripping everyone else off –'

'You know you don't mean that. *Low* and *Heroes* are the two most innovative albums of the past year . . .'

'Brian Eno out-take albums. Turgid. Unlistenable.'

'OK. Suit yourself. We won't go.'

'Oh yeah – and have you hold it against me for the rest of our lives!'

'We won't go.'

'Look. We'll go. But I just want you to know that I can't – ever – come to terms with all that fascist shit. OK?'

With his first night at Bingley less than a week away now, Nicole hadn't so much cooled to the idea of Bowie live as revolted against him. With Danny repeatedly playing the albums – and in particular *Station to Station*, *Low* and *Heroes* – Nicole had decided Bowie was a fascist, and a talentless one at that. This was in no small measure a self-defence mechanism to bolster her newly revealed devotion to Bob Dylan. This had perplexed Danny. Seemingly, her Dylan worship had come out of nowhere. He and Nicole met before a Wire concert. They'd spent their courtship, more or less, in underground clubs listening to alternative music. They liked the same things – more or less. It had never been articulated, but there was an understanding between them – they were complicit in the same indie pact that held that all hippie music was to be ridiculed, condemned and buried for ever. That basis for progressive living had mainly gone unchallenged between them – until the Dylan festival was announced.

He recalled it all too clearly. She'd come bouncing in through his front door one day, brandishing *Sounds*, barely able to get the words out: Bob Dylan was to play his first live UK show in years. Blackbushe Aerodrome, 15 July 1978. Danny had rarely seen Nicole so excited.

'We've *got* to go!'

'*Dylan?*'

'Bob fucking Dylan, man! We *have* to be there . . .'

In truth, Danny was not intimately familiar with the Dylan canon. He'd heard bits and pieces, formed the opinion that he was old and boring and sang through his nose and that was that. He hated Dylan. He was a hippie. Nicole waved *Sounds* in his face and said the wrong thing.

'Danny. Bob Dylan! Here! Roberto Zimmerman! The godfather of protest! Are you completely fucking ignorant?'

Reflexively, Danny went on the attack.

'He's boring.'

She turned away, then turned back to him, dumbfounded. Her mouth fell open but no words came out. Instead Danny grinned at her, held his nose and whined, 'Heeeeeeey Mister Tam-boring man, bore us all to death!'

'Oh, fuck off!'

'You fuck off!'

'You know what you are? You're a caveman!'

Danny leapt up, angry too now. 'No! *He's* a fucking caveman! That fucking dead-as-a-dodo folkie hippie dino-rod you want to see!'

She sat down, eyes blazing. 'Come on then. Tell me. Explain to me what's so bad about wanting to see Bob Dylan.'

Already he knew she was baiting him, coaxing him into her lair, but this time he felt ready. He had right on his side. And this time he didn't lunge in. He stood back, and reasoned with her.

'I'm surprised at you.'

'Why? Because I like great music? That surprises you?'

'I didn't know you were into all that hippie shit . . .'

She shook her head in despair. 'Hippie shit . . .'

'I mean, what else do you want to admit to? Are you secretly into Camel?'

'Fuck off, Danny! We're talking Bob Dylan, here. Is he a hippie? I don't know! I've never fucking thought about it. If he is then he is –'

'He's irrelevant. That's what he is –'

'And Leonard Cohen isn't?'

'Leonard's cool.'

'Why? Because he's on the jukebox at Eric's? Because they programmed you to think he's cool?'

'Don't talk daft, girl. "Famous Blue Raincoat". End of debate.'

'An acoustic guitar and a tone-deaf "spiritual" bird wailing in the background, if memory serves . . . that's not hippie shit?'

'Nic. You *love* Leonard. Don't start acting like you don't dig him. Tell me this. Does your little sister play your Leonard Cohen records?'

'Course she doesn't.'

'Can she sing you five Bob Dylan songs?'

'Jesus! So you're using elitism as your acid test, now? Come on then, Danny – let's go all the way! Are you going to tell me you don't like the Beatles?'

'The Beatles? Fuck, no! They're shite.'

'Oh. Dear. Me. You really are a prick, aren't you?'

'Hey, hey – hold on! I'm just telling you I don't personally like this overrated band that every Tom, Dick and Harry's into. How does that make me a prick?'

'Because you *do* like them but you won't admit it because you don't think it's *cool*!'

'I don't! I genuinely do not like the Beatles!'

'*Everyone* likes the Beatles!'

'*I* don't . . .'

The amnesty was frail. As June slipped by, scorching hot and slow, and Bowie's Bingley shows drew nearer, Danny knew she'd be a reluctant companion. He tried to seduce her with tales of his innocent early youth. While all the other lads in his class were getting into Slade, he was tearing out the full-colour pictures of Marc Bolan and David Bowie from his sisters' *Jackie* magazines. Aged only eleven, and plastered in his mother's Avon face-cake, he'd stolen in at the stage door of the Liverpool Stadium to witness what he could of the Ziggy Stardust show. Spellbound, he'd fallen hugely for the glamour of Bowie, forsaking all others to follow his idol. In sharing his first crush with her he hoped she'd relent, but it was looking bleak. His *Revolver* performance complete, the Thin White Duke was still smiling his crooked smile on the telly, looking away from the lens, knowing exactly where it was.

'He is *not* a fascist!'

'Don't get me started, Danny . . .'

'Bowie's now. Dylan's then. End of story.' He glared at her, surprised at how hurt he felt. 'What else would I expect from a girl from fucking Blackburn, anyway.'

The moment the barb left his lips, he regretted it. She stood dead still, staring at him for a moment, then dropped to the couch, silent. He reached for her wrist, but she tugged it away. Danny shuffled closer.

'Look. I'm sorry. I didn't mean that. You know I didn't.'

She turned her head away from him.

'We'll go and see Dylan, yeah?'

'No. We won't. *I* might . . .'

'Nic. I'm being nice here . . .'

In her heart of hearts, she knew she'd started the fight. It was up to her to end it.

'You've got to *want* to see him.'

'I *do*.' He shuffled up closer still, and put on his adenoidal Dylan voice again. 'I really *really* waaant to see Baaaab Dylan!'

She allowed herself a peep at him. She allowed herself a chuckle. And they were friends again.

'But if I'm going to Blackbushe with you, you've got to come and see Bowie with me.'

'*Bowie*? Bowie's a fucking fascist! I'm not going to see David Bowie!'

Nic's constant griping had started to wear him down anyway, and the essence of her detractions left a residue with him. *Was* Bowie a magician or a fraud? Was he still the Thin White Duke, or was he a pale and empty führer? And this big, huge, massive world tour: was it *really* the shock of the new, or just a gigantic piece of advertising? Did Bowie *matter* any more? She'd got to him, too true. But his decision to sell the Bingley tickets came all in a flash, all by himself. He was listening to John Peel in the way that he did – that is, half listening, half reading. He'd never really read before. He'd read *The Outsider* because he heard some Arties arguing over it, years ago – and when he picked it up at the library he was immediately sucked in. He'd looked at some of her course books and found them impenetrable. But she'd come good on her promise to lend him *The Thief's Journal* and he was loving it. It was full of queer episodes and madness, but it had a real passion, too – so throbbing with filth and energy and a lust for life. It was perfect for nights like this, radio on, only turning away from the page when something new grabbed his attention. A track came on, and it didn't just sit him up. It snagged his heart. It was all bass, the wiry guitar stabbing away above and beyond the song itself. And that voice. Everything about the song was, in the best of ways, soul-destroying.

> *We've been moving round in different situations*
> *Knowing that the time would come*
> *Just to see you torn apart*
> *Witness to your empty heart*
> *I need it. I need it. I need it . . .*

It was rough, badly recorded, pretty badly played. But that voice just haunted him.

'*I need it.*'

In ways he hadn't known in a long time, he was moved by music; the urgency, the hurt, the anger, the anguish all combined to take hold of him and stand him still.

'That was Joy Division. These are Throbbing Gristle.'

Danny's first thought was to leg it out to the phone box and tell Nicole all about them, tell her to get the radio on in case he played them again. Something held him back though, made him want to keep it to himself, for now. Peel's next pronouncement set it in stone. The band had a couple of dates coming up. Just the two, for now – in Liverpool and Leeds. The Liverpool gig was set for Eric's, on 15 July – same day as Dylan's Blackbushe jamboree. In an instant, Danny's mind was made up. He'd be attending neither the Bowie nor the Bob Dylan mega-gigs. He had other plans. He was going to be at Eric's to see this Joy Division.

The Deep End

She lay on her side, stroking his wet hair.

'You're getting freckles.'

'I've always had freckles.'

'You're getting more.'

'Make you love me more then, hey?'

She looked around the crowded terraces of the lido.

'Sure it's OK to skin up in here?'

Neck tensed, he raised his head an inch from the ground, shielding his eyes from the glare of the high sun. He scanned the peeling art deco arena of the pool and lay back down again.

'Yeah,' he drawled. 'They're not arsed here.'

He tuned out from the rustle of the grass and the sticky whip of the papers in her hands and listened to the babble of children and, further away, the whining protest of a speed-boat's engine, ploughing on through the choppy sea. A tinny transistor radio banged out Plastic Bertrand's summer hit, surreal in the context of New Brighton's open-air pool with scores of reddening mums and toddlers humming along in ill-heard French. The last droplets from his swim dried on his chest as he exhaled, happy – calm and happy to be lying there in the sunshine with his girl. He breathed in deep, sucking up the sweet smell of sinsemilla, and took the spliff from her hand. She ruffled his hair again.

'So, genius. How does it feel?'

'It feels good, babychild. It feels fucking ace.'

'I told you you'd walk it.'

'Still. Can't take nothing for granted, hey?'

'*You* can! You should start believing in yourself more. Anything you want to do, Danny Boy, anything at all – you can do it.'

'Yeah . . .'

She sat up again, eyes shining.

'I mean it! You don't seem to know how *good* you are!'

'Well. One thing at a time, hey? I'm in. That's the main thing.'

'Well, it *shouldn't* be the main thing. I think it's ridiculous making you do that stupid course . . . How's that going to improve you as a painter?'

'What if I *want* to do the course though?'

'You don't . . .'

'I might . . .'

'Two years being told Michelangelo was a half-decent painter and decorator?'

'Well . . . it is what it is. I do the foundation course, I go the art school . . . it's not the end of the world, is it? It's not like I'm having to do applied maths or something.'

'No. Just . . .'

'What?'

'I don't know. I'm just worried about them schooling all the brilliance out of you, I suppose. You're brilliant. You know that?'

He passed her the spliff, then sat up against the low wall.

'Wanna know what I know?'

'You absolutely love the living daylights out of me?'

'Yeah-yeah-yeah-yeah-yeah!'

He tickled her ribcage, taut and still wet through her swimsuit.

'Know what else?'

'No. What?'

'It's all I've ever wanted. I mean it. Long as I can remember, all I could ever picture me doing was going to that art school. The foundation course is just a part of it. It's a *good* thing, Nicole. I know we all want to get on with our lives and all that, but this is . . . it's *good*.'

She kissed him on the nose and whispered in his ear: 'I know it is. I just like things the way they are . . .'

He took another toke, and turned his head as he blew the sweet smoke up to the clouds. He could feel her staring at him. He turned to look at her, and her eyes were filmed with tears. She gripped his head firmly above his ears, looked into his eyes.

'Tell me you love me.'

He looked right back at her, stared into her beautiful wet eyes. He was looking at the girl in the Grapes all over again.

'More than anything in the world.'

She held his stare a moment longer, before getting up and going towards the diving boards. A big, cage-like structure dominated the deep end of the pool, a series of ladders leading up to platforms, each one higher than the last, each with a diving board jutting out abruptly over the azure-blue drop. Most of the skins and hard-knocks, the lads from Leasowe and Moreton and the North End, would venture halfway up, make a big thing of beating their chests and give a Tarzan wail before bombing off the boards into the thirty-foot depths. Nobody had been off the top board all day. Danny watched her climb; he thought she'd jump in off the first board, but she bypassed the first three platforms by heading straight up the middle ladder. From there, she could take one of the halfway dives – or go straight on up to the very top. She continued to the top board. A ripple of anticipation went around the poolside now, as people started to sit up. '*Ça Plane Pour Moi*' gave way to 'Let's All Chant' on Radio 1. Danny half stood, squatting by the low wall and eventually perching on its rim. He'd ribbed Nicole about her prim, matronly swimsuit all morning – now all he could see of his girlfriend was her bright blue costume.

'She's not gonna . . .'

A skinny lad with a blond flick swept his fringe out of his eyes for a better look.

'The last fella to go off there overshot the pool and splatted himself all over the café roof . . .'

His tattooed mate warmed to the subject.

'I heard about that. And the aul' fella what got caught in a big gust of wind and got blown back into the shallow end. His brains was all floating on the surface. Lifeguards had to mop it all into buckets . . .'

'She's not going in . . .'

Nicole stood perfectly poised, her back straight, her toes clutching the lip of the diving board like talons. She raised her arms above her head.

'Jesus! She's not even bombing it! She's gonna dive . . . she's gonna *dive*!'

'She's gonna *die*!'

Of all the craning onlookers, Danny alone remained dead calm. He knew Nicole was a keen swimmer – it had been her idea to spend the day with a picnic at New Brighton Baths. And, while they'd never discussed high-diving or underwater swimming or anything specific to the feat of audacity she was contemplating, he knew this about Nicole Watson: if she set her mind to something, she'd do it. He had not a shred of doubt that she'd execute the dive beautifully, and safely. With hardly any backlift, she launched herself up and out from the platform, leaning forward at a ninety-degree angle and plummeting quickly, only tipping herself forward into a full dive as the placid surface of the pool rose up to meet her. Plosh! She sliced into the water with minimal noise, emerging a few moments later slightly breathless and slightly embarrassed at the applause ringing around the terraced crescents of the open-air pool. She tried to suppress the smile that wanted to light up her face as she sat down next to Danny again.

'Me too,' she said.

He took her hand and pulled her down, closing his eyes until the attention died down.

Shadowplay

The two of them sat in front of the portable like they were waiting for news of war. Two weeks before he'd taken her down to Eric's to witness for herself the new obsession in his life. Nicole, too, had been blown away by Ian Curtis's frantic, wild-eyed dancing, his tender melancholy and the pain, the sheer monumental angst of his performance. He'd seen them three times since that night in July and they just got better and better. Tonight they were making their first telly appearance, on *So It Goes*.

'Look at him,' whispered Nicole.

'Shhh!'

'But look at his eyes. Such . . . *fear*.'

'I know. Shut up, will you . . .'

They watched the band in awed silence. Just the one song – 'Shadowplay' – but the intensity of the performance paralysed them.

'*To the depths of the ocean where all hope sank searching for you . . .*'

Even when Tony Wilson came back on, they sat still. Nicole took a huge, deep suck of breath, exhaled slowly and pushed herself up from the sofa.

'Do you want a cuppa?'

Danny nodded dumbly, eyes still fixed on the screen, and she went down the hall. They were as good as living together now, Danny spending most nights at her flat in Greenbank Road. With Ninna not so good he made regular guilt trips home, but his mother made it plain she could cope. More than that, she *wanted* it to work out, him and Nic. To Mrs May, Nicole was an integral part of Danny's making the most of his talent and his life. She could not have made it easier for her boy to leave home. Nicole returned with two steaming mugs of tea.

'You know – they could end all the stupid theories just by playing Brockwell Park.'

'How come?'

'God, Danny! You know what the Joy Division *was*?'

'Course I do!'

'Go on then . . .'

He grinned over the lip of his tea mug. 'Dunno!'

She flopped down, sighing out loud for extra significance. 'They were a specially selected squadron of prostitutes, reserved for the exclusive pleasure of the SS.'

'So? It's just a name, isn't it?'

'Yeah. So's the National Front.'

'Jeez! Does every band I'm into have to come with some sinister Nazi health warning?'

'I'm not *saying* that –'

'You have to read mad things into everything you, don't you?'

'I'm just pointing out the obvious, Danny. It's a dangerous game. They could do themselves a lot of favours by aligning themselves with Rock Against Racism.'

He took another slurp of his tea.

'I know what you're saying, but . . .' He, too, sighed deeply – but his was out of frustration. 'It's a hard one to put into words. But . . . thing is with Rock Against Racism and that . . . it's a bit . . . it's not that cool, is it? Do you know what I mean? Sham 69 and Elvis Costello – it doesn't exactly sit right with Joy Division, does it?'

'I don't see why not.'

He blew into his cup. 'I'm going to write to them.'

Her eyes lit up. 'Are you?'

'Yeah. Deffo.'

He met her eager look.

'Not about that, like. Not the Brockwell Park thing. I'm gonna see if I can do a sleeve for them.'

'Seriously?'

'Couldn't be *more* serious, girl.'

She just stared at him, eyes wide, grinning.

'Ah, Danny. That's just fantastic! I'm so –'

'Hey–hey–hey! They haven't said nothing, yet! Just because I'm writing to them don't mean I'm gonna get the nod.'

'Don't be so negative!'

'I'm not. Just saying – it's a long shot, isn't it?'

'But the fact that you're doing it . . . oh, Danny Boy! I could *eat* you!'

And between them they sat up and composed a letter to Mr Tony Wilson, care of Granada Television, Quay Street, Manchester, announcing the existence of Daniel May, artist to the stars.

Camera Lucida

The letter came the morning after the Dalek I Love You sofa gig. Thursday nights had evolved into something of a local band night at Eric's, with members getting in for nothing and a healthy clique of bands, real or imaginary, starting to throng the back bar, each vying to outdo the next with ever more elaborate and esoteric names – Echo and the Bunnymen, A Teardrop Explodes, Wah! Heat, Pink Military. Big In Japan were recording a live EP that very weekend, but even they, with their magnificently dirty stage act, would have their work cut out to trump the previous night's Dalek show. They'd trooped on to the tiny stage, lights out, no announcement, and this tinny, metronomic drum machine had kicked in. It sounded great, weird and other-worldly, but perfect for Eric's. Then gradually you could make out the band – sitting onstage, on a sofa. As though they'd suddenly noticed there was a crowd present, they got up, went to their instruments and started into 'Freedom Fighters'. He loved it, Danny. Nicole went along with his gushing excitement all the way home, curbing her tendency to challenge him right until the key grated in the crunchy front-door lock and only then just to quieten him down.

'They weren't *that* good, Danny.'

'I'm telling you, doll. These are the ones. Out of all that Eric's crew, these are gonna go all the way.'

'We'll see.'

'We will. Believe it.'

They stared at the letter and turned it over and over, searching for clues before carefully slitting it open. It was dated 6 December 1978 and it came from a Manchester-based company, Peter Saville Associates. He felt faint. He passed the letter to Nicole and sat down.

'Go 'ead then. Give us the bad news.'

For a moment she said nothing, then let out a high-pitched whoop.

'Danny!'

'What?'

'They *love* you!'

'They don't!'

She clutched the letter tight, jumped on top of him and smothered his face with kisses.

'Oh, Danny, Danny, Danny! Listen!'

He wanted to stay calm and savour the moment, but he couldn't keep the grin off his face.

'Come on then!'

Beaming, she stood up, cleared her throat and did her best to execute a newsreader's gravitas.

'*Dear Daniel May, We are retained by Factory Records, who passed me your letter and work samples for consideration —*'

'Fancy!'

'Shhh! Listen!'

'My apologies for this late response to your proposals, which were passed to me by Rob Gretton some weeks ago, but subsequently misfiled. We are always keen to view the work of the region's best young artists, and there's no doubt you have talent and ideas in abundance.

'Did you hear that, *Daniel May*?'

'Oh yiss-yiss-yiss! I heard it all right! Move over, you – here comes Danny Boy!'

'Talent and ideas in *abundance*!'

'Is that it then? Is that all's they're saying about us?'

'Shut up, bighead!'

She continued. *'Here at PSA we are currently working to a graphic/photographic aesthetic –'*

'A what?!'

'– graphic/photographic aesthetic, so it is unlikely we'd pursue your ideas as laid out here. However, we'd certainly be interested in meeting if you should find yourself in Manchester in the future, especially if you were to come with concepts that fit closer to the PSA ethos. I am returning your file and wish you well with your work both now and in the future. Sincerely, Peter Saville.'

He looked up at her. She grinned back down at him.

'Waaaaaaaaah! Waaaaaaaaah! Woooooh!'

He jumped up, grabbed her round the neck and flung her round and round, screaming for sheer joy.

'Oh my fucking God, la!'

She gripped him by the ears, staring madly into his eyes.

'Danny! You've *got* to go and see them!'

'Not *now*!'

'No, no, but, baby – go soon, yeah? Go while they're hot for you!'

'I haven't got no what-d'you-mah-call-it . . .'

'What?'

'The design aesthetic thing. What'd I take with me?'

She circled the mottled rug by the two-bar fire.

'Yes!'

'What?'

She took his hand, excited now. 'Remember the photomontage guy I was telling you about? John Heartfield? The anti-Nazi guy . . .'

Danny chewed his lip. 'Remind us . . .'

'Oh, Danny, I *knew* you wouldn't go. They had an exhibition at the Open Eye in the summer.'

'I was *revising*, weren't I?'

'Well, listen, listen . . . Heartfield's just perfect. Nobody's used him at all. And with that kind of subverting Nazi imagery thing that Factory like to play with, I mean . . . God, Danny, it's perfect! You take along a mock-up of one of Heartfield's images, put a classical, *really* serious font over it . . . What's up?'

He'd ceased the manic grinning and sat down again.

'It's not my idea, is it? It's your idea . . .'

'What does it matter who thought of it first? It gets you through the door, doesn't it? That's the main thing.'

'Yeah but, babychild, I know you're wanting to support me and all of that, but I've got to do it myself. Do you know what I mean? It's got to be *me*.'

She was stung, but let him be. For three or four days the letter wasn't even mentioned. But on the last day of term, drunk after a Christmas tipple with her tutorial group and professor, Nicole stumbled in to find Danny hunched over a collection of photographs on their rickety dining table.

'What d'you reckon?' he muttered, not even looking up. She could hear the pleasure in his voice. She leaned over his shoulder. There were sixteen prints laid out, austere images of gravestones, a sandstone crucifix and other religious icons. Most were dappled with a queer sunlight, freckled through the trees and leaves. They had a dignity and timelessness she found impressive and moving.

'My God, Danny . . .' She took a closer look. 'Did *you* take these?'

'Yep!'

'My. God.' She straightened up. 'But, Danny, I mean . . . what with? Where d'you get the camera? How did you *do* this?' She let out one sharp, astonished laugh. '*When?*'

He got up from the table, pleased.

'Fella from the college lent it us. He's all right. Runs the photography course, night school mainly. Said I wouldn't mind having a go. Could only afford a little roll of black and white, like, but they don't seem to mind that at Factory, do they? Seem to prefer it, if you ask me . . .'

'Danny – they're going to *love* this work! My God, boy – you are a fucking miracle! Come here! Let me touch you, O chosen one! Let me kiss your feet . . .'

She crouched down on her knees and he had a sudden flush of euphoria, a flashback to their first night together, Nicole on her knees in the Casablanca, smelling his damp shoes. How far they'd come already – and how much his life had changed. He felt dizzy with happiness, a warm and general well-being that sprang from deep within, giving out a tingling, thrilling optimism. He was going to do it, all right. He was going to make it! Him and Nic, they were going to the stars together.

'So. What d'you want for Christmas?'

She threw her arms around him and kissed him hard.

'Nothing. You.'

'Oh. You won't want this, then?'

He dived behind the couch and pulled out a flat, board-shaped package, beautifully wrapped with silver bows and a plain silver gift tag.

'But . . . it's not Christmas yet!'

'I know, I know. I've got you loads! I just wanted to give you this one now . . .'

She shrunk her head into her shoulders.

'Are you sure?'

'I'm sure I'm sure!'

She gave a little whoop and a clap of her hands, snatched up the parcel and flung herself down on the couch.

'Wow! This is so naughty, opening prezzies when it's not even time . . .'

'Be assured, you will pay the ultimate price in Purgatory . . .'

She went to give a clever answer, tore the last strip of wrapping from the package and sat back, stunned. Danny had created a collage, a likeness of her so real that it could almost talk. He'd glued hundreds and hundreds of shreds and scraps of paper on to hardboard, subtly shading each element, until, painstakingly, he had her. It was uncanny. It was Nicole. She had never gazed on anything so beautiful and so frightening in her life. For a full minute she let her fingers run lightly across the rough surface before remembering he was with her. She looked up, shocked and humble.

'Danny, I . . .'

Half out of awkwardness, half to rescue her from this dumb and grateful stasis, he tugged her up by the hands.

'Come on then! What have you got *me*?!'

It was an altogether different calibre of shock that surged through Danny as he tore open his box to discover a Bullworker as his prize. He hugged her close with all his heart nonetheless.

1979

The Master Race

'You've got to admit it – from a design point of view, that's a brilliant logo!'

'It's . . . simplistic, yes. There's a lot to be said for simplicity.'

'Specially when your target group are a gang of deadheads who probably can't even *spell* NF!'

She snorted a half-laugh and threw the leaflet down again.

'Well, whoever they are, they're having no trouble getting *that* all over the place. I'm worried, Danny. I really think they'll do some major damage, you know –'

'Nah! No fucking way! It's the same few divvies going round spraying it everywhere. They've got no chance of getting in.'

'I know they won't get in – but they could really divide the vote. Gordon reckons there's five thousand expected on Sunday –'

'Five thousand! As if.'

'He's deadly serious, mate. They've got moles inside the National Front and they reckon they've booked over a hundred coaches to get them all in to New Brighton –'

'I will absolutely fucking eat my deerstalker if they have more than two hundred fat lads on the day.'

'Well, we'll see, won't we?'

'We will.'

'Danny – we *are* going?'

'Too right we are. I know how much all this means to you, babe. I wouldn't let you down.'

She thought about upbraiding him, reminding him that this wasn't *her* cause, but one look at his eager, obliging face and she caved in. She kissed him on the cheek.

'We need manpower as well as goodwill. If there's any handy lads you know from round Tocky and that . . .'

'They'll all be there, mate. I only seen Billy Adu out with his megaphone the other day.'

'I do hope so . . .'

'Count on it. Mork doesn't have to shit hisself. All hands'll be there.'

As the election drew closer, she'd got more and more deeply involved with the SWP again. They, more than any other organisation, were taking the threat of the NF's Easter Sunday rally at New Brighton Baths deadly seriously. It irked him to hear her coming home, spouting Gordon's latest conspiracy theories verbatim, but it kept her from rattling his cage about his art, work, Factory, ambitions. He'd never heard back about his photographs but at no stage did he get down about it. These were artists, not business people – they'd probably lost the package in the Christmas post. He'd *told* Nicole they should wait until New Year, do it as a fresh start, but she wouldn't hear of it. That very next morning she'd marched him to Smithdown Road and stood over him while he posted off his pictures. Every so often she'd ask him if he'd heard anything, even volunteered to telephone them, but now Callaghan's inevitable calling of the election pushed it right out of her mind. Three times a week at first and, this last fort-night, every single night she'd been out with Gordon and the unit, pamphleting, heckling, selling the magazine and trying to drum up support. She was excited, he sensed. She was gimlet-eyed and motivated. She picked up the NF leaflet again.

'Maybe you should send *that* to Factory.'

He pulled a sarcastic smile and screwed the flyer into a ball.

By nine o'clock on the Sunday morning, the café by New Brighton Station was packed tight – but there were precious few people on the streets outside. Persistent drizzle and rumours that the entire exercise was a National Front decoy to deflect police and protestors away from their true venue combined to damp the vim of volunteers. But it was early in the day, and with the NF convoy not expected until midday at the earliest, there was time yet to muster a more impressive mob. A tall, strikingly handsome black man with a Zapata moustache came in and clapped Danny on the back.

'All right, lad? So – do we reckon the fash are gonna show?'

'No fucken chance, la. One sad coach at best.'

'Bit early for them, hey? Couldn't picture too many early risers in that shower.'

Nicole over-laughed at this, eyes shining up at him, waiting to be introduced.

'Do you know me girl, Billy? This is Nicole. Nic, this an aul' mate of the family, Billy Adu. Done a lot of good work for the area, Billy has.'

'Has he fuck! Pleased to meet you, girl.'

She almost swooned as his huge hand smothered hers with a surprisingly gentle grip.

'Well, fellas, ta for turning out. Can't be too careful with these twats – pardon me, darling. I don't usually swear but there's something about these *fucking Nazi bastards* . . .' Again, she contorted her face with laughter, covering her mouth self-consciously. Billy clapped Danny on the shoulder again.

'I'll keep youse posted, kidder. Tara.'

'See you, Billy, man.'

Billy loped back towards the door. By the wall, Gordon

was earnestly trying to make eye contact, first with Billy as he passed by, then with Nicole.

'He seemed nice,' she said.

'Good lad, Billy A. One of the best.'

Gordon loomed over them.

'Friend of yours?'

Without quite knowing why, Danny had taken against Gordon severely. For Nicole's sake he was polite, but his dealings with Gordon had become terse, accompanied by minimal eye contact. Right now he could feel Nicole willing him to be nice, to give Gordon the feedback he was craving. But Danny couldn't do it. There was something sly and opportunistic about Gordon's basic demeanour, things he might not have been able to control or adjust, but at base level he made Danny anxious, and angry.

'Known him a while, mate, yeah.'

'And may I ask the comrade's name?'

'Billy.'

'Billy . . . ?'

He waited for Danny to fill in the gaps. Nicole kicked him under the table and flashed a smile up at Gordon.

'Billy Adu, his name is, Gordon. He's a community leader round the Lodge Lane area . . .'

Danny could feel the pique in her voice and moved quickly to appease her.

'Granby, he's from. Does a lot of work down the centre.'

'The centre. Right.'

He stood off, hanging behind them, hoping for more, but Danny bent back to his *Sunday Mirror*.

'Careful of that rag, son,' laughed Gordon. 'They call themselves socialist, but I don't see much between them and John fucking Junor.'

'I only read the sports pages,' lied Danny.

Nicole could have stabbed him with her fork, she was so cross with him. Why did he have to act like this whenever her friends from the party were around. He'd even programmed her to cease calling them 'brothers' or 'comrades' by virtue of his puerile sniggering every time she did so. She swallowed her bile, took a deep breath and decided they'd have to confront this properly once they got back to the flat. Right now, there were bigger battles to fight.

Danny paced up and down outside the station, whistling softly, tucking his hands under his armpits for warmth. He smiled to himself all of a sudden, belatedly recognising the tune he'd been whistling – 'Jilted John' by Jilted John. How weird, the way the mind kept ticking while the brain was taking a nap! He gave a little chuckle and stood back to get a proper look at the turnout. There was a much bigger crowd now, with some hard-looking fellas in donkey jackets standing back on the main road, looking down the hill towards the promenade. Nicole was huddled with the *Socialist Worker* sellers under an ornate cast-iron lamp-post. Danny had read her face and recognised the warning signs all too well. This was not the time nor the place to ask her how many of her new friends actually *worked*.

The clatter of footsteps and panicked shouting preceded the sight of about twenty or thirty young punks, some of them faces he knew from Eric's, running up the hill towards them. Behind, truncheons drawn but in sluggish pursuit, was a phalanx of red-faced policemen. A girl with large round spectacles jumped into the road, fists clenched. She turned to face the crowd and, face distorted with rage, screamed: 'Pigs! Get the fucking pigs!'

A roar went up and, as though this were the signal they'd all been waiting for, the majority of the mob surged down the sloping road. Some of the younger lads stooped to pick up bricks, bottles, anything they could launch at the police, but as glass started exploding at their feet and the police began to back off, Billy Adu ran out up front with his megaphone, three or four of the donkey-jacket crew by his side.

'Yo! Stop! Quit the fucking madness, will youse!' He pushed a couple of hyped-up black boys back up the hill. 'Youse are playing right into their hands! These Babylon twats are just *itching* for this! Just one of them bastards gets a cut hand and they'll have the whole fucking SPG down here, just like that! They're waiting round the corner now, just *waiting* for us to give them a excuse . . .'

The donkey jackets nodded. A fat lady in a kaftan came and relieved Billy of the megaphone.

'Brothers! Sisters! Who's the real enemy here?'

Some young lads started smirking at each other.

'The filth!'

'Plod!'

'The fucken bizzies!'

'You are!'

The woman continued. 'Who have we come here to tell, in no uncertain terms, that their presence is not required on Merseyside?'

Nicole's voice rang out: 'The fascist scum!'

Then it was Gordon. 'Smash the National Front!'

Rallying together, the *Socialist Worker* gang struck up their familiar chant: 'The National Front is a Nazi front . . . SMASH THE NATIONAL FRONT!'

Down below, more and more police were arriving, piling out of specialist Transit vehicles and lining up right across the bottom of the hill. The punks were in earnest conversation with Billy Adu, gesticulating wildly and pointing down the hill. A Lambretta screeched round the corner, skidding to a halt. Another purple-haired punk jumped off, along with a kid in a parka.

'Here y'are!' shouted the punk. 'They're here!'

The crowd began eddying this way and that, all trying to get close, tense to breaking point. The police line continued its way up the hill in a slow, very deliberate march. Billy snatched up the megaphone again.

'People. Thanks for waiting. We're getting word that the fascist coaches are making their way *under armed police guard* . . .'

More bottles flew through the air with chants of 'Filth! Filth! Filth!' One livid punk spat hopelessly into the wind. Billy held his arm up.

'As youse can see, we have company today. Our friends here from race relations . . .' He bowed theatrically at the police line. '. . . are keen that our welcoming committee shouldn't actually get to say hello to the *fucking NF scum*!'

The crowd began pogoing on the spot, fists beating out a rhythmic chant.

'Scum! Scum! Nazi scum!'

The police line was now within a hundred yards of them. Billy had to shout to be heard.

'Everybody! We're going to have to use our heads here, as well as our fists and boots – God willing. If you'll all follow our fast music-loving comrades here, they'll show youse through the backstreets down on to the prom. Listen up! I'll tell you now, people – there's gonna be bloodshed down there. Some of youse are gonna get nicked. Anyone who wants to bow out now, youse are all still heroes. But from the moment we get down there, this is us against them. Are youse with me? This is a fucking war!'

And that was it. A blood-curdling scream went up from the girl in glasses, and she charged out into the street, flinging herself head first into the police line. The shock of the attack put them on the back foot momentarily, and the punk squadron – led by the prattling Lambretta – skewed off down Victoria Road and left then right, left then right, weaving in and out of the backstreets and alleyways of New Brighton, through ornamental public gardens and down on to the once-grand esplanade. Up ahead, the heavily escorted trail of coaches was being dragooned into columns directly outside the main entrance to the swimming baths. Nicole arrived by Danny's side, breathless.

'Bastards!' she panted. 'How fucking dare they!'

He looked down at her flushed face and angry, sparkling eyes and he wanted nothing more than to kiss her. The look she returned was tender, though shot through with fear.

'You gonna be OK, honeygirl?'

She took a deep breath. 'I'll be fine. Yeah.'

'Well – just stick close to me.' He kissed her on the nose. 'I'll knock 'em down, you stamp on their big fat heads!'

'Scumbags . . .'

'Probably won't be able to get anywhere near 'em. Look at that!'

More and more police piled out of unmarked vans, linking arms in the middle of the broad main road. Nicole clung to Danny's arm.

'I just want to see what the bastards look like,' she muttered. Danny leaned into her ear.

'They have one eye . . . thick, butchers' wrists . . . and *very* tiny penises!'

A brick zipped through the air, crashing down on the roof of a police van. The line of coppers held firm, hardly registering any reaction at all. More and more bricks and bottles whizzed and crashed, the bottles giving off an unearthly looping wail as they spun and wobbled in flight. The police line took a step back, then another, taking themselves out of range. The younger element in the mob burst forward, running into the coppers with kicks and blows, making little real impact. Suddenly a lad in a combat jacket started jumping up and down, almost foaming at the mouth.

'There he is! There's the bastard! Fucking . . .'

The sheer venom of his fury wiped him out, rendering him mute with rage. Nicole gripped Danny tight.

'Fuck! It's Webster . . .'

It was him. Ashen, eyes darting around scared as the police

escorted them from their coach, Martin Webster and company seemed dwarfed by the attention they'd generated. Webster kept his eyes firmly on the floor as his guard pushed him on towards the main entrance. Slow and flabby, and dressed in a nondescript V-neck jumper and slacks, he was nothing if not perfectly ordinary. He shuffled on, getting ahead of himself, eager to get inside, away from the baying nasties hurling abuse and bottles from beyond the police lines. But as he got closer to sanctuary he couldn't resist a quick glance up and around him, his fat lips smirking back at his right-hand men.

'*That's* the fucking leader?'

'Looks like George Roper!'

A ripple of laughter greeted Danny's quip, but the good humour lasted seconds. Bringing up the rear, Webster's bullish minders turned, and began to give the crowd their Nazi salute from behind the safety of the police ranks. That was it. The protestors poured forward in waves, piling into the police to get at the NF. Even women with pushchairs took their chances, getting right into constables' faces.

'Why you protecting them? Why you looking after that scum?'

No answer.

'Who's paying for your overtime? *I* am, that's who!'

One fresh young copper couldn't resist a smirk. 'Thanks, ma'am. I'll toast you in the pub later on.'

She slapped his face hard and ran back to her child, as though regaining contact with the hands of her pushchair would make her safe. Other mothers and fellow protestors tried to swallow her up in their mass, but the police were playing to different rules. Waiting for the nod, a snatch squad dived out into the crowd and pulled the woman back, dragging her away from the pushchair, away from her frightened infant.

'Hey! Hey!' The woman in the kaftan ran after the arresting

officers. 'You can't do that! That's her baby there! You can't separate a mother from her child!'

Two young constables checked around and about, then took an arm each.

'Fuck off, Mama Cass! Just watch us!'

'If *you* don't fuck off, you'll get it too . . .'

They flung her back towards a knot of angry, powerless mothers. The child was screaming wildly now, distressed by the commotion all around.

'*You* look after the little bastard!' shouted the first copper. 'Your tits are big enough!'

Pleased with their work and their wit, they rejoined the ranks, by now coming under serious attack from three sides. Webster's brief appearance had fanned the flames, but with the NF now safely inside the baths congratulating themselves on a well-worked operation, it was the police, not the fascists, who were in the main line of fire. Nicole dragged Danny to one side.

'Shit! Danny!'

Three, then four, then five coppers were in the middle of the boulevard, trying to drag Billy Adu to the ground. One officer punched him repeatedly in the ribs, while another swiped him across the shoulders with his truncheon.

'Can't we *do* something?!' shrieked Nicole.

'Fucking right we can . . .'

Danny flew across the road, launching himself into a near-horizontal jump kick. Both feet crashed into the copper's back, sending him sprawling to the ground. Danny stood back and booted him again, then turned to pull another of them off Billy's back.

'Get down, nigger! Lie fucking down!' the copper was shouting. With each insult and each threat he truncheon-whipped him hard across the back and shoulders. Nicole jumped up and down in front of him.

'Fascist! Filth! This is fucking police brutality!'

She spat in his face, neat white spittle speckling his ginger moustache. Before she could draw breath again a fist slammed into her cheekbone.

When she came to, Nicole found herself on a deep sofa in a big, airy house with huge sash windows, open wide. Outside, she could see three lone stars, and hear the call of seabirds. Danny was sat over her, holding ice cubes wrapped in a face-cloth to her eye.

'Is it bad?' she whispered.

'Bully Beef,' grinned Danny.

She winced. The kaftan woman came in with camomile tea and home-made brandy.

'For the heroine of the hour,' she smiled, pouring a small measure of the brandy and holding it to Nicole's lips.

'How's Billy?'

'He's sound. He got away.'

Nicole nodded, recollections coming thick and fast now.

'That poor woman with the baby?'

The woman withdrew the glass and mopped Nicole's lips like she'd just taken communion.

'She's out. The police have dropped all charges against her – so long as she makes no complaint against them . . .'

Nicole jerked her head, then winced. 'Bastards! She's not standing for that, is she?'

The woman shrugged. 'She's got a family. These things take up time. Got to be realistic about stuff like this . . .'

Nicole sat up. 'Well, sod it then! *I've* got time. Get me to hospital for a full report. I'm suing those bastards!'

The kaftan woman's face lit up. '*That's* what I like to hear!' she beamed. 'A victory for common sense!' She leaned over and kissed Nicole on the forehead. 'A victory for democracy. And a victory for the man in the street!'

But as they drove towards Mill Road Hospital in the woman's 2CV and Danny regaled her with tales of the wreckage they'd wrought on the NF coaches, it didn't feel much of a victory

of any sort to Nicole. Her face ached madly and her mouth –
and her world – tasted vile.

The Iron Lady

It was a downbeat Danny queuing up for the Amnesty
International gig at Eric's. Nicole was bugging him on two
counts. Firstly, she'd taken to wearing this huge, badly made
orange badge that said BLONDIE IS A GROUP. The more he
ribbed her about it, the more devoutly she wore it. Worse,
though, she'd started to develop a real downer about the election. The queue pushed on slowly, but Nicole never let up.

'We may as well face facts now, Danny Boy. She's in. That
woman is fucking *in*. And that's curtains, you know. That's the
end of the State. Yeah?'

Danny, speaking low and almost to himself, muttered into
her ear. 'I know, I know, I *know*. But come on. In day-to-day
terms. In ways that's going to touch you and me. For once,
honeygirl, just think on this: what real difference is it going
to make if she *does* get in?'

She shot him a look but said nothing.

'Is it going to stop you loving me? If Thatcher gets in, is
she going to ban us from seeing each other?'

Unusually, this seemed to mollify Nicole. For the past fort-
night the entire election question had engulfed her, taking over
her life to a point where she couldn't even study. With key Year
Twos coming up she needed to be cramming, but each new
Thatcher utterance, every Keith Joseph smile and Norman Tebbit
glare threw her into a tailspin. In particular, she couldn't cope
with the idea of ordinary people falling for Thatcher's line.
She'd burst through the front door in tears at least three times
that week, having taken some gnarled pensioner or some over-
burdened mother to task on the bus, and being left in no doubt
that she was an unwanted, over-privileged nosy parker.

'Fuck off, you, you woolly back!' one hard-faced checkout girl shrilled at her when she butted in with what she saw as a simple dissemination on monetarism. 'Who the fuck asked *you*?'

She snuggled into Danny's side.

'You're right, you know. Come what may, May — we'll always have each other.'

He squeezed her hand tight and shuffled closer to the door. This was their third night here in a row. Tuesday had been Nicole's Philosophy Department's May Day bash with the Passions and Those Naughty Lumps. The previous night was a free Here & Now roadshow, and tonight, on the eve of the general election, it was the Amnesty International benefit gig: seventy-five new pence for Fireplace, the Passage and Joy Division.

'How come the Passage are headlining, anyway?' murmured Nicole.

'He's on the telly, isn't he? That Dick Witts. On Granada all the time. Smiling.'

She chuckled and pinched his bottom. 'He can smile all he wants. Everyone'll go home once Joy Division have been on.'

Danny shot her a sly look. 'Got to be up early to welcome Maggie in, hey?'

She jabbed him in the ribs. 'That's no laughing matter, Danny. That woman is going to sail in tomorrow and turn our world upside down. Believe it. This is like the *Titanic* going down! These are the final few hours of the age of reason!'

He smiled faintly and, backlit by Eric's dim entrance lamp, kissed her with all his heart.

'Come on. Let's see civilisation out with a bang!'

By any standard, the Joy Division show was explosive. Every gig they'd seen had been better than the last, but this was a leap forward in every sense. The band seemed wired, electrified, different and more cocksure than before. They were aggressive, abrasive, sinuous and utterly mesmerising – and they played exactly five songs before Ian Curtis keeled over exhausted at the side of the stage. Stories of his epilepsy had started to filter into write-ups in the *NME* and *Sounds*. Nicole shouted into Danny's ear.

'He *is*, Danny! He's doing it to himself! He's willed himself into a higher fucking state out there! Call it the ecstasy of performance – seriously, he's just worked himself up and out of his body . . .'

Danny laughed and hugged her close as the crowd clamoured for more. 'Yeah-yeah, ecstasy of performance! More! Wooooh!'

She struggled free, eager to ram her point home. 'Call it what you want, my darling, but that guy has just brought a fit on himself. I mean it. He's effectively imitated all those throes and convulsions to the point that it's almost fucking killed him.'

'Well, if he *has* – wooooh! More! Yes! Yeeee-yay-ess!' He turned and looked into his girlfriend's eyes. 'If that's what he's done then he's even more God than he was half an hour ago . . .'

The band didn't come back on and, forgoing the pleasure of the Passage, they strolled back up Bold Street with every intention of stopping off at the Casablanca. But up ahead a mob of Checkers girls were dancing right down the middle of Hardman Street, shrilly belting out the chorus of 'Ring My Bell'. Danny and Nicole ducked right at Chaucer's to avoid them, taking the short cut past the Pilgrim and through the art school's grounds. Danny stopped and looked up at the great Georgian edifice.

'This time next year, honeygirl!'

'Fifteen months, to be precise – *if* you get in!' she teased.

'Well, if I *don't* . . .' He pulled her into a kiss.

'What?'

'Nothing,' he said. But the thought refused to go away. What if he *didn't* get in.

Laughable. Impossible. Unthinkable.

They sat in dumb bafflement, watching Mrs Thatcher arrive at Number Ten. Gone was the prissy Women's Institute look of before and in its place the new, blue-clad dominatrix. She was encased in a violent-blue dress, hair sprayed bigger and yellower than ever, one arm extended to the crowd in an almost Nazi salute. Her husband stayed behind her, eyes apparently glued to her arse, as she approached the ranks of reporters.

'Is that *booing*?' asked Danny.

Nicole ignored him. There was definitely booing amid all the cheers and celebrations. Angry, persistent booing came through loud and clear, and Thatcher seemed shaken for a moment.

'Shhhh! Let's hear what the witch has to say . . .'

Thatcher composed herself and, head cocked meekly to one side in a show of compassionate, maternal concern, she launched into her greeting to the nation.

'Where there is discord, may we bring harmony. Where there is error, may we bring truth. Where there is doubt, may we bring faith. Where there is despair, may we bring hope.'

Nicole turned to him. 'Can you believe her?'

'I wouldn't, like, if I hadn't just seen it . . .'

She turned back to the TV screen and watched Britain's first female prime minister saluting her public.

'I don't like it, Danny. I really don't like it at all. She scares me.'

Danny nodded, but part of him was already back to wondering whether Ian Curtis would be all right.

Browsing Penny Lane's singles and imports racks just a few weeks after the Amnesty gig, Danny very nearly emulated Curtis's death throes. Flicking through the new releases he found Siouxsie's latest, 'Metal Postcard'. The sleeve, protected here by a plastic folder, featured a sinister black-and-white photograph of a family, gathered at the dining table, preparing to swallow their cutlery. Heads held back, they dangled spoons and forks above their gaping mouths, awaiting the awful moment. He was shocked – suddenly full of bile, and a pain so dull and throbbing he could barely think. But there it was. It was the John Heartfield picture Nicole had urged him to send to Peter Saville Associates. In the end, he had never done so. He'd sourced the image at the Bluecoat, thought about how he'd use it, how his own lightness of touch could turn this into a classic Factory sleeve. But he'd stopped right there. He'd changed his mind, put the print straight back down again, and left. He wanted acclaim for his own ideas. He didn't want to fall back on collage and archive, no matter how cleverly implemented. But in spite of all that, he felt sick.

Ecce Homo

Lingsby stood back again, her head cocked admiringly to one side, eyeing up the painting. She shook her head in disbelief.

'This is just . . . *stunning* work, Daniel. It's . . . I'm stunned. Lost for words.'

He was pleased, but no more. He *knew* it was good. Four consecutive weekends he'd planted his easel outside Owen Owens, blithely sketching the street scenes, waiting for that one special subject. Since *Quadrophenia*, town had become overrun by more and more mod revivalists, hundreds of them rampaging through Church Street hoping for some kind of action. With all the two-tone stuff, the Specials and Madness and Selecter leaping out from the underground and into the charts, and bands like Purple Hearts and Secret Affair chiming in with the sort of anthemic pop the Jam had been honing for years, the city centre was a confusion of match-heads in balaclavas and training shoes, nouveau mods in pristine parkas, and hybrid rude boys in their cardigans, brogues and pork-pie hats. More than a style, though, Danny had been on the lookout for a face, a spirit – some special entity who could project an attitude way, way above and beyond the clothes on their back. And that fourth Saturday, he'd seen her. He couldn't say she was beautiful, or even pretty – not with those teeth. But her face, her poise, her aggressive narcissism stood out from the crowd. Hair cropped in a scalp-tight ginger crew cut, she had violent, narrow-slit eyes darting wildly above swollen, almost bruise-like cheekbones. Her face was pale, pale white. If she weren't so short, she could have been a catwalk model. She was five foot three, no more, slender to the point of being too thin, and she wore a lemon Fred Perry under-neath a jade-green tonic mohair suit. She looked amazing. She was what he'd been looking for – that special spirit of the streets. Knowing how odd it would sound, Danny stopped her nonetheless.

'Er, listen . . . sorry, bit of a mad one, this. Can I paint you?'

'What?'

'Can I paint a portrait of you?'

She eyed him slowly, up and down. 'You gonna try and shag me?'

Danny smiled and half turned away. 'No!' He looked her in the eye. 'I'm not, no. I've got a bird.'

She swayed her hips lightly, hands dug deep into the jacket pockets. 'How much?'

'Oh – no, no, no! It don't cost nothing . . .'

The girl snorted. 'I mean how much are you gonna give us, like? If I let you paint us?'

His face fell. 'I'm a student. I'm skint.'

She shrugged and looked him up and down again. She offered a twisted grin, more of a snarl than a smile. Her teeth were tiny and stained nicotine brown, yet on this girl it was some-how not repellent. The brown teeth were her, a part of her, part of that easy and insolent self-possession that made her so striking.

'Don't look skint. If you're asking me to sit still here while all kinds take the piss . . . got to be worth a fiver, hasn't it?'

'I'd love to, girl . . . What's your name, by the way?'

'Michelle. Fiver, or it's no go.'

He sighed hard. Since moving in with Nicole he'd as good as given up on the sketch work. Very occasionally, if he needed money for presents or special occasions, he'd put in a stint at the Lucky Bar, but the truth was it was getting hard to find time for everything, and although money wasn't exactly tight, they certainly weren't throwing it around. Five pounds was money he simply didn't have.

'Tell you what. Let me just sketch you, right. Just get the outline, the likeness. Won't take me more than five minutes, yeah? I'll take that home with us, right, and what I'll do is, I'll do one for you, too. How does that sound?'

Chewing slowly and deliberately, she pierced him with her gimlet eyes. 'Shit.'

He was about to give up when she started laughing. Danny was surprised by the powerful surge of attraction that charged through him. Under that suit was a great, nimble figure and in different circumstances he'd have loved to find out more about her. She winked at him.

'You're all right, lad. I've got no use for a picture but if it's only gonna take a few minutes, go 'ead. Make a cunt out of me . . .'

He smiled, placed his hands together in an oriental thank-you and set to work. She'd made her mark on him. Somehow, even in sketch form, he brought that cruel, clever light to her eyes, and in the thrust of her hands in the suit pockets, he picked out her strength and defiance.

Back home, he brought Michelle to life. With his trade-mark background of wild, swirling browns and yellows crudely pasted on with the brush strokes and track marks left in, as though smudged straight from the tube, he stamped his deft individualism all over the painting. When Nicole came home laden with Kwik-Save bags and asked, half in admiration, half out of envy, who the young savage was, he said: 'Rude Girl.'

And that's what he called the picture. Elaine Lingsby – Lingsby, as his art teacher liked to be known by students and colleagues alike – was blown away by *Rude Girl*.

'I want to get this seen. May I, Daniel? Do I have your say-so to show this to a few people?'

Danny shrugged. It didn't make much difference to him one way or the other. He knew he was good. Fuck it, he knew he was *special*, and whether it took a week or a year or ten years for the world to cotton on, he felt a deep and soothing certitude that his future was assured. He just knew it – that was all. So when Lingsby came back to him the day before Halloween and told him she'd been offered a hundred pounds for *Rude Girl*, he hardly blinked. But when she said the purchaser wanted to talk to them about an exhibition in the new year, he could barely hold back the rapture. He found himself spinning Lingsby round and round by the hands, squealing madly in her face: 'Yiss-yiss-yiss-yiss-*yiss*! Oh, Danny Boy! Danny *Boy*!'

Lingsby laughed and laughed, desperate to get her breath. 'This is just the start, Daniel! This is just the start . . .'

Walking away from the Transalpino office, tickets tucked safely in his inside pocket, he saw her up ahead, crossing Grove Street towards Myrtle Gardens. He went to shout to her, but couldn't remember her name.

'Mikey! Marie! Damn!'

He put his head down and sprinted to catch up with her. She was disappearing through the arch into the well of the flats.

'Rude Girl!'

She stopped and turned to face him. Wearing tight jeans

and a washed-out Lois sweatshirt, she looked agitated, angry. Danny willed all that away in his pleasure at seeing her again. He checked for traffic, dashed across the road and pulled up a few feet away from her. There were still the carcasses of spent fireworks – burnt-out bangers and rip-raps, somehow beguiling and still wondrous, though damp and flattened – on the ground.

'Hey!' He leaned down, rested his hands flat on his thighs while he got his breath back. 'Guess what?'

'I haven't got all day, lad. If you've got something to say . . .'

He was stung, but not fatally. He looked her up and down, nodded at her jeans as he spoke. 'You look different –'

'Likesay, kidder – I haven't got time to gas with you –'

'Look all right, like. Look even better in your suit . . .'

The quickest flicker of something shot through her, bringing a sting to her cheeks. She bit it back, fought it, swallowed it.

'Suit's gone, la.'

'Shame.'

'Isn't it, though? Sold it. Life goes on.'

She held his gaze a moment then turned to walk away.

'Hey! Know the picture? The painting I done of you?'

'What about it?'

'I sold it.'

She turned back again, raked his face all over with that sly, calculating look, reading him for signs of weakness.

'Good. You can give us that fiver well, can't you?'

He grinned broadly, truly believing it was a joke. Her pale face creased in an angry scowl.

'I mean it. Give us the fucking dough you owe us!'

Danny held his hands up. 'Hey! I just wanted to say ta and what have you. Share the good news with you.'

'Good news! Good news for who?'

He shook his head sadly and moved off back towards the hospital. She caught up with him and hissed in his ear.

'Listen. I'll give you half.'

'What?'

'You can come back to mine and we'll do it in together.'

'*What?*'

She came right up close and put her hand between his legs. Her breath smelt foul, stale and brown and acidic, as she tried to play him, crooning into his ear.

'You give us the dough, yeah? I'll get the gear and we'll go back to mine. You might get lucky, darling . . .'

She licked his neck, and no matter the acrid breath and the too-tough maul of her hand, he was aroused.

'See? I'll have you like that all day, la. You buy the gear and I'll suck your cock all afternoon . . .'

'*Whoa!*'

Danny jumped backwards, arms held aloft, face set in a foolish grin. 'Listen. I'm –'

'Don't be a fucking letdown, lad. I'm not gonna tell your bird, am I? Let's just have a good time . . .'

They stood a yard apart staring right at each other, neither flinching. Once again, she had her hand on her hip, swaying slightly, jutting her tits out. Danny couldn't prevent himself eyeing her up, his artist's eye taking in every pout and curve of her body. But it was he who spoke first.

'I'm not interested, girl. See you.'

'You don't know what you're missing, lad,' she shouted after him.

He couldn't say whether she meant the drugs or the sex, but even though he didn't turn round, even though he quickened his pace to put real distance between them, he still could not get Rude Girl out of his mind. When Nicole was asleep that night he crept into the bathroom and wanked himself off into the sink, crazed by thoughts of Michelle's breasts. Looking at his weak and drained face in the mirror he was laid low with a new horror of himself, terror of the depths that lurked within.

Love Will Tear Us Apart

Exactly a week before the Bains Douches concert he led Nicole into their snug front parlour, eyes blindfolded, and sat her down.

'Can I look yet?' she shrieked.

'Oh . . . go 'ead then!'

He stood back smiling, anticipating her excitement. He'd decorated the little table with doilies and decorations he'd made himself. In the centre of the table stood a bottle of Beaujolais Nouveau he'd bought and stashed a few weeks before. A white envelope inscribed with his scruffy, spider-like hand leaned against the bottle.

'Waaaaagh! Wow! Wow! Wow!' she squealed, covering her mouth in belated acknowledgement of the din she was making. 'Danny, this is *sooooo* cute! Did *you* make these?'

'That I did, my babychild! Oh yiss!'

'Ahhh – it all looks *gorgeous!*'

'Well, sit back and take a sip of le Beaujolais while I bring in le Grub.'

'Is this what I think it is?'

'All depends what you think it is . . .'

'Don't tease, Danny Boy! Have you been cooking . . . ?'

He tried to keep the grin off his face, failing the moment he started to answer her. 'Aha, well . . . I must confess I *might* have invested some of our hard-earned moolah on a plump, succulent turkey from good ol' M&S. See? I'm learning!'

'Oh, Danny! This is just . . . *ace!*'

'Well – wait until you open your prezzie . . .'

He nodded at the envelope. Her face fell.

'Ah, *Dan* . . .'

'What?'

'We said no early presents this year. Remember?'

He placed a kiss on the end of her nose and handed her the envelope.

'We did indeed. And don't panic, I'm not expecting nothing from you. This is a present to the both of us. It's not something that'd really keep till Chrimbo, if you follow my drift. Just open it up and all will become clear . . .'

She turned the letter over and over in her hands, suddenly enjoying the drama of the moment.

'Hmmm. Know what I want to know, Danny May?'

She reached out and pulled him towards her, holding his hands to her lips as she gazed up at him, adoring him all over again.

'Tell me quick – before the turkey burns!'

Her eyes sparkled and played with him. 'I want to know how . . .' She kissed his left hand, then his right. '. . . how these hands, which *throb* with such skill, such magic that they create works *so* amazing that folk are prepared to give hundreds of pounds . . .'

'Ahem. *One* hundred pounds. Once.'

'*So* far . . .'

She stood up, wrapped her arms around his neck and looked into his eyes.

'How can these hands that weave such magic . . . write like *that*! Hey?' She held the envelope right up to his nose, laughing. 'That, Danny May, is the scruffiest, scruffiest, *scruffiest* handwriting I have *ever* seen!'

He laughed and kissed her again.

'Just open the fucking thing, will you, or we might miss the train –'

'Train? *Train?!*'

She tore open the envelope, tipping its contents on to the table. Two Transalpino rail tickets. She snatched them up.

'Where to, where to, where to? Where we *going*?!'

'Guess!'

'Can't! Fuck! Can't read the damn thing!'

She scrutinised the waxy ticket, running her finger along the faint print and reading out times and numbers, but still she could not make out the destination.

'Where does it *say*?'

'Want me to put you out of your misery, honeygirl?'

'Oh God, Danny, please! Where are we going? *When* are we going?'

She was shivering and gurning and jumping up and down on the spot. He'd never seen her more wired, more anxiously excited, more childishly wrapped up in the moment. He'd never seen Nicole happier. All background sound and vision seemed to fade out as he smiled with his eyes and said the word.

'Paris.'

At first she just stood there, eyes wide open, smiling massively, but in utter silence. Danny stepped forward.

'We're going to Paris next week to see Joy Division.'

She carried on staring at him in stunned silence.

'Oh, Danny. Oh my God. Thank you.'

And then tears started trickling freely down her cheeks.

'This is just . . . I *love* you!'

As cold as it was, even after the endless, seemingly hopeless trudge along the banks of the Seine in that freezing, sleeting rain, their first glimpse of the little hotel was a moment of pure, radiant joy. Arms wrapped around each other as his numb fingers struggled to keep hold of their stinging, sopping wet rucksack, they headed back up again from the Pont Neuf and crossed towards the only side street they hadn't yet tried.

'Surely, surely . . . *please* let it be this,' stammered the blue-lipped Nicole. They turned into the narrow neck of the Place Dauphine, silent but for a drunk on a bench, bellowing with laughter as the rain soaked him through. The tiny, naked square was a timeless gasp of the romancer's Paris, stripped and slender trees presiding over a watercolour scene. The bloated December sky cast spectral shadows across the deserted *boules* pit, yet the sight of a lone waiter setting tables in his cosy neighbourhood bistro gave them warmth in their hearts. Splashing past a dim-lit cellar bar, they started to sense that this, at last, was the place. There was nothing about the shabbily elegant town house to advertise itself as Hotel Henri IV, but they stopped and caught their breath and, both at once, started giggling.

'Oh, baby,' whispered Nicole, 'this is just . . .'

He squeezed up to her and kissed her lightly.

'Magic,' he said. Shivering, wet through but fastened on the notion, Nicole dredged the Instamatic from the side pouch of the rucksack and snapped Danny, joyous, outside the hotel.

'Let me take one of you,' he laughed – but she squeezed up close to him and, heads together, held the camera straight out in front of them and shot.

'Let's get warm,' she said.

Nicole was childishly delighted by the croaking hot-water pipes and the other idiosyncrasies of the hotel, and Danny found it hard to coax her back out into the night.

'Come 'ead, beauty child . . . the club's not all that far away. We'll suss out if there's gonna be a queue and all that, then we can go explore!'

'Yes! Let's just dive out into the night and see where we get blown!'

He stood right in front of her, straightening the broad red hairband dividing her lustrous bob.

'Well. So long as it blows us to Les Bains Douches, hey?'

She smiled her compliance, yet somehow felt thwarted. Bent against the rain again, that cloying sense of dread stayed in the pit of her stomach for the entire walk to the Etienne Marcel district, only vaporising as they settled on to tall stools at a narrow, smoky bar and hooked their arms together and sipped on warming brandies. Sucking on her third Gauloise and loving the thick, musky decadence of the smoke, she could not now pinpoint her anxiety. They'd been travelling all day – National Express to Victoria, boat train to Dover, overnight crossing to Calais and another train into Paris Gard du Nord. With all the aimless wandering in search of the hotel, Nicole was ready to lie down, have a long soak in the corridor's sole, ancient, crackle-glazed tub, rest up for an hour or two and plot out the beats of their adventure. But it was Christmas, it was Paris – and it was Danny. Danny was burning up with excitement, eager to soak up every little droplet. They'd flung themselves on top of the bed and fornicated – truly, they had gyrated, urgently, both eager to come – and Nicole drifted off on to a different plane. Since he'd sprung the tickets on her they'd spoken of little else but Paris, where they'd go, what they'd do. Montmartre, the Eiffel Tower, the Louvre, Père Lachaise Cemetery – the highlights chose themselves and it had all been easy enough to fantasise about. In her subconscious she'd dreamt of pastis and ganja and revolutionary discourse with Left Bank intellectuals too, without ever stopping to wonder whether there'd be time – they could only afford one night there – or whether Danny would crave the same slug of Paris. But the brandy was swooning through her and, once again, her soul was soaring with a vague but swelling sense of well-being. She leaned across to Danny for a kiss, smiled at the diminutive barman watching them, and tried to resist when he topped up their glasses.

'For lovers,' he beamed.

He hesitated, went to say something else, conspicuously checked himself and, instead, leaned over to light Nicole's fourth cigarette in half an hour. Intoxicated by just being there, with Danny, in a little Paris side-street bar, smoking strong cigarettes, she felt a surge of love for the boy sat next to her. What she felt was a tingling sensation, a growing sense that it was all there and the best was yet to come. Dizzy, she turned to tell him what thoughts were galloping through her mind.

'Darling? Know, like . . . we're in Paris?'

He grinned, carefully kissing her top lip, then her chin, eyeing her serenely, as though for the very first time. She looked fantastic in her cropped sheepskin jacket, tight 'London Calling' T-shirt underneath.

'I'd noticed, yeah . . .'

She sucked hard on the Gauloise, trying to arrange her thoughts.

'Like . . . Sartre talks about this. I think. Barthes says it best. Remember the book of essays I gave you? *A Lover's Discourse*?'

'Did it have pictures?'

She slapped him fondly. He winked at her.

'I won't have read it then, will I . . .'

'All he's saying, is . . .'

She finished the cigarette, stubbed it out, blew the smoke out through her lips and her nose as she finally reined in the slew of ideas and notions coursing through her clever, hot-wired head.

'I mean, if you're thinking one thing, and you know your lover's thinking another? You want something, he wants the other thing. You love each other, you're mad on each other, you'll do *anything* for each other – but by thinking the opposite thing to him, by even allowing an idea that you know might not make him happy . . . Here's the thing. Do you tell him, knowing it might not make him happy? Or do you think, he loves you so much, he'd want to know? Would you, in fact, be cheating by allowing him to think that you were in accord when perhaps you weren't?'

She paused, then reached instinctively for the crumple-pack of Gauloises, her need heightened by the brandy and the situation. But she didn't light one. She fiddled with the tip, slid it back into the packet, leaned forward and took Danny's hands.

'Does that make any sense at all?'

'No,' he smiled.

Now she took the cigarette out and lit it. And as she exhaled, she confessed.

'I don't think I want to go to the gig.'

It ran Danny through. He swallowed, smiled back at her, but the stone in his guts had dropped, hard. She'd said this to him. Why? Even if she had good reason – say she didn't, after all, love the band as he'd believed – this had been the surprise Danny had lined up for them. Telling him she didn't want it – it was wrong.

'Let's not go then. What d'you want to do?'

She was grief-stricken, instantly.

'Oh no, no, no! Darling! Look at your face. Oh, baby . . .' She smothered his face and neck with kisses. 'Oh, God! I'm so sorry . . .'

He pulled back, smiled again.

'Hey! Don't be. This is both our trip, you know?' He managed to kick some laughter into his voice. 'Let's do something we both want to do!'

She examined his face, his eyes, looked at the floor, holding his hands, looked back up again, met his stare.

'Are you *sure*, Dan?'

'Sure I'm sure!'

'God . . .'

She started swinging her leg, kicking the base of the stool with her heel.

'It's just . . .' She leaned right into him, wanting to take him along with her passions. 'We're here for *two days*. I mean, I love Joy Division, really I do . . . but, fuck! I'd *love* to go drinking on the Left Bank. All those basement bars by the Sorbonne, all the places we've read about and dreamt about. Can we?'

'Course we can!'

'Really?'

'Why not?'

'Promise you're not cross with me?'

'Not cross. Not at all.'

She jumped up off the stool, clapped her hands. 'You mean it?'

'I solemnly swear that, here and now, I wish nothing more than to drink cheap wine in student bars . . .'

He was starting to believe it. As they made a dash for the Métro station, Nicole already felt confident in the strength and the wisdom of her stand.

'We can see Joy Division any time,' she gasped.

Not here, thought Danny. Not in Paris, with the love of your life.

But he ploughed on, holding her hand and jumping puddles.

He was no lover of jazz anyway, but this was excruciating. A knot of smiling African men crowded on to a tiny semicircular stage, limbs clashing as they pounded out a frantic, skittering fusion of electro-jazz and highlife. To Danny, it was actually painful to listen to. Nicole sat there, eyes alight, tapping her hand on the table, nodding her approval at total strangers, loving the carnal, cosmopolitan atmosphere. She snatched at Danny's hand.

'Come on!' she gasped.

'What?' he murmured, hoping against hope she'd had second thoughts about the gig or, better, had been stricken with lust and fancied one up against the wall outside.

'Let's dance!'

'To this?'

'Yeah, baby!' She bit her bottom lip and gave him an eyes-screwed, party-girl face, pummelling the air wildly with her fists.

'You can't dance to *this*!'

She gave him a momentary once-over, briefly registered

her disappointment in him and, certain he knew he'd let her down, stroked his hair, once.

'Well, *I* can! You don't mind, do you?'

He shrugged. This was bad. Since the plan had first roosted with him, he'd lived their one night together in Paris in his head, over and over. At no stage had it involved spending ten francs a pop for a small carafe of rusty red wine and the horrors of the Parisian intelligentsia twisting gaily to Nigerian jazz. It was as though the band were making a silent pact before each new song – 'Let's see if we get them dancing to *this*!' – then launching into another jerky, arrhythmic ensemble piece. Not that Nicole seemed to care. Hands raking through her hair, hips swaying like a mambo queen, she was getting down and distinctly intimate with the Sorbonne's finest. One gawky youth in particular, a Buddy Holly doppelgänger who, to Danny's dismay, was wearing the collar of his shirt outside the neck of his jumper without sign of censure from Nicole, had taken an evident liking to her. As Nicole laughed and shimmied, so Buddy Holly got closer and closer, until he was rubbing his bottom against her hips. All the while he grinned stupidly, clicking his fingers and, like Nicole, clamping his teeth on his lower lip and letting his left eye droop. It was sickening – not so much that she was dancing with another man, but that she was loving this whole phoney scene so much. He was furious. The more he watched, the more Nicole stopped catching his eye, the angrier Danny became. He slugged on his wine, swallowing another bitter mouthful. On the other side of the Seine, his blessed Joy Division were about to take to the stage. And here was he, a gooseberry, a misfit, a peeping Tom, looking on at his girlfriend's treachery. If the dance floor had been less crowded he would have vaulted the little balcony and volleyed Buddy Holly up the backside. But he didn't. He left silently, biting his own lip too, now – but biting back tears of anger.

★   ★   ★

Tears of sheer relief poured down his smiling, helpless face. He slumped down on the top step of the short run leading to the bar and, in succumbing to the floor, succumbed also to the pent-up emotions now spewing forth. A couple of girls turned away from the stage and checked him over with mild concern but Danny's forceful, lunatic grin convinced them he was OK. Joy Division were four songs into the set and everything was fine again. This was like a massive overdose of the Thrills, jump-starting the very valves of his soul. He was devastated. He was ecstatic.

He'd found the elegantly tiled former bathhouse a sumptuous but alien place for a rock concert. The sprung dance floor and galleried surrounds would make a fine setting for live theatre or a tea dance or a night of flaming tango. But for the mutant melancholia of Joy Division, the place needed shrinking – or the arrival of at least a hundred more hopeful souls than those gathered reverentially to either side of the mixing desk. At forty francs a ticket on a vile, wintry night it was a tribute to the band, and to the hip young Parisians' love of rock'n'roll that so many had got there at all, but the turnout still looked sparse. Small clusters of bedraggled fans stood back from the stage, while the traditional smattering of sexy rock chicks and nervous, friendless boys hung closer to the front, though still leaving a few yards of spotlight between themselves and the amplifiers.

Danny took a swig of his Kronenbourg and sauntered with confidence and a heart full of fearful hope to the very front and the very centre of the stage. Following his lead, and not a little miffed at his getting there first, an odd assortment of nutters and diehards built themselves in around him.

The band came on. Danny wanted them to clock that he, an English lad, was there to see them.

'Come on! Yiss-yiss-yiss!'

He wanted everyone there to understand that precisely one week before Christmas he was there in Paris as the ultimate act of devotion to the ultimate rock'n'roll band. He stuck his fingers in his mouth and whistled hard and shrill. Peter Hook half looked up from his bass, then Steve Morris bent over his kit, picked up his sticks, beat out the rapid-fire intro to 'Disorder' and that was them. They clicked right into the groove of suddenly becoming Joy Division, just like that. For Danny, it was like the first time all over again. It was extraordinary. The music coursed through him, gathering him up and possessing him in a way that made him weak and giddy. Yet something about the urgent intensity of Curtis's delivery went straight to the core of Danny's psyche. In some strange and wonderful way, the band sent him mad. He began to flail his arms around, forcing those around him to dance too or move away. No taboo restrained him, he was barely aware of the crowd around him, ones and twos starting to throw themselves into the music, watching keenly as Danny jerked and jacked, totally gone.

'*Feeling-feeling-feeling-feeling-feeee-ling!*' howled the singer, his head slumping at the final note. Danny opened his mouth to join the shouts of encouragement, but nothing would come out. One of the band shouted something to a technician as Hook devoutly tuned his bass, plucking the same two notes over and over. Again the one-two-three-four count-in of the drumsticks and again Danny was swept away, beguiled by the stripped-down purity of the new song — its thin, eerie keyboard swirling around and beyond this plaintive, hymnal song of loss and regret. He'd never heard this one before. Its chorus drove a stone-hard lump to the back of his throat.

'*Love, love will tear us apart again.*'

Swallowing the words, understanding them, he stood back now. He stopped flailing and backed away to the steps and listened. The song was so simple, and so very sad. It was him and her. It was as though the whole world had been peering through the window at Danny and Nicole's troubles, and put them to music. He watched, and wondered. Not pausing for applause, the band went straight into 'Insight' and this time the words ghosted right through him, clamping his heart tight:

> Guess your dreams always end
> They don't rise up, just descend
> But I don't care any more
> I've lost the will to want more . . .
> But I remember – when we were young.

He was overwhelmed by a sudden crushing sense of loss. The band were there, mere feet away, and he was there watching them, but a flickering kinesis of dislocated images now danced in front of his eyes. It was him and her, Danny and Nicole, snags of memories and past times, frame by frame. It lasted a minute, no more, but it felt to Danny as though he were watching an archive – as though he or she had already died and all that remained was the cine-reel, the flashback. That faint and general heady sensation swooned up fully now, rocking him backwards. He was drunk, he knew that – and he was exhausted, emotional, drained. His head was spinning and he was both manically happy and stiflingly sad – and he needed to sit down. They were doing 'Shadowplay' now. He stumbled back up the three or four steps towards the bar, sat down on the top step and burst into tears.

'They're emotional, *oui*?'

A pair of green suede ankle boots stood a foot apart, and a foot from Danny. Slim calves clad in black denier made him look up, briefly. It was one of the girls who'd been watching him. She stood right over him now, concerned. He didn't reply. He was lost in thought.

'Emotional? It's right?'

Danny looked up at her again. She had an open, pretty face, framed by an asymmetric bob which in turn was adorned with an electric-green bow. Clever brown eyes studied Danny quizzically. He managed a smile.

'Emotional. Yeah.'

She crouched down. She had a perfectly round, full mouth and his immediate instinct was to kiss her. Reflexively, he moved his head back, out of temptation's way.

'You are sad?'

He smiled again.

'I don't know. I'm not exactly happy.'

'*Tant pis*. That's too bad.'

'I'm not exactly suicidal either. I'm just thinking.'

'You want to come out to some bars with me? Think in loud?'

Danny pulled himself up so his eyeline was level with hers.

'What's your name?'

'Hilda.'

'Hiya, Hilda. I'm Danny.'

'*Enchantée*, Danny. So. We go?'

He looked at her feet, then back up to her face.

'That's what I been thinking about, see. I wasn't kind of, like, taking it for granted that you'd come and talk to us, but I was just thinking about that whole thing. Strangers in the night and all that . . .'

She grinned at him. 'You are Danny the *romantique*!'

He laughed. 'Nah. Just me being me. I batter me little head with all kinds of madness. Do you know?'

She just stared at him and gave a delightful, dismissive shrug. Danny laughed again.

'I'm saying, I think I think too much!'

The first trace of artifice from her came as she lowered her eyelids for effect, so that when she opened them again she was staring right into him.

'I don't like so much to think. I prefer to live.'

He loved the way she said 'prefer', rolling her *r*s, but he carried on doughtily, putting his point of view.

'I *have* to think. Otherwise I'd just *do* . . .'

'What you think?'

'I think that I'm new, you're new. That straight away makes

us . . . *new*. Do you know? It follows we're going to be . . . attracted. I think so, anyway.'

'I think so also.'

'So it's the easiest thing in the world to just, you know. Just get on with it. Isn't it? Maybe it's the best thing in the world, too. Nobody knows.'

She shrugged again and let him see she was not just confused but getting vexed with him.

'So . . . ?'

'So, there's no truth to it.'

His calm eyes met hers. A flush of anger flickered in her.

'No truth? Then how –'

'Not when you've got a girl, there isn't. I could fall in love with you. Easy. But I've got a girl, see?'

She held his stare a second longer, shook her head and walked away. He felt bad, felt he'd rejected something good, but his instinct told him all was well. He knew he'd done the right thing. This was what he'd been trying to work out: even if he'd just gone for a drink with her, what did that mean? It meant he was beguiled by someone else. By heading off into the bars of Paris with a brand new soul, however innocently, he'd be exploring her, finding things he might not find in Nicole. Whether their association lasted for one drink or several hours, for that time he would not just be replacing Nicole, he'd be preferring another girl to her. He didn't want that. He couldn't do it. Encouraged by his resolve and strangely inspired by what had just happened, or just by being in Paris, or by some potent mix of everything he was discovering there, he wanted only to find Nicole and make everything good again. He jogged steadily through wet and narrow streets, vaguely sure he was going the right way.

It must have been around five when Nicole crept back into their bed. He'd lain there, wide awake, all his love and hope slowly dissipating as he watched the clock tick on. He got back

to the hotel at a quarter past one. All the way back he'd imagined she'd be there, in bed, hurt and cross with him, and it
would be he who had to plead with her for indulgence. Finding
the room empty, he dug the little alarm clock out from the
rucksack and, thwarted, lay back on the bed, arms behind his
head. After three his fond thoughts, all the things he'd wanted
to say to her, turned to sour delusion. Reckless images
tormented him – images of Nicole, eyes dancing, sucking the
student's cock. He found himself aroused by the idea of her
going back to his attic and acquiescing to him, letting him do
whatever he wanted to her. He imagined the delight in Buddy
Holly's spastic eyes as she stood before him in her Clash T-shirt
and he realised how perfect she was, would be. He felt Nicole's
eyes on himself as she writhed under Buddy's touch. Lying on
that hotel bed, he was utterly certain that at that precise moment
Nicole was betraying him with another man.

Disgusted with himself as much as with her, he clenched
his eyes tight, shut out the demented thoughts and visions
and willed sleep upon himself. His head was pulsating with
snatches of songs, barbs of conversation.

'*I remember – when we were young.*'

'Emotional. It's right?'

He blinked back the tears. At no point did he rue his rejection of Hilda. Fatigued now and with his mind thumping
hard and lurching from thought to fragmented thought, all
that remained of the episode was a deep conviction that he
had done right. Hilda had gone one way, Danny the other.
For his own part, he'd done right. He fell into a jagged sleep,
never at rest but not quite conscious either. Then he was aware
of her coming down the corridor. Although switched off, he
could tell that she was trying to walk quietly, perhaps with
her shoes off. He sensed the light on his face as she creaked
the door open, felt her brush against him as she slipped under
the sheets. He even felt the weight of her decisions – whether
to kiss him, even whether to see if he was awake. He was

awake. With his back to her, staring at the window, Danny found one biting question on his lips. It had taken him over, this thing, and it was all he could think about, all he wanted to know. It was in his heart, on his mind.

'Did you fuck him?'

But he couldn't say it. He lay there facing the window and said nothing at all. Whether she'd done it or not, things were not the same now. Something had broken.

Unable to sleep at all and suddenly ravenous, he roused himself, trudged to the window, watched the road sweepers pick the square clean. He turned to look at his supine, treacherous girlfriend. Heavy-hearted and sick of this place, he nonetheless found his every consideration revolved around Nicole. He had every intention of getting out of there, fast – but would she have sufficient money? Did she know how to get to the Gare du Nord? Would she be all right? But fuck it, he thought – and fuck her! He left her three of the remaining Métro tickets from the *carnet*, emptied her belongings from the rucksack and headed off into the morning.

Several strong cups of coffee and a *croque monsieur* lifted his mood slightly. Perhaps she hadn't *slept* with anyone at all. It was bad enough that she'd thought fit to sit around smoking with strangers all night, talking shit, but he could forgive her for that. He'd forgiven her almost as soon as he left the hotel. Already, he was envisaging their passionate reunion on the boat train back to Dover. He couldn't wait that long. He just wanted her there, next to him, sharing all this. The coffee was hot and thick, but the whole thing of sitting outside in the middle of December, watching one of the world's great cities creaking into life – it was something else. He was loving it, and he knew how much she'd love it, too. Somehow, it wasn't as good without Nicole.

Feeling that he couldn't quite slink back to the hotel – it was up to her to find *him* – he traipsed around the general

Pont Neuf neighbourhood, crossing the river and perusing every art shop, every bookstore, every stall. Artists and traders, hunched against the cold, nodded pleasantries as they set out their pitches, hoping to catch the Christmas trade. Danny didn't spend too long with any of them. He knew from experience how disappointing it could be – especially when you needed the money badly – to have your hopes raised then crushed by a lingering punter. Besides, there was some truly *bad* art here! Cod oriental birds perched on silver branches; paltry pastiches of Monet and Renoir; and, for him, worst of all, trite scenarios of lovers loitering over Ricards at some hazy pavement café. This was the cradle of artistic *élan*? Perfect! He need worry about nothing. Once or twice, finding himself under the gaze of a lively-looking art dealer, he felt like stopping and looking them in the eye and declaring himself an artist. A *painter*. He wanted to hear himself say it, wanted it known that he, too, was a painter.

Ambling down the steps to the river, he mused on the likelihood that one day, maybe a hundred years from now, some other lovelorn teen might pad these same streets and stalls, eyeing up lost masterpieces by Daniel May. He felt better. He felt good. Torn between continuing on past the *bateaux-mouches* as far as the Eiffel Tower, or hitting the Métro to Père Lachaise, he fixed upon the latter. The Eiffel Tower was not a place to be alone, and he knew she'd think the same, too.

Entering the cemetery at its grand main gate, Danny was immediately lost, wandering from grave to elegant grave. Huge, ornate sepulchres bore graceful testament to the lives and legacies of long-dead muses – Colette, Haussman, Faure. He came to the squat cubic tomb of the Monument to the Dead and again he found himself pining for her. He stood back and took in the intricate carvings, submissive, naked figures offering themselves up. Nicole would love all this. She, more than anyone else he'd known, appreciated the silent dignity of a lonely place. Somewhere like this, she'd just sit there and soak it all in. How he hoped she would find it.

He mounted the mossy steps to the upper part of the cemetery. Signposts pointed off down different footpaths to different graves: Edith Piaf, Isadora Duncan, Sarah Bernhardt, Maria Callas. Everywhere, even in the form of her dead heroes, Nicole's presence haunted him. Oscar Wilde, Proust, Gertrude Stein – he'd heard her rhapsodise over one and all, and here were the paths to their graves.

The path became loose and flinty, overhung by ancient trees in this remote part of the park and, without light now, somewhat dank and eerie. He kicked on, losing his bearings but content just to go where the trails led him. In their squabbles and plans for the Paris trip they'd agreed that a pilgrimage to Jim Morrison's grave was a must-do. Notre-Dame and Montmartre if possible, a boat trip down the Seine if time and budget allowed – but ten minutes at Jim's graveside was a priority for both of them. Now, though, he didn't really care if he saw it or not. This enormous decadent sprawl of a cemetery was awe-inspiring. Just taking his time, passing each memorial to each great life, gave him a perspective, but also the urge to do great things himself. He'd have liked to have seen Jim Morrison's grave with Nicole, but, without her, he was starting to look forward again now, thinking how little he'd done with his life and how much he had yet to commence, let alone achieve. He meandered on along a more formal path and found himself next to Chopin's vault. He stopped still, and couldn't stem the fantasy of being thus remembered himself. What would you have to do? Just how *great* would you have to be to deserve a sarcophagus like that? It was mind-bending even trying to take it in, how one person could make one choice, one decision, that took his life on an epic journey. 'I shall continue with my piano lessons.' Something like that. Another person might make another choice, and end up anonymous. He kicked a stone, unsure what he really thought about all this. Wasn't it just as good to be happy? Was he happy right now? He couldn't say for sure, couldn't pinpoint anything with any certitude. He was pretty sure he wanted a tomb like Chopin's, though – or at least a life that deserved one.

He started to notice that the more mundane gravestones bore scribbled graffiti: *JIM*, with arrows pointing back towards the cobbled perimeter walk. Curious, Danny ambled in that general direction, marvelling at the love and the work and the detail that had gone into the place. Hitting the outer circle of the cemetery, he found a greater concentration of graffiti, along with formal signposting to *Robertson* and *Jim Morrison*. Why allow himself to be called 'Jim' anyway? thought Danny. Not one single other person in there went by a shortened or bastardised name. Surely the very fact of residing in Père Lachaise signalled timelessness, a classic life, fittingly appreciated. What if James Joyce had shortened his name? Would his greatness still reverberate if he were Jim Joyce? Could Munch still be his hero if he was Eddie? He scuffed along the perimeter path – more of an avenue, it was so broad, so grand – further and further lost in his puzzles, and drifted without thinking towards the silent gathering ahead and to his right.

Realising he'd stumbled upon the Morrison grave, he was simultaneously surprised and dismayed at its modesty. There was no carved tomb, no monument, no watchful statues, not even an urn or a vase for flowers. Jim Morrison's grave was just that – a small, sad patch of earth with a small headstone, simply marked:

JAMES DOUGLAS MORISON – 1943–1971

James! Yes! He was ridiculously pleased. Underneath, in the same, plain capitals, a short inscription in Greek:

KATA TON DAIMONA EAYTOY

He knew he should ask one of the solemn bystanders if they knew what that meant but, lost in their own private reveries, no one looked at all approachable. Even if they had, he wouldn't have asked them. The plot was small, unimpressive, hemmed in and overshadowed by neighbouring graves, but it had something none of those had: a fan base, a congregation of mourning acolytes – and it was bedecked with mementos from visitors far and wide: syringes, empty bottles of Jim Beam and Jack Daniel's, candles, prayer cards, one damp cigarette. A group of about fifteen Doors fans stood there quietly. Perched on top of the grave was a large, white bust of Jim Morrison's head – or it had been white, once. Every inch of it was covered in scrawled messages: *The End. Alfonso, Austin, 3/27/75.*

Some faded messages had been obliterated, too, by a new (Danny was quite certain it was the very newest) piece of graffiti: *Joy Division.*

He couldn't keep the smile off his face.

'Love that French spelling of Morrison, huh?'

He jerked round. All his plans and pledges to himself, all his determination to play it cool, to let her make the running, were forgotten. His face lit up with the joy of seeing her again. He threw his arms around her. Playing the moment through his mind months and years later, he could see she was holding back. But at that moment he saw none of that – he was blinkered by love and joy. She gave him one chaste kiss and a rueful smile.

'The guy that made that bust claims Jim Morrison came to him in his dreams and urged him to go to art school. So folklore has it . . .'

She studied Danny's questioning face, already bracing himself to be teased. She was suffocated with love and regret, but she felt strong.

'I think he was from Yugoslavia. Maybe Albania. Whatever, Jim Morrison comes to this guy in his dreams and he gives him the strength and the vision to return to his art. This is the guy's lasting tribute to him.'

She grazed the sculpture with her fingertips, noticed the latest addition and turned back to Danny.

'Were Joy Division good?'

He couldn't repel the hurt that the memory stoked. He looked away.

'They were amazing. Yeah.'

He pointed to the Greek inscription on Morrison's headstone. 'Any idea what that means?'

She didn't reply, but gave out a faint, almost involuntary laugh. Not even a laugh – it was one, short, stifled guffaw. He felt her come up behind him, hook her arm through his.

'Come on. Let's walk.'

He knew it in his heart, knew this was going to be deadly. It felt like the end.

They strolled back towards the main entrance, dawdling self-consciously, neither in any hurry. Nicole was unnatural with him, joshing him how she'd never be cool enough for him. Suddenly certain that she'd come here only to break up with him, Danny could stand it no more.

'Did you?'

She stopped, looked away from him, took a deep big breath.

'The guy with glasses?'

'Yep.'

She exhaled hard. 'No, baby.'

A mighty gale of relief nearly knocked him backwards. He was ready for tears, anticipating the very worst. Now he turned to her, eyes wet with the joy of an unexpected reprieve. So pathetic was his happiness that she nearly swallowed the awful truth. But she had to tell him – not for honesty's sake but, in her heart of hearts, because she still felt she could justify it.

'Not him.'

Up to this point in his life Danny May had never truly known grief. Now it hit him with full force. He covered his face, turned away from her. She'd thought she could be strong in this moment, even fancied she could guide him through the worst of it so he'd understand. Seeing his crumpled, distraught face, etched with disbelief, she could only turn and run away. Not even remotely caring how he should act, but enraged beyond control by the act and the sight of her running off, Danny sprinted after her, pulled her back by the wrist and slapped her face, hard.

'Who was it?'

She faced up to him, eyes red.

'Oh, Danny, baby –'

'Don't fucking *baby* me, you slag! Who the fuck have you been with?'

She looked away, chest heaving, as though still unsure what to tell him, what might hurt him least.

'It was one of the musicians.'

He found himself in free fall. He opened his mouth to speak. No words came out.

'What? Why's that so bad, Danny? Why's that worse?'

She was backing him down, already seeking out, if not the high ground itself then at least a route to it. Eyes wide open, wide with shock, he walked right into it.

'The *African* guys?'

'Yes.'

'You let an African fella fuck you?'

Whatever she thought she was going to say deserted her. She burst into bitter tears and flung herself on him.

'Oh baby, baby, baby! I . . . I'm *so* –'

He threw her off and ran towards the gate.

Do It Clean

The day her letter came, Danny was moving out. Had she not thought to write it, not taken the train into Liverpool on Christmas Eve and hovered around outside the flat, changing her mind with every sharp blast of the wind that scattered the last remaining leaves across Greenbank Avenue, not held her breath as she shoved it through their letter box, then run, head down against the gust, and hunched herself down into the hollowed base of a broad oak tree; had she not done this, they would have split, for ever.

For his own part, Danny wanted her back, badly. One hour after she'd left for Darwen, he pined for her. But there was no way he could tell her that. It was not for him to beg a reconciliation. She had killed him with her confession. She had broken his heart. But for every day she'd been gone, he conjured no end of tearful reunions, soul-stirring endgames in which he'd be walking, lonely, by the lake at Sefton Park; or, without hope and with nothing left to lose, he'd abscond to Paris and exist from day to day in a shabby garret; he'd be painting some shallow likeness in the Place du Tertre and there she'd be, Nicole, staring at him from the other side of the square; the locations might vary wildly, but the outcome was always the same. She, breaking down in front of him, shattered with remorse and regret, pleading for one more chance; he, giving it.

Whether consciously or not, he'd tried to bring it about. They'd travelled back from Paris – totally separately, same trains and coach – overnight on 19 December. By the evening of the 20th she was back home in Darwen. There were things they'd dreamt of doing that Christmas, things they'd planned to do, and Danny found himself going through the motions, hoping she'd show up. On the 23rd there'd been the Eric's Christmas party – Echo and the Bunnymen and Teardrop Explodes co-headlining, a night they'd looked forward to as being the climax of their Christmas festivities. At eight o'clock Danny was still moping at home with a quarter-bottle of Captain Morgan, hoping she'd appear at the front door, knowing she would not. Even with his ticket he knew he'd struggle to gain entrance to the party if he left it much later. He held the bottle up to the bare light bulb and made a pledge to himself. First, he was going to Eric's, right now, and he was going to enjoy himself. Oh yes! Second, and he had to admit it – he really, really hoped she'd be there and that, if nothing else, they could talk. He'd have to allow that he'd been churlish over her Parisian tryst. She'd tried and tried to sit him down, tried to talk him through it but each time he'd run away. Really, he'd left her with no option but to pack a small bag and slink back to Mum and Dad's. But the third thing he vowed to himself was that, if this was it – if he and Nicole were no more – then that was something he'd have to start facing up to. So he was pretty well resigned to it. He'd go to Eric's, get up tomorrow, gather his things and start moving back to the Close.

He didn't see her at the gig. The joint was absolutely rocking, packed to bursting with an atmosphere so unhinged it was almost orgiastic. Truly, he'd never witnessed the like – girls necking each other passionately at the bar, clay-faced gothics smoking heroin in the back room, everyone skinning up, dabbing speed, sniffing poppers, downing brandy and dancing, dancing their nuts off, dancing to everything, each song greeted more ecstatically than the last: Television – 'Marquee Moon', Gina X – 'No GDM', Dillinger – 'Cocaine', the Only

Ones – 'Another Girl, Another Planet', Suicide – 'Ghost Rider', Lou Reed – 'Vicious', Devo – 'Whip It', Magazine – 'Shot by Both Sides', the Modern Lovers – 'Road Runner', Human League – 'Being Boiled', Silicon Teens – 'Memphis, Tennessee', Iggy Pop – 'The Passenger', the Normal – 'Warm Leatherette', Mink DeVille – 'Spanish Stroll'; it was like an Eric's hit parade, with even the most reserved of the regulars belting out the words to Wah! Heat's 'Better Scream' in a glorious, ramshackle singalong. Caught up in a knot of punk-ish, spaced-out Wirral girls, Danny declined, in order, seven spliffs, four lines of coke, two heads of smack and a three-some in Rock Ferry with two willowy, utterly smashed blondes. He said yes to the ciggies and yes to the vodkas and didn't wholly resist when one of them put her hand down his jeans during the Bunnymen's amazing set. It was easier just to let her do what she wanted. For one blind second he was going to turn round and start kissing her, but he couldn't – physically, he was packed too tight to manoeuvre, anyway – he just couldn't do it. He was in their place. When he was back in the flat he vacillated between the compulsive desire to go out and meet a girl, and a real dread of letting go for ever all that had been so good. More than anything he craved company. He was a talker, Danny, a dreamer who liked to romance out loud, spitting out half-formed views and ideas, one after another. He missed that – the way Nicole would sit, head cocked as she listened, always ready to hear him out. More often than not she'd scold him for his naivety or analyse his changing world view: one day he was a Naturalist, another day he'd be an Existentialist. Now she was gone. And never did he feel that isolation more than at night, in their bed. He almost felt like asking the girl back with him, just to not be alone. But he knew he wouldn't. He was nowhere near ready for new adventures yet – let alone in their Eric's playground. It hit him like a thunder flash that it was time to go. The Bunnymen were fantastic, the place was wild, but something was calling a halt to it, calling him back home. He gave the girl an apologetic grimace, shuffled sideways and backways, squeezing himself, little by little, to the stairs. It barely seemed to register with the doped-up blonde that Danny and his pliable dick had gone. The band was playing 'Do It Clean'.

Christmas Eve, heavy heart. He'd got back there, lain down on the bed, drained the last dregs of rum and smoked his last cigarette. Even at 2.17 a.m. in the small hours of 24 December, there was a fat fly squatting on the wall, watching him fail to rest. He hurled the bottle at it and regretted it at his leisure as the insect spent the next hour waiting for him to pass out, then buzzing in his ear. Being alone in bed was bad enough, but being alone with a bluebottle was torture.

He got up, neither alert nor with any purpose, but because he was bored of just lying there. He had little appetite for Christmas now. Ninna always made a huge fuss and, more so than any of her young offspring, contrived to have a merry time of it. For his part, Danny was used to being a willing cog in her merriment, fetching and carrying and making eyes and over-giggling at every joke, every coarse remark. He'd told them nothing of his dolours and the closer the time came, the more he delayed going back there. They weren't expecting him and Nicole until Christmas dinner anyway, thinking they'd go to Darwen first – her being the girl and all that. But Danny knew that in her heart of hearts Ninna would not be able to avoid a tinge of disappointment if her only grandson failed to pop in there sometime on Christmas Eve and indulge her with a game of housey-housey and an amble down to the Croxteth.

He sighed hard and drew himself up to face the music. He'd leave the formalities of moving out until after Boxing Day, so, deciding he'd put off all bad news until the very last possible moment, pretending he still had a girlfriend, he pulled on his Campri jacket, dug the gloves out of his pockets and trudged two flights down to the inner hall door. If he hadn't dropped a glove he might have missed the letter altogether, numb and preoccupied as he was. But there it was – a letter addressed to him. All it said on the envelope was 'Danny'.

He tore it open, heart thumping, wanting to gallop ahead and devour its contents all at once. The words slowed his heart right down though.

> *It's four in the morning, the end of December*
> *I'm writing you now just to see if you're better.*

It was the opening few lines of 'Famous Blue Raincoat'. Blinded by tears, he couldn't read on. Whatever grief he'd been nursing came powering forth now, and he slumped down the vestibule wall until he was sat there, flat on the cold tiled floor, sobbing. He was overjoyed. This, more than anything she could have written, told him why she was the only girl for him. Whatever she did to him, he could never, ever let her go. He dabbed his eyes and sniffed hard, and read on. She was outside. She was over the road, waiting in the woods!

> And so, my thin gypsy thief, it comes down to this. Yes or
> no? I'll wait here until I know, one way or the other. I love
> you. Whatever happens now, never forget that I loved you.
> Nicole

One kiss underneath, as always. He threw the door open and bolted across the road to find her.

Nausea

'You've had her, haven't you? You've *fucked* that old boiler!'

Danny was struggling to see the funny side. They'd made it – just – through Christmas, though they managed to argue, savagely, about every little thing; his refusal to dance to the Dickies; her insistence on calling anyone under the age of thirty 'kids'; his wanton use of back slang whenever they bumped into anyone from the university; her blatant overspending on his sisters' Christmas presents when ten Number 6 would have done just fine. They bickered and made up, fell out and kissed it better, but the more they tried to put Paris behind them, the more she started into a new tack of wanting to justify her fling.

In the few days before New Year's Eve she'd become increasingly obsessive about the subject, doggedly bringing up the concept of fidelity again and again, looking to dissect and debate the issue to a point where he was ready to concede, sign a treaty, let her see whoever she wanted. He couldn't stand talking about it and couldn't comprehend why she'd want to hurt him with it, all over again, so soon after the event. Sitting there in their cosy room, both dressed up and ready to go and see the new year in, she couldn't resist one more hack at it.

'I'm not *saying* it's going to happen again, darling. That's not what this is all about. But look – if you and I are going to make it, we have to face up to some harsh realities. Yes? Neither one of us has even *started* to fulfil their sexual potential. You know? It's just unrealistic to think that two good-looking kids like you and me are going to go through life without even *looking* at anyone else. Don't you see that?'

'I see it. And I know it. I'm not fucking stupid, you know? But for me, like . . . that's the fucking *challenge*!'

'It shouldn't *be* a challenge. You know, that stupid little affair in Paris . . .'

His head dropped. She insisted on calling it an 'affair'. She reached for his hand.

'No, please, darling, please – hear me out . . .'

She squeezed his three middle fingers as though filling him with the strength to stand up to this latest dose of Harsh Reality. He felt miserable.

'All I did wrong . . .' She sighed deeply. 'I *know* I shouldn't have. I know that. But at that moment, at that crystallised point in time, I needed to be free to follow my own *will*. Is that so wrong, baby? Do I have to feel guilt for that? Do I have to feel shame over an act of free will?'

Danny said nothing. He looked at the floor as she continued.

'Kierkegaard teaches that –'

This, of all things, enraged him. He jerked his head back up.

'Look! I'm not arsed what some cunt with a mad name from the olden days thinks. I want to know what *you* think!'

She was shocked into silence. He dropped her hand and stood up.

'I want to know what you stand for, Nic . . .' He walked to the door. 'I want to know what *we* mean to you.'

She jumped up and ran to him. 'Oh, baby! I've done it again, haven't I? I didn't mean . . .'

He turned to her, tears in his eyes. 'Look. Let's leave it, la. Can we just go out and get fucking bladdered, please? I'm sick to death of all this . . . *talk*!'

They walked briskly along the Avenue towards Peter Kavanagh's alehouse. With the steam of their breath gusting against the cold night air and a jet-black sky sprinkled with thousands and thousands of stars, there was a glimmer of their magical past. Danny looked for his star, but it was nowhere to be seen. Understanding everything though, she pulled him close, kissed him tenderly.

'Remember the lake? When we went skating?'

She wrapped herself around him as they walked. It felt good. To both of them, it felt good again.

The warmth of the pub along with abundant beers and brandies only increased this deep-seated sense of cheer – faith in themselves, and real hope for the coming year.

'You with your painting and me finishing my degree – we can start living, Danny Boy!'

'Yiss,' gasped Danny. 'Once I get started proper at the art school . . . it's going to be sound. Just you see . . .'

Nicole leaned towards him and grazed his nose with a kiss. A woman was looking over them.

'Who *is* that, Dan?'

He turned, saw her and his face lit up.

'Ah, nice one! That's Lingsby, babe.'

She recalled the name, but placing Lingsby was proving elusive.

'You know! Who got me the painting gig and that . . . my thingio, you know – my tutor, at college. Come 'ead! I want you to meet her.'

He started pushing through the crowd, concentrating on getting there rather than on Lingsby herself. Nicole's eyes never left her, though. There was something not right about her, she thought. All her intuition told Nicole that Lingsby's presence, or more particularly her demeanour, was bad news for them, and her abrupt departure only confirmed it. She saw it all. Lingsby seemed emotional as Danny made his way towards her and, as he got within touching distance, she clamped her hand to her mouth, turned and ran out of the pub. Danny just stood there, speechless. He turned to Nicole, bemused.

'What was all that about?' she asked, not especially kindly.

'Fuck knows. Did you see her?'

'I saw her all right.'

Danny was too busy puzzling it all out and digging for cigarettes to take in the expression clouding Nicole's face. He sparked one up, offered the pack to her. She batted his hand away.

'What I saw was a besotted middle-aged woman whose fantasies had just been shattered.'

'You *what*?'

'Come on, Danny! Please don't play the innocent with me. She saw me with you and realised your affair was going nowhere.'

'*Affair*? What the *fuck* are you on about?'

'She was *devastated*, Danny! She couldn't look you in the fucking eye!'

He floundered around, suddenly feeling guilty by association. 'She's probably feeling bad, isn't she?'

Nicole said nothing – just watched him, as if watching an experiment to which the outcome was already known. Danny blustered on, angry, but knowing he needed to make some sense out of this sudden madness.

'Look. She said she'd get us a showing in a gallery, didn't she? She said her mate could sell loads of paintings for us. Maybe she's just feeling last that it never come off . . .'

She prepared her *coup de grâce*. She took a step back so she could examine his reaction to it.

'You've had her, haven't you? You've *fucked* that old boiler!'

Danny found himself chuckling at the absurdity of it. He laughed, but he was struggling to see the funny side.

'Jesus Christ, Nic – you're obsessed! You've got cheating on the brain! Cheating and scheming and lying and people doing the dirty on each other – it's all's you want to think about! Fuck's up with you, girl?'

160

'I *saw* her, Danny. All that fucking cleavage! What's she doing going out like that anyway, at her age . . .'

Danny held the cigarette to his mouth but didn't smoke it; indeed, he seemed to forget it was there. He sighed and took her hand.

'Look, you. You've had a hard time. We've both had a hard time. Now, maybe it'd make life easier for you if I'd done something bad, too. Hey? Maybe it evens up the score. But I haven't. Right? I wouldn't. That's it — top and bottom of it. I wouldn't do that to you. Not just to you, Nic — I wouldn't do it to *myself*. And I really need you to get all that shite out of your head, please. We've said we're putting it behind us. We've said we're moving on — so let's move on. OK?'

She nodded, once, but her eyes betrayed no love. They danced in Catherine Street at midnight and they kissed and made promises to each other, but the sordid end to their year was already dragging over into the new one.

1980

Stars are Stars

All was not well with Lingsby. Glassy-eyed, she'd drifted through the class on autopilot to such an extent that Danny started allowing room for Nicole's theory. When she asked him to stay behind afterwards, he was almost certain what was coming. Nicole was right. Lingsby was going to ask Danny to move class for these last, crucial months. He could see it in her moist eyes – she was smitten with him. She motioned him towards her own seat and remained standing herself. Nervous, he found himself grinning up stupidly at her.

'Wassup, Doc?' he said.

She sighed hard and shook her head. 'Oh, Daniel. I'm just no good at this . . .'

He got up, still radiating what he knew would be, if he glanced in the mirror, a daft, simpleton's grin.

'Look. If your mate at the gallery's changed his mind, it's no big deal. Their loss, hey?'

She turned her back on him and stared mournfully out of the window.

'It isn't that. If only it were that simple.'

'What, please? What's so bad?'

Now she turned to him, eyes wet and red and puffy.

'It isn't fair, Daniel. It simply isn't right. They're centralising all the fine arts degrees.'

He blinked back at her. Nothing she'd said seemed that bad. It didn't sound like anything to do with *him*. Yet he could see from her face, her eyes, her abject misery that this was *all* to do with him.

'Tell us straight, like. How d'you mean?'

Her shoulders slumped. She managed, just, to look him in the eye.

'They're closing down the art school.'

She held his gaze a moment longer before her face collapsed. Danny hardly took it in. Three questions shot through his mind: *who* is closing down the art school? Why? When? But none of these questions was voiced. A bolt shot through his heart and left him dumb, and dead. His mouth fell wide open. He stayed rooted to the spot, stunned, mesmerised. He looked at her mouth, which had delivered the verdict, and her eyes, which had given it away. He turned and stumbled from the building, and staggered out on to Myrtle Street, gasping for breath. He'd seen it in films and on television and never thought it looked real, but here he was sat down at the roadside, clawing at the tight top button of his small-collared shirt, suffocating. He completely lost the next segment of his existence. He found himself sitting on the steps of the bombed church – no recollection of getting there and no interest in it, either. He didn't know even vaguely what time it was. The skies had fallen in on him. All he'd ever wanted, everything he'd ever dreamt about was being taken away from him. They were closing down the art school.

He took his time walking back, starting to think through his next move. He couldn't even picture himself finishing his foundation course now. It was all to fuck. What would be the point in any of it? Lingsby was advocating Sheffield, but that completely missed the point. He couldn't leave. He didn't want to. He might as well just get back on the Scream and start trawling the Toxteth fleshpots again, looking for marks. Turning into Upper Duke Street a whey-faced lad clocked him and, as he passed, gave the faintest nod, his fearful eyes kept lowered to the floor. The greeting was mute and wary, seeming to expect rejection yet still flickering with some remote flake of hope. Danny nearly didn't recognise the wraith, so slight had he become, so keen and bony his head. It was Brian Tremarco, emaciated and shivering in a thin, ragged Harrington jacket.

'A'right, man.'

'Danny?'

Danny squeezed some life back into his voice. 'How's it going, Bri?'

Brian took a step back towards him. Accustomed to being shunned by acquaintances and strangers alike, he was unused to such consideration. It took him a second to abuse it. Danny's gentle enquiry came alive to Brian, laden with possibilities. Eyes suddenly shining with invention, he reached out to him.

'Got caught in a fire. This place I was staying –'

'Shit! Is your mam all right? Did youse all –'

'Not there, la! Haven't lived there since I spewed the Postie . . .'

'Never even knew you'd spewed the Postie, Brian . . .'

'Soft lad's still there, like . . .'

They eyed one another carefully. Brian took one more step and made his pitch.

'Just, like – everything went in the fire. Me Judy's in bits, la. Weren't insured or nothing. Just going the soshe now, kidder, see if they'll give us a by-hander and that . . .'

'Bad one, man . . .'

He gave it a second's more thought, then went for it. 'You haven't got a flim have you, Danny, la? Just till later. Till I get me giro?'

Danny shook his head. 'I haven't, kidder. Skint myself.'

'Have you got a nicker, well?'

'Got fuck all, la. I'd be on the bus if I had poke . . .'

Desperation returned to Brian's stale eyes. His mind lurched on, still plea-bargaining for any gift, anything at all.

'You seen *The Wall* yet, la?'

Danny shrugged. 'Not into them, man.'

'Ah man, you don't *have* to be into them. You wanna see it, la, it'll wreck your fucken head . . .'

'Probably will do, Bri. Anyway . . .'

Danny was tiring of this needy, scatterfire chat. He stretched and made a silent yawn and started nodding towards the great elsewhere, ready to make his move. Brian saw it and blocked it.

'Here y'are. Come with us! Come and see the fillum, kidder man!'

'Ah, dunno, Brian . . .'

'Come 'ead, la! I know the girl at the ABC. Be easy . . .'

Danny could hear the words in his head, but he was too tired and too dejected to argue with him. He didn't care either way any more. What difference would it make whether or not he went? Of course he shouldn't go. He knew that full well, and he knew it'd be easy enough to fob the lad off. But the pulse of damnation beat hard in his ears. Whatever seemed good, he only wanted to tear down. All these people pushing past, excited to be going to Chinatown or Kirklands or just to be going home for the day – he detested them. More than anything, he detested himself. How could he have ever thought this was going to work out for him? Did he ever really, truly believe those big dreams could come to life? He gave a nasty little chuckle, revelling in the inevitable cruelty of fate, of life. What difference did it matter if he went with Brian? And who exactly gave a fuck anyway? But no – he wouldn't go. He'd clear his throat and pat him on the back and make his excuses, go on his way.

'Catch you again, kidder,' he smiled, the finality of it making its mark even on Brian's frazzled psyche. He winced and scuttled away, head craned forward towards some wholly illusory finishing line. Danny kicked his lugubrious path back up the hill. Up ahead, he came to the streets at the back of the art school where he and Nic had kissed and saluted his glorious future. Rage coursed through him, obliterating the sadness and the dull ennui. He stopped, sized up the beautiful old building and turned on his heel. He spotted Brian up ahead and went after him, trying to keep pace with his jerky speedwalk.

The film was a revelation, not for the mastery of Gerald Scarfe's vision alone, but for the pungent fug of drug smoke in the stalls. The ABC was rammed to the rafters for this mid-afternoon showing and every single punter was under the age of twenty and stoned out of their box. Down by the emergency exit, Brian mithered and harangued a skin-thin wretch in a green Peter Storm. Browbeaten, the lad unzipped his chest pouch and delved inside, handing over a wrap and moving the pathetically grateful Brian along so the next lad could speak to him. Not so long ago, a film like this would have brought in the corduroy-clad, bearded Arties, the roll-your-own students from Preston and Leicester who Danny so devoutly looked up to. But this matinée was populated by bleary-eyed scallies from the Dingle and Scotland Road, killing time in town before the pubs opened up again. Brian slumped back down, grinning.

'Now then!' he gleamed, checking around reflexively, while straightening out a length of KitKat foil. 'Here we go.'

He sprinkled a gritty powder into the nape of the foil and flicked open a Zippo, running the flame up and down the silver, quickly and efficiently. Biting on his inner cheek, he felt around for something then swooped, a little stainless tube clamped between his lips. He inhaled, held the smoke deep inside and sat back, suddenly serene. For a moment he said nothing at all, just turned towards Danny, eyes pinned, trying to smile. He slumped down, eyelids drooping heavy, and the weight of his head fell forward, waking him. Confused for a split second, he turned to Danny, offering him the kit.

'What is it, like?'

'What is it?'

'That's what I said, la. What is it?'

A merry snort burst from Brian's lips and nose. He lurched his head around and about, as though appealing for any one of about four hundred witnesses to come forward and tell the mook what was what. Instead, he grinned right into Danny's face.

'Try it. You'll like it.'

'What is it?'

'You. Will. *Lllilllove* it.'

'Is it smack?'

'It's heaven, la. It's the moon. It's fucken beautiful, man.'

Brian scraped the foil and set about building another head for Danny. He warmed it with the Zippo, waited for the fumes to rise and, eyes now drilling deep into his reluctant accessory, handed him the pipe.

'Come with us. Come and see the stars, la. You haven't had nothing like it . . .'

Danny looked at him, looked at the gently sizzling foil and took the steel tube.

Brian hardly seemed to register that they were going their separate ways. He just carried on walking, eager and agitated. Head and shoulders leaning forward so that he was almost toppling over, he tottered away into the night, already prospecting for his next opportunity. Danny watched him lurching along the middle of the Avenue, head jerking this way and that, then continued back to the flat.

Being and Nothingness

'Darling. You've got to snap out of it. You've still got time, you know – but you've *got* to start going back to college.'

'Why?'

'You *know* why.'

'What's the point?'

She sat him down again.

'The point is, Danny May – you're a fucking genius. Whether you go to Liverpool or Manchester or Glasgow to show yourself off, I don't really care. I'm there with you, little man. But you've got to *do* this for yourself. Don't just buckle, Danny baby. *Please* don't give in to them!'

He turned to face her.

'You really don't get it, do you?'

'*Tell* me . . .'

He stood up, shaking his head in sullen fury, and stumbled to the door. She ran after him, trying to block his way.

'Danny!'

He fled down the stairs.

'Danny!'

She ran back inside, flung open the heavy casement window and stuck her head out. He hovered at the side of the road, waiting for a break in the traffic.

'You're being a fucking *baby* about this, Daniel!'

She heaved the window back down and, with a heavy heart, returned to her dissertation.

Peckish after two hours' grappling with Kant, she went to the fridge and, finding nothing at all titillating, let out a sigh of dejection and hooked up her bag from behind the door. She'd benefit from a break anyway. A walk down to the Kwikie, coffee, milk, beans, bread – perhaps a packet of Bourbon biscuits – and she'd be ready for Round Two. She fished out her purse. Odd. She racked her brain, tracing back their movements last night. Yes, they'd stopped on Smithdown Road for ciggies but she'd definitely, definitely, *definitely* paid with a tenner. Neither of them had been out of the flat since, yet her purse was empty but for some loose change. There should have been a fiver and at least three if not four pound notes. She turned the purse upside down, probing it now for flaps and zips she might have overlooked. There were none. It was empty. They'd been robbed! A lead weight dropped inside her as she checked the door, the windows. The horrid thought occurred to her that, while they'd sat here arguing, one of their neighbours had slipped inside and stolen her money. The idea seemed worse somehow than a burglar breaking in from outside. There'd been a spate of incidents in the area – students getting held up at the new cash dispenser, flats getting ransacked – but with Danny there she'd always felt immune. Now she was sick with worry. She paced up and down the front room, glancing out of the window sporadically, willing him back home. This was just more bad luck, and she wished that the tide would turn and refloat them and let them start their trip again.

Back on the trundling train out to Darwen, he was chirpier than she'd seen him in a long time. The art school at Wigan had survived the latest round of cuts, and she was ardently weighing up the pros and cons of moving them back to Lancashire as soon as she graduated. It was far from being ideal, but he seemed a different Danny out here.

'Look at that! Did you see that, honeybaby?'

Those silly little pet names he used to make up. Even they were making a comeback. She leaned towards him, as though craning to hear the first words in months from a sick loved one. He grinned at her.

'Look. That's a fucking kestrel, that is!'

'You sure about that, Dan?'

She didn't want to burst his bubble, but neither did she want him getting into an in-depth conversation with her pernickety, birdwatching father.

'Didn't know we *had* kestrels round here.'

'Old Kes is no different to you and me. He responds to human hardship. Well . . . birdy hardship and that. He goes where he has to, to make a living.'

She studied his lively, clever face and her heart vaulted with sheer adoration. Why *shouldn't* they live out here? It'd only be for a few years, and if it helped get Danny back his lust for life . . .

'Might be a kite though, mind you. Or a hawk. What's a kite look like?'

She could see his lips moving, but she didn't hear him. Her face melted into a vague, peaceful smile as she watched his happy chatter. He was chattering again, and that was good. How different from last night. After the raid, after the police had finally searched every purse and pocket and made their arrests and kicked every last soul out into the night, Danny had declined every single suggestion of hers to keep the night alive. They'd trudged back home in the drizzle, in silence, until she could take his sulking no more. She stopped in the middle of the park, arms folded.

'Look. They'll have to reschedule. You'll see your precious Furs.'

He stopped, too.

'You think I'm arsed about the Psychedelic Furs?'

He shook his head bitterly, letting her see just how trivial her concerns were. He took her by the upper arms as though ready to force her backwards, but instead he gazed into her eyes.

'Don't you see, Nic? That's it. That club'll never open again now. That's the fucking end of Eric's. That's another place closed down.'

And although she'd never stopped to think how much she loved the place, she was stricken with a sudden sense of loss and threw her arms around him, clinging to him tight.

'Oh, Danny baby, no. Don't say that!'

But she knew he was right. Watching him prattle on now about birds of prey and their nesting habits and the prospect of seeing young kestrels take to the skies, it seemed like a different Danny. For the first time in a long while she recalled their early days together, panging for each other the moment either had had to leave. She cherished the thought, and bowed her head at the recollection of his recent woes. There had been times over the past few weeks when she'd sifted through his drawings and half-finished paintings and wondered if he'd ever find his zeal again. She laughed at something he said. She didn't hear it, but knew from his smiling delivery that a chuckle was required from her in return. She sat back and watched the trees and fields whirr by, and she vowed to herself that she and nobody else could help Danny back to his feet, and his easel.

As the girls bickered, Danny winced at Mrs Watson and excused himself. Harriet had become tipsy quickly and started aiming ever more suggestive remarks at him. It was all in jest of course, but there was a knowing undertone to her play. There could be no denying it – Hattie Watson was growing into a beautiful and sexy young woman, and her hormones were in riot. As Danny took the stairs two at a time, he could hear Nicole hissing at her sister. 'For God's sake, Hattie – wipe your chin! Oh sorry – that *is* your chin . . .'

He pissed, wiped the toilet seat, treble-checked he hadn't left a single splash anywhere and made to go back downstairs when something caught his eye. It was a well-worn Harris tweed jacket, hanging on the edge of the Watsons' bed – and there was just a suggestion of wallet peeking out. He made up his mind in a trice.

The buzzer made both of them start. It was unusual, if not unheard of, for either of them to have visitors at night. She went to the window.

'Who is it?' drawled Danny, sleepy. Nicole didn't answer at first. Of course she regretted losing her temper with her sister now, sending her running to her room in tears at Nicole's mention of her spotty chin. Harriet had not re-emerged before their departure – but that was no reason for her father to show up at their door at that hour.

It was unclear whether Mr Watson had expected, by simple virtue of his sitting there in abject silence, Danny to break down and confess. Whatever, it was an uncomfortable hour for all of them, Nicole in particular trying to mediate between the two men in her life. Her father beat around the bush, airing a general grievance that thirty pounds had gone missing from his wallet sometime that afternoon, rather than coming out and grilling Danny about it. Danny remained calm and relatively cheerful, though the longer his charade continued the more Nicole started to believe he might have done it. She couldn't pinpoint how she'd expect him to act under circumstances where his future father-in-law suspected him of theft, but she knew in her veins that he wouldn't behave like this. It just wasn't her Danny. It wasn't him. The Danny who had delighted her so on the train up to Darwen would have got upset, perhaps – marched off or slammed the doors or even just sat there, silently fuming. But this Danny now was almost smug in his polite concern for Mr Watson's plight. He was too smiling, yet too remote, the light behind his eyes burning with a provocative, teasing insolence. His eyes seemed to say: 'You think I did it? Well, maybe I did. Now prove it!'

In the end Mr Watson got tired of the game. He stood up. Danny remained seated. Nicole implored him with her eyes to pay her father a respect that neither she nor Danny felt. He opened his eyes wide to her, feigning non-comprehension, and stayed exactly where he was. Mr Watson scowled at Danny one last time, accepted a chaste hug from his daughter and let himself out. Nicole stayed in the doorway, watching Danny. She watched him as though looking at a snake or a crocodile at the zoo, interested, yet appalled. At no stage did he turn towards her. He gazed up out of the big sash windows, picking out the stars in the sky and smiling, faintly smiling to himself. She turned and went to the bedroom.

The End

Tired, dirty and badly in the grip of the pangs, Danny glanced anxiously down the track as he paced the platform. Sunday service was hit-and-miss these days, but he couldn't think of a better score. He knew from Nicole that the Watsons were away, knew there was a fighting chance they'd left the key in the usual place, too. If not, that patio window at the back was criminally easy – a hefty stone wrapped in a jacket would bust one of those tiny panes out with hardly a noise at all and he'd be in there. He'd get whatever he could easily carry – jewellery, cash, any valuables – and if there were bigger things he could sell off at Seth's, he could always come back in a car with Brian or Robbie. It was a clear, bright, mid-May morning, so still he had to strain to hear the distant sounds of traffic. Twice already he'd felt the warm glow of anticipation as the rail tracks spat and crackled, announcing an impending arrival, but neither had been his train. He sat back down by the kiosk, picked up a discarded *People* and grazed the headlines. Unemployment had topped two million. She'd barely been in a year and already, this. Nicole would be unbearable. A slow vibration trembled through the platform seat, and this time he was on. He took the paper with him.

As eager as he was to cash in and get fixed up, he stood back and watched the house for a moment. The car was gone, but something about the place still seemed lived-in. There was no telltale milk outside, and the grass was already unkempt by their frigid standards. No, the Watsons had definitely gone on holiday. As casually as though he lived there full-time, Danny sauntered up the path and groped underneath the big plant pot. Nothing. Shame. Having to break in would only slow him down. He spotted another big planter and put his back into shoving that to one side, gritting his teeth as it grated against the clay tiles. He hadn't moved it completely, but there was clearly nothing there either. Panting, he straightened his back.

'Hey!'

His heart nearly stopped dead in a blast of panic. Yet, even as his pulse was still lurching from the shock, his subconscious was on the mend, absorbing the surprise, the happy and slightly cheeky thrill in her voice.

'What on earth are *you* doing here?'

Danny was quick to recover. He stood up, flirting with Harriet with his eyes.

'What do *you* think?'

There was little or no jousting. From the sudden drop of her eyeline, the stylised kicking of her leg and her artful toying with her hair, she told him straight away it was Yes. She was young, she was bored, she was naughty. Of course she was letting him come in.

'I don't know, Daniel. What could you possibly be doing out here so early on a Sunday morning?' She held on to the door frame and swung her head and shoulders, in and out. 'Unless you've come to rape me and rob the house.'

He shot her his best filthy smile. His face was stretched tight across his cheekbones, giving his eyes a dazzling, drugged-out intensity. Long gone was any trace of dimples. He was all dramatic, jutting bone and brilliant, crazed eyes. He fixed both lamps full on her.

'Well, I'll be quite honest with you, babe. Your sister's kicked us out. Just one of them silly things, but I'm out on the streets. And I just thought to myself – where can I get a wash? Who do I know in this world who'll take us in?'

She pulled the door back wider and nodded him inside. He saw now that she was wearing only very brief knickers and a vest. Her tiny bottom twitched with every stride of her slim white legs. He followed her up the stairs to the landing, soft underfoot with its bottle-green carpet, patterned with tiny gold diamonds. She signalled for him to wait, and went into the bathroom. He heard the plug go in, the slug of the water piling down into the tub. He heard her brush her teeth, then she was at the door again, beckoning him inside. Her breasts showed through the fabric where she'd splashed water down her front. He extended a hand and felt out for her tits, eyes locked on to hers. She put her hand on his wrist, held him back for a moment then let herself lean back against the bath-room door. She seemed troubled by doubt for a moment but then she bucked her hips out from the door and pushed her chest out slightly, willing him to grope her again. Danny's cock was pulsing hard in his skinny jeans. He started to feel her breasts again, more roughly this time, pushing them together and moving them around under her vest. She let out a moan.

'Danny, no . . .'

He tugged at her knickers. She pulled them down and stepped out of them, kicked them to one side and parted her legs. He put his whole hand over her mound, soaking up the heat of her fanny. She closed her eyes and let her head fall back, thrusting her fanny sharply against his palm as he leaned forward to kiss her. She brought her face up to meet him,

175

impassioned, biting out at his tongue and cheeks. She jerked her head back from him, eyes flashing.

'God, you fucking stink!' She tugged at his zip. 'You dirty fucking bastard!'

He dragged her vest up hard, snapping the shoulder strap, engorged with lust at the sight of her, naked, wanting him. He lay on his back, bucking his hips to wriggle his tight jeans over his throbbing cock – and pulled her down beside him.

It was not without remorse that Danny kissed her narrow back as she slept, and crept from the bed. He stood and watched her for a moment, bitterly sad about what she'd wake up to yet queerly detached from it. It was as though he were removed from the picture and was looking on at two completely different people. For his part he had been thrown awake by a fearsome, gnawing pang in his guts, a craving to be fed. He kissed Harriet lightly, regretting everything – but what had passed was past. For Danny it was all now, furious now.

He dressed silently and, knowing the Watsons would have left her ample living money, let alone emergency funds, he set about seeking it out. Obvious places – her chest of drawers, the vase on the kitchen table, the bureau in the dining room – turned up nothing. It never ceased to amaze Danny how unimaginative people were when it came to concealing cash. Of course it wouldn't occur to most people, ever, that they might be robbed – and they tended to want easy access to their dough. Like everybody else, the Watsons would have put the cash somewhere really, really stupid. How much? he wondered. Twenty quid? Thirty, perhaps? They were only gone for ten days and Harriet was supposed to be revising for her O levels, but she'd still need at least twenty rips. He opened up a kitchen cupboard, and bingo! Among the clear-glass jars with their cork stoppers, jars containing muesli, pasta and rice, was one containing banknotes. Lots of them. Nimbly, he went on to his toes and, head back, eased the jar down from its shelf, prising the bung out and emptying the notes out on to the worktop. Quite a few fivers and *plenty* of pound notes. And – yes-yes-yes! Was this a tenner? It was. There must be close on fifty quid there. He could kill himself on that! Self-consciously checking around to reassure himself he was still alone, Danny scooped up the money and let himself out at the front door. He had all the way back to count it and to plan how to spend it. There was enough there to get down the art shop, get some new brushes and get himself working again. He could get himself a little second-hand Pentax too, start going out taking pictures. He had the eye and the feel for that – not as a job, maybe, but for himself. He liked developing them and seeing how they'd turn out. He was still technically a student at City College – he'd get into the darkrooms again, easy. And he'd *definitely* get Nicole something – that big thick book on Trotsky she was always thumbing in News From Nowhere, and some nice clobber for summer. If they got the money together for the InterRail pass, she was going to need clothes. But first of all, there was a house in Windsor Street he had to visit.

'Baby! Oh you poor, poor thing . . .'

Danny, grey and clammy, had been sitting with his back against their door, unable to face her. Hollow-eyed and hopeless, he looked up at her now. She got her hands under his armpits and tried to haul him up.

'Come on, you. Let's get you inside.'

He put an arm around her shoulder and let her help him into the front room. She shuffled him across the floor to the sofa, laying him down and propping his head with a cushion. She ran her fingers through his clotted hair.

'You look dreadful. When did you hear?'

He tried to plug back in and offer something back to her. Nicole kissed him lightly on the lips.

'You must be shattered. Radio 1 have had it on all day. They're saying he hanged himself . . .'

He managed to drag his head up, then his shoulders, until he was sitting. As though the heroin had worked as a proving agent, he knew immediately whom she meant. He nodded to the radio, once again perched on the window sill though he'd told her a dozen times to leave nothing on display.

'Put it on, will you?'

She gave him a pitying look, walked over and snapped it on. She came back and sat beside him.

'Were you absolutely distraught, baby?'

He nodded. She ruffled his hair again.

'Look at you . . .' She gave him a tender smile, leaned to brush against his cheek. 'Pooh! *Smell* you. What have you been drinking, Danny May?' She jumped up. 'Come on. Let's run you a bath. To hell with the gas bill . . .'

She bounded off into the bathroom. He felt utterly, utterly wretched. Their bell went. He knew exactly, to the precise pitch of every hurt and angry note, what was coming next. Nicole's girlish voice trilled from down the hall.

'You stay there. I'll get that.'

He heard the little dimpled window go up as she checked outside. He heard the delighted gasp as she saw who it was.

'Wow! Hang on, Hatt . . .'

He lay back and fought against the lump in his throat. He could hear Nicole padding innocently down the stairs, thrilled to think her sister, lonely and perhaps a little scared in the house on her own, had come to spend an evening with them. He could hear the big front door creaking open, too warped and heavy for its sticky frame. By now, Nic would have seen Harriet's face. Over the next thirty seconds, her world would be turned inside out. All her worst suspicions; all the times he'd found her staring at him, unable and unwilling to think it; all the dreadful conclusions she'd swallowed and buried – they were now being laid bare in front of her. Harriet was down there, in their vestibule, telling her sister all about the man she was living with. The radio broke back into Danny's consciousness.

'This is one of the very last songs Ian Curtis wrote. Listening to it now, you can't help but believe it was his epitaph . . . Ian Curtis, who died at his own hand last night, aged twenty-three.'

He could hear the footsteps now, coming back upstairs. Harriet would be stung, angry, self-righteous; he'd fucked her then robbed their house. Too fresh to bunk the train, she'd probably scraped the fare together from her wary neighbours, who'd be unsure whether they were helping finance a trip to some sultry discotheque. Nicole would still be hanging on by a gossamer thread, hoping against hope. There was a chance her puckish sister had made this whole thing up. There was a chance, still a chance . . .

But when they walked into the room and Danny was standing by the window with his back to them and when he didn't even turn round or speak, just stood there, looking out at the park, she knew it was over. Giddy, faint, viciously angry and cheated all at once, she still could not speak. In her mind she could hear, clearly, how her voice would sound – weak, silly, pathetic. She went to pack her bag. Harriet remained in the room. From the bedroom, but with devastating clarity, came Nicole's desperate, whimpering cries.

'Happy now?' said Harriet.

Danny turned, briefly, but he could not meet her eye. He turned back to the trees across the road. Curtis's baleful aubade rose from the radio:

> *People like you find it easy*
> *Naked to see*
> *Walking on air . . .*

He sensed Nicole right behind him, about to say something. She said nothing. She put something down on the table, something light, paper, a contemptuous farewell note. He heard her walk away. He heard her stifled sobbing. He heard the door open and close.

Walk in silence
Don't walk away . . .

He tried to get the window up, lacked the strength to move it. Helpless, he saw the sisters emerge below, arms around one another, walking away. The finality of it smashed into him. He sucked the breath down to his lungs, trying to rein it all back in but no, no, no, no, she was walking away. She was gone.

The Planet is Glowing

For the remainder of that summer he tried to get himself moving again. It was slow and deadly, each positive move marked down by some hateful aberration. His sole and faithful answer to every personal crisis was the bag. He'd have a good day, two good days, but the moment the crabs came crawling he'd take refuge in that merciful nest of oblivion. The day he went back to the flat to clear it of all he held dear, he nearly passed out at the vehemence of his own self-loathing. Nicole had taken almost nothing. It was as though she had gone in there, started to pack, but been unable to hold herself together long enough to complete the task. Or perhaps she wanted to leave it all as was, a vacuum-packed elegy to better times. More killing than anything, she'd left the portrait he'd done of her, their first Christmas together. Weary and disillusioned, he collapsed on to their bed, his animus warring between total obliteration and this time, finally, taking things by the scruff of the neck.

He was back at his mother's, but it was an awful place to be. With Vera herself laid off from the factory and not one of the girls even working part-time, she accepted Danny's presence and his plight with a stoic but utterly silent resolve. Not even Ninna could relieve the leaden spirit of the May household. Lost in time and increasingly confused, Ninna had taken to walking out of the front door, often to be returned hours later by a neighbour or a relative who'd found her clinging to the bus stop, crying out that the road was tipping up, while schoolkids looked on, sniggering. He couldn't stand this for very much longer. His mother continued to feed them all, but the house was dead quiet. If not for himself then he'd have to get out for her sake, start to do some good again.

Through September he kept it clean for a week, ten days, eking out a living selling watercolours to the antique dealers down Allerton Road. Yet it always seemed just a matter of time before his next fall. Any slight, any knock-back, any new sense of the injustice of this harsh new world led him back to Windsor Street, and wipe-out. He thought of Nicole constantly. He couldn't quite believe that she wouldn't still love him. Three days in a row he sent her rambling, mewling letters, hardly aware what he was saying or asking. Without her, he was lost. He'd known it then, but he understood it now. With her, he was always looking forward. That, he had come to realise, was all he wanted from life – to still have dreams. Without Nicole he had only days and nights to live through, and live out.

With the last of the autumn sunshine came a new resolve. Biting down hard, swallowing back an immediate and virulent nostalgia, he pulled out his rusty old bicycle, turned it over on to its seat in the backyard and set about cleaning it up with Duraglit. Just working away on his trusty old steed, polishing its spokes, brushing out the rust and touching up the paintwork, made him feel better. He took the seized-up chain right off and, link by link, scoured away at the rust and the dirt until it was slick and ready again. Finally, and with a faint smile, he took up his finest brush and a tin of green enamel and, with tiny strokes, went over the faded name he'd given his bike. By teatime it was the Scream again. And when the students came back he drew himself up, forced himself across the threshold and set up on the campus outside the Augustus John, sketching new arrivals for a quid. Whether they truly thought the likeness was good seemed not to matter. What they were queuing for was the memento – the immediate rush of something of that elusive bohemia they'd been dreaming of, encapsulated in the form of a mute and remote young artist and the three magic words on their sketch: *Liverpool, Autumn 1980*. That was them, locked in time, for ever.

He did well those two weeks, yet it made little difference to Danny himself. There were records he could have bought – lots of records he'd heard or heard of, but nothing really moved him. He didn't even get *Closer*. The shops were full of cool new winter modes. Harold Ian had an elegant leather wolf jacket he would have killed for a year ago, but though he saw it in the window and noted it, he'd forgotten about it by the time he got home. Neither did the various notes and smiles of the student girls who fell for him make much impression. The less he said in answer to their questioning, the more they were fascinated by him. But nothing could get beneath him other than the constant beguiling lure of another hit. He could turn his face away, but it was always there, pricking at him.

This time he felt he was winning, though. All he was concentrating on was home, his suddenly-ageing mother, and how to make things right for her again. Everything he earned from his drawings he took straight back, put it into her hand. The first week she'd hardly thanked him, though he could see even from her sharp and almost aggressive turn away from him that she was grateful for the relief the money would buy. By the second week in October and with Danny still bringing back anything between a tenner and twenty pounds a day, she was not so dogged, starting to regain a flake of her previous vim.

But on the Thursday that all changed. Unusually buoyed by the mild autumn sunshine, Danny felt stirred by spirits and feelings he hadn't enjoyed in a while. Simply, he became affected by an uncommon joie de vivre that had started with the girl at lunchtime and stayed with him all day. All that had happened was a girl he sketched had made him laugh. That's how it started. She made cross-eyes at him, pulled a face and put on her best Margaret Thatcher voice:

'Young man. You are a credit. You are a shining example to the wreckers, the work-shy and the wanglers . . .'

He couldn't help himself. He chuckled out loud, making the girl smile, too. She got up to take a peep at her picture. She had a game, slightly tomboyish gait. She liked the picture and paid up her pound. She winked at Danny.

'Hope you're declaring that, mate!'

Wow! He thought. She's *lovely*. He winked back at her.

'I'm one of the two and a half million, girl . . .'

They both paused, both understanding that the next bit was where Danny asked her out for a drink, she'd demur a moment or two and then say yes. He took a deep breath. This was it, then – back on the road. The girl glittered back at him – pretty, and nice, and lovely. They'd get along well together. They'd be perfect. He pushed back his shoulders to help the words out, and spoke.

'Suppose I'd better get off, then . . .'

It had been the last thing she'd expected. She made a fair job of masking her dismay, but her shrug and her rueful smile and the real hurt in her eyes gave it all away. Danny started to collapse his easel, trying not to look as she ambled away. He wanted to run after her, give her back her pound and assure her that she was going to have the very best of times and, who could say, it might well start that very evening – but not with him. Sorry. Instead he felt unconscionably alive and chipper, and decided he was going to damn well spend some money on himself.

He bounded down the hill to 81a, and rummaged through their tweed jackets and Bunnymen-style overcoats. Since *Crocodiles* came out with McCulloch on the front in a long tweed Crombie, Kirklands had been full of young fops in raincoats, trenchcoats and all manner of tweedy tramps' overcoats, with just a few dissenters trying to look cool in Julian Cope pilot's leathers. None of that would do for Danny. Down and out or on the up, he could never quite bring himself to embrace second-hand chic. Standing there now made him nostalgic for his spats with Nicole, him standing firm for his modernist principles, she telling him to lighten up and let his hair down.

He wandered down to Probe, picked up a second-hand gatefold album of the music from *Apocalypse Now* and idled in the Armadillo, half reading the sleeve notes, half listening to Bowie on the radio. He sipped at a peppery, hot pumpkin soup. 'Ashes to Ashes' was overwhelmingly Danny's favourite Bowie track of all time – better than 'Drive in Saturday', better than anything, absolutely no doubt in his mind. He put down his soup spoon and closed his eyes for a moment, letting the song soar through him.

'*I'm hoping to kick but the planet is glowing . . .*'

He squeezed one last cup of tea out of the pot. That earlier rush of well-being had subsided, but he was feeling fine – strangely calm, and quite certain again. There was always that craven itch, biding its time to steal up on him and stab him in the back, but Danny was sure that by the time he got back home and gave his ma her spends he'd have other things to occupy his mind. He finished his tea and set off back up the hill for another night convincing Ninna there was no goblin knocking on the window.

Passing the Philharmonic and quite content to meander back on foot, he heard the chanting and he knew straight away she'd be there.

'Maggie, Maggie, Maggie! Out! Out! Out!'

For all Danny knew, Nicole was living in London or Manchester or Darwen, but his heart told him she'd be right here, just around the corner with the rally. He was aware from sketching so many students that day that a convoy of coaches for the big Right to Work march would be leaving from the campus. It was not unlike much of the information that drifted through him during the course of a day's graft – interesting enough at the time, instantly forgotten. He wasn't even certain where the march would take place. Brighton? Bournemouth? He pulled out his *Echo*. It was Brighton. The Conservative Party Conference had started, and would be gatecrashed tomorrow by tens of thousands of dissidents, protesting about unprecedented levels of unemployment. His heart skipped a beat. The coaches would be leaving soon. Nicole was there! She'd be on one of those coaches, heading for Brighton – he knew she would. If he was quick, he might just catch her. Just a word with her, let her see how much he'd changed. Even if she didn't want him back, surely they could be friends. And if they could be friends, with time, little by little . . . He stifled a big fat grin and set off down Hope Street at a jog.

As he passed the Everyman, it was as though Nicole herself were berating him. He smiled inside at the familiar and agreeably facile catechism.

'WHADDA WE WANT?'

'*More jobs!*'

He could almost picture Gordon with his megaphone, and dozens of keen Nicoles waiting to respond.

'WHEN DO WE WANT 'EM?'

'*NOW!!*'

There were six coaches backed up as far as the Catholic cathedral. He could see as soon as he crossed the road that all but the back two had filled up. A clutch of students and organisers stood with clipboards, ticking off names, handing out placards, window-stickers and badges. A girl in a striped

Peruvian blanket lowered her placard diagonally as she went to get on board. 'If the Tories Get Up Your Nose,' it said, 'Picket!'

Danny's heart sank as it all came racing back to him. The tiffs, the arguments, the abject failure between him and Nic to find any common ground. How he would have howled with laughter if she'd brought home a slogan like that. How she would have roasted him for his imbecility. Was there *any* point his trying to find her? He brushed past the girl in the blanket, who turned sharply and scowled at him. She wore a big badge with bold black lettering: 'HOW *DARE* YOU ASSUME I'M HETEROSEXUAL!'

He shuffled past, averting his eyes from her accusing glare, almost convinced he must have fallen into a trance for a second and unwittingly groped her placid breasts. He jumped up every few steps, checking each window for Nicole.

She was on the very last coach: that is, the one at the head of the convoy. His pulse throbbed hard in his head, then seemed to stop altogether as he saw her. For a second he just stood back and watched her, her nose in some magazine, lost to herself. She became conscious of someone outside, staring at her, and put down her paper to see Danny May beaming up at her. Her first reaction was to smile, massively; her second to clamp her hand over her mouth. Danny stood closer to the window. He went up on tiptoes, a futile attempt to get close to her. He tried to touch the window of the coach, but overbalanced and stepped back on to the pavement. Her eyes gave off a dozen different emotions, of which doubt was uppermost. Danny found himself taking *Apocalypse Now* out of the Probe bag and holding it up to her, mouthing at her: 'Have you heard it?'

As though they were still together. As though they'd last spoken an hour or so ago. The coach's engine started up and gradually, almost imperceptibly, it began to pull away. Danny walked quickly alongside her window, trying to keep up with the coach without breaking into a sprint. Eyes red-rimmed now, she held his gaze for a moment and gave one small, sad wave of her right hand. It was hardly a wave – she held up her fingers and bent them towards him, once. Absolute, debilitating sorrow dragged down on his heart, sagging his face. He held up a hand to wave back to her but he could barely muster the will. So he stood there, empty and alone, one arm slightly raised in farewell, watching the coach disappear up Mount Vernon.

Danny had felt purged by writing the letter, but now he had real doubts as to whether he should send it – *where* he should send it, for that matter. He reread the final paragraph, his crabby handwriting toppling over backwards as though someone had pushed the first word into the second, sending it all tumbling back to the right.

> I'll never forget the look on your face as that coach drove you away from me, for ever, I think. You looked so beautiful, so sad. Your face seemed to be saying I love you but look what you've done to me. It kills me, over and over again it kills me. Remember how we always loved that song by Leonard? It kills me to know that, whatever I do now, I can't take it back. I can't take the trouble from your eyes. But think back to when we used to play it. Remember? When we used to argue about how long it took him to write a letter? Whatever happens, that'll always be me and you. I'm putting a little snip of hair in for you. Think of me sometimes and try to think of good things, not the wrong I done you. Try and think of me when I had smile dimples.
>
> Loving you. Always.

It said what he wanted to say to her. Sorry. Think of us now and then. It wasn't always so bad. Stay free. He took a deep, deep breath, signed the letter, folded it and sealed the envelope. He thought of her – adamant, compassionate, full of conviction, off to fight the latest battle. She'd be well on her way now. She'd almost be there. He switched on the news, hoping against hope he might see her. Mrs Thatcher was bringing the house down. Dressed now in her trademark fighting-blue, she was imperious as she mocked the handful of protestors who'd managed to infiltrate the conference hall.

'Come on in! It's always better where the Tories are . . .'

But at the flick of a switch her eyes turned cold again as she shouted down the dwindling band of dissenters in her own party.

'To all of you waiting with baited breath for that favoured media catchphrase the U-turn, I have only one thing to say. *You* turn if you want to. The lady's not for turning!'

A thunderclap of laughter and wild applause greeted her. She was back in the driver's seat again, steering the runaway truck. Danny stared at the TV screen, and it all made sense. Everything that was happening to him, it was all out of his hands now. There he was, there she was. He tore up the letter. He got up and went to find succour.

1981

All You Need Is Love

A doer by nature and by habit, an optimist who for so long had ploughed ahead, sure that his blend of talent and application would see him through, Danny had started to greet each new day with a mighty ennui in his heart. His sap was dying as his dreams were hung out to dry. If not exactly bitter, he became realistic about his prospects. He came to accept his lot in the grand scheme of things. And his scene with Rowena was getting darker and dirtier. Really, it was only a matter of time before something dire happened. Something had to give.

He met her the day John Lennon died, or the day after, to be precise – the day the news broke big. It was getting on for Christmas, a couple of months after he'd last seen Nicole. He'd been drifting to and from the house in Carlingford Close, chasing the dragon, going clear then getting himself dragged back into it again. Vera had given up on him since he took the Marie Curie box. He knew he was going to have to do something, move out, give his ma a break so that, at the very least, he wasn't there as a constant reminder to her of what might have been and what would not now be. He had a vague thought that he'd get Christmas out of the way then try and look up Lingsby first thing in the new year, see if he could maybe finish off his foundation course and go from there. But the day everyone was lighting candles for

Lennon he found a flim in Sefton Park and headed off to score.

Cutting along Linnet Lane he passed a face he half knew heading the opposite way, back towards Lark Lane. Who *was* that girl? Not yet twenty, he was becoming hopeless at remembering the simplest thing. He'd stand there trying to link the associations together – 'Come 'ead, Danny, la, you *know* him, used to go to St Bernard's, name's like a fruit or something, red-headed lad, Peter, Patrick, *Paul*! That's him – Paul Curran!' The way it happened, he'd often get the hardest part first, the rest of it following easily after that. But this girl – he just couldn't place her. Such a wave of heady, altogether pleasant wooziness did that brief glimpse of her pale face trigger, though, that he turned on the spot and automatically started to follow her. She turned right on Lark Lane and, somewhat jerky and preoccupied, crossed over the road and disappeared into the Masonic. This gave Danny a problem. If he went into the pub he'd have to buy a drink – possibly one for her, too. That, in turn, meant breaking into his fiver and that would put paid to his pleasure plans. Whoever he went to, it was a five-pound bag or nothing these days – even more so with it being the season of good cheer and half the city wanting to get ding dong mellow and high. He had a choice to make.

So powerful was the aftershock of the fleeting encounter that he still felt her good vibrations as he stood outside the pub. Whoever she was, whatever she'd meant to him, it had certainly been something wonderful. He craned his head inside the door, hoping for a better look before making his final decision, but the girl was already making her way from the bar to an empty table. A group of lachrymose students swayed in the corner, arms around each other, belting out 'Imagine' with all the tone-deaf pathos they could muster. Untogether, they were one. Lennon's death was going to mean weeks of this shit, but at least he wouldn't have to buy her a drink now, which was one good thing. He took a deep breath, sauntered to the bar and ordered a large rum and Coke.

It was hard to get a good look at her without staring blatantly, and every time he thought he might steal a glimpse she seemed to sense it and look up, staring him out until he looked away. He finished his drink quickly and went for another, getting himself a pint this time, hoping it might last longer. She sat reading a paperback, glancing up every now and then, seemingly anxious. Her face was alabaster white, framed by a limp shag of dirty auburn hair. She looked tired and worried, yet her face was still alluring without being beautiful; it was spoilt by her oddly bent, almost doubled-back nose. The lager was tinny and gaseous, but he finished it and took himself off to the toilet, racking his mind for just one bit of inspiration. He came back to the bar, nicely warm and half drunk now, and ordered another large rum. He stood at the bar sipping it, convinced he was a sip away from recalling just who the fuck she was. He studied the meagre slice of lemon in his glass and, with half a mind to suck on it, dipped a finger in to isolate it against the glass and retrieve it.

'Excuse me. I'm sorry. I saw you looking at me . . .'

'I . . .'

He turned to face her, oddly uncomfortable. His ears stung slightly and it felt like he might be blushing.

'I'm Rowena.'

He was staring right into her face now.

'Did, er . . .' She thought twice about it then pushed herself over the edge. She forced an apologetic smile. 'Did Sammy Macca send you?'

Two things hit him, both at once. He knew exactly who Sammy Mac was, though he found himself strangely saddened at such a well-spoken student girl asking after the South End's nastiest smack dealer. The other thing was that this was not the first time the girl had smiled at him. She'd smiled at him twice before – and she hadn't meant it then, either. Take away the auburn hair and the trouble in her eyes, keep the twisted nose: it was the Girl With Blue Hair.

The morning of the accident they'd had sex for the first time in a week. Danny awoke with a hard-on and Rowena, still half asleep, on her side with her bare back to him, raised her leg just enough to let him fuck her from behind. After, he shuffled through to the front room, instinctively certain there were enough vultured ciggies there to raise a little rollie. Once that was gone, they were fucked. No bag, no baccy, no nothing. Three days in a row she'd looked into his eyes and sworn blind she had no money, nothing left in all the world, then somehow conjured something out of thin air when her need was greatest. It was one reason he stuck with her when his last thread of conscience told him they were killing each other. She only had to call her parents and tell them she needed materials, and cash would arrive courtesy of the Royal Mail. She wasn't even lying when she told her folks that – they laboured under the grand delusion that their precious, talented girl was on the verge of recognition from the art world as she persevered in her Sefton Park garret, determined to do it her way, make it on her own with just the occasional grant from her parents to help. Once or twice the sound of the postman had filtered into Danny's scattered slumber and he'd dragged himself up to intercept the rescue parcel. There'd be trouble, but she always seemed ready to take him back. The very first time he clapped eyes on her, all those years ago, he knew in his heart she was special. And he was right. The more they cheated and scammed each other, the more they couldn't do without each other. And, by and large she was good for him, too. One time he'd come in to find a brand new easel, paints and canvas waiting for him. They'd talked over and over about jump-starting him, just forging that little bridge that might get him back on his feet again, but for his part Danny had assumed that neither of them really meant it. 'People like you find it easy,' he was fond of singing to her. He'd started a portrait of her, all yellows and browns, but as soon as she went out he'd packed it all up, taken it down to Seth to see what he could give him for the lot. Not even Seth would take a chance on art paraphernalia so, listless, he'd dumped the lot in his ma's backyard and knocked at the door, hoping to blag some cash from her. Emotional but firm of jaw, she opened the door to him, looked into his eyes – and wouldn't let him over the doorstep. It meant nothing to him.

He finished the rollie and, while his head was still more or less on, got himself dressed and went for a walk. An idea was starting to form. Two buses later he was up by Everton Library, heading for Sir Thomas White Gardens. Last time he'd been to score off the Yellowman he'd seen how he left his little porthole window open, even at that time of night. They'd had sunshine these last few days and the only thing in Danny's head was that open window and all that bag inside. He turned into the courtyard of the flats, deserted except for a bitch patiently waiting while three mutts queued to bone her. He found the ground-floor window shut. Or was it? He couldn't be sure if it was just warped or badly fitted, or whether it was, after all, still open just a crack. He checked over his shoulder then went on to his tiptoes, prising his fingers under the minute gap. He forced as much power through his fingertips as he could muster, pushing forward with his thighs and shoulders, trying to transmit that last final thrust that would lever the thing open. Something caught his eye, a flash of movement behind him.

'Hey! Smackhead!'

Across the forecourt a vicious-looking man of thirty or so, a long scar running from his temple to his chin, walked towards him with menace. He had thinning, greasy red hair cut in a bad mushroom wedge, and a straggle of red moustache. Worst of all, his tattooed hand strained at the sinews to restrain a thick, stainless-steel leash at the end of which was a snarling pit bull terrier.

'Fuck off out of Tommy White, you robbing smackhead twat!'

A flicker of a smile as he unclipped the chain from the dog's collar and set him free. Danny turned and sprinted, heart thumping in his ears, terrified. Surprisingly, his motor, the voice in his head that was now guiding his immediate well-being, remained calm. He raced right out across the main road and started heading for the steep steps leading down past the park towards the Piggeries. He'd been there with Rowena to score bag a few times and he knew the warren of side streets and jiggers well. Getting past him and cutting him off like any other rat he'd cornered, the pit bull sprang low on its front paws, its jaw almost touching the pavement as its wild eyes gleamed at Danny, ready to leap up and tear out his throat. Shocked out of his wits and genuinely scared for his life now, he turned back, blocked by the dog, then back again and, panic-stricken, flung himself down the steps, out on to Netherfield Road and straight under the wheels of the Transit van Mickey Mo was driving.

Mickey was out in an instant, supporting his head and checking him out for fractures.

'Fucking lucky, lad! Fuck you doing running around here this time of a morning?'

Danny managed a feeble grin. He felt nauseous.

'Could ask you the same question, Mickey, la.'

'Hey! Trying to make a honest living here. Doubt I could say the same for you, going by the kip on you . . .'

He opened up the back doors of the van and jumped inside, clearing cellophane-wrapped sweatshirts and jeans. Then he jumped out again and helped Danny to his feet.

'Come 'ead, sunshine. Let's get you up the hozzy, get you checked out.'

Supporting himself on Mickey's shoulder, Danny hobbled

to the back of the van and hung on to an open door. Mickey took his weight and helped him inside.

'Just try not to crease the swag too much. I was on my way to Greaty with that little lot . . .'

Danny sat down, eyeing the treasure trove of designer gear. 'Fuck's all this?'

'Ask no questions, lad . . .'

'I hope it's all paid for, mind you . . .'

'Every last nasty little knock-off . . .'

Danny picked up the nearest packet. It contained an emerald-green Marc O'Polo sweatshirt. He held it up, smiling.

'Jarg,' grinned Mickey. 'The whole lot of it. Lacoste, Hardcore, Edwin – got the lot there, kidder. Everyone knows it's jarg. Fiver a piece. They don't give a fuck.'

Danny whistled and grinned at Mickey. 'I'm in the wrong business, aren't I?'

Mickey looked at him, stern and slightly sad. 'You are, kidder.'

'It's down to yourself, Danny, la. This ain't something no one else can do for you. Do you get me?'

Mickey was driving, Danny in the middle, his mother to his left, all squashed on to the bench seat of the Transit. They'd kept him in the Royal for observation and now it was time for his lecture. He nodded.

'I *do* know what you mean, Mick. Fucking right I do.'

Mickey addressed him through the rear-view mirror, even though he was sat right next to him.

'Well, it's down to you, kid. You look fucking terrible. Your ma's in bits. Everyone's fucking grieving for you like you was already dead. Know what though, la? You've gone nearly two days without shoving that fucking shite into your veins –'

'I don't inject –'

'So you say. Whatever . . .'

'He *is* a bit thingio about needles, Michael. Always was –'

195

'Listen! I don't give a fuck if he's injecting the shite, smoking it, sticking it up his fucking arse . . . It's killing the kids round here. Are you with me? Your Daniel's meant to be one of the bright ones. Wouldn't fucking think so to look at the little quilt right now, would you?'

He shook his head, wiped the sweat from his top lip. This time he jerked his head left and tried to look at Danny properly. He gave him an embarrassed punch on the arm.

'You're not beyond help, Danny lad. And you can help other kids like you an' all. But you got to sort yourself out first, kidder. You got to stand up against this thing.'

They pulled into the Close and parked up. Mickey turned off the engine and put his arm round Danny, pulling him towards him.

'Get yourself off to bed now, yeah? Your mam'll see you right. And soon as you can – tomorrow at the latest, la – come on down to the centre and let's see what we can sort out. Come here . . .'

He held up his hand for a ghetto high-five, Danny meekly obliging. Getting out of the van, he couldn't say with any certainty whether he'd be back with Rowena that night, or sweating it out with the crabs at his ma's.

Ashes to Ashes

'Was you really at Cockney Rebel? How old was you!'

'Thirteen, la! Fuckinell! Been going to gigs for years by then!'

'Remember the riot?'

'Dunno that I'd call it a *riot*, man. Same thing used to happen every gig . . .'

Mickey pushed back on his chair legs, tilting himself backwards.

'Way I remember it is it was a fucking riot and the bouncers got legged out the side exits! The first couple of rows got up, didn't they, tried to rush the stage soon as Harley says all right and that . . .'

'Well, they was mainly just trying to dance, weren't they . . .'

'And all through the gig the fucking bouncers keep pushing them back down . . .'

'And then they played "Come Up and See Me" . . .'

'And the whole fucking place went up!'

'Fantastic! Remember? Every fucking last one of us was up and running down the front, la! Them grocks just couldn't keep the tide back!'

'Like I say though, Mickey – whatever gig you went to, that always used to happen. You'd hardly call it a fucking riot!'

'Well, I wouldn't know about that would I, la. I weren't a sweat like you.'

Danny laughed and left Mickey's hot chocolate on his desk. With unemployment the way it was, the Meth was now as busy by day as it was at night time. The small team offered advice on social security, housing, abortion, grants, and drug and alcohol rehabilitation programmes. And more and more lads were coming in to see Marcia about the police. It had been bad around there as long as Danny could remember, but with the sus law getting questionable results for the Ulster Constabulary the worst elements of the local plod had been using it as an excuse to stop and search anyone and everyone around L8. It was mainly young black lads coming in to see her, complaining of drug plants, racial abuse, even sly beatings where they'd been hauled off the street and worked over in the back of a Maria. While the pool table and Pac-Man just about earned their keep, Marcia was desperately underresourced.

Mickey had secured a small grant for Danny to work as a community artist, based at the centre. It was embarrassing for him at first, with no set hours and no specific role. Mickey kept an eye on him but made it clear the gig was to be what he made of it.

'You gorra mind what that George Orwell said, kidder. No cunt's past salvation if you catch 'em young enough. Go and fuckin' catch 'em, la!'

Danny felt like a gooseberry, sloping over to huddles of young lads with a fixed grin on his face and a charcoal stub in hand. With time, though, he treated it as no different from his former life roaming the youth clubs up Lodge Lane, sketching and painting the kids and street scenes he saw. They all took the piss – but they all wanted to see their picture when he'd finished.

He was mainly relieved, and only a little bit piqued, to find Rowena gone. He knew they were going nowhere, he and she – it had only ever been a liaison of the neediest mutual convenience. And beneath the skin, when it all came down to the very fabric of it, he didn't even *like* her that much. She was spoilt. She was fussy. She was deluded. But, the more distance he put between that time and this, the more Danny recognised the good in her, too. She was a giver, Rowena, and above all else she believed in him, hugely – smack notwithstanding. He wanted to square things off between them. If they could maintain a friendship, great. If it was just not to be, then at least he'd thought to try.

But having rung and knocked at the door without answer, he turned and walked straight into Willie from the flat below. As always, he looked at Danny warily.

'She's gone, lad. Gone a while, now.'

There was awkwardness between them, and Danny only stayed long enough to get the basics. Rowena had been unhappy, crying a lot – all day, all night, really. She got ill. Her mother and father came for her, packed all her things into this big, big car – and that was her, gone. Trudging back to the Meth, Danny's clearer conscience was muddied only by the vaguest sense of injustice – and even that was something new to him. It was Marcia. Each and every comment was underscored with a bitter, world-weary irony. Time and again she'd point out little things to Danny; the postman would be late with his delivery and she'd cluck at Danny and say: 'See, Dan-Dan, people like us don't get our post in the morning.'

He didn't like to hear it, but it was making its mark on him. Cutting up Devonshire Road, past the big old houses he'd once adored, he couldn't quite stifle a flickering resentment. When it'd all got too much for Rowena, she'd been able to pick up a phone and make it go away. Marcia was right. People like the Girl With Blue Hair found it easy. For people like them, it was always going to be a fight.

One steaming hot July day she edged over to him, real doubt written all over her face. Even though she was thirty-five, older maybe, Danny had a massive thing for Marcia. She seemed stern, always very serious, but there was something about her that made his balls ache for her. She always wore a suit to the centre, always with a white blouse underneath. She was slim, which he liked, but not outstandingly pretty. She had quite a long, equine face and, unsurprisingly in this heat, with so many folk thronging the place, she had a mild BO. He couldn't explain the attraction — it just *was*. He'd been thinking about her a lot and her presence now made him self-conscious. Did she know? Did she feel it, too?

'Danny, love. Can I have a word?'

She beckoned him away from the vending machine to a quiet corner. She looked him in the eye.

'I believe you can take a photo?'

'What?'

She actually smiled at him, making his heart shuffle. He'd read that your pupils enlarged if you were attracted to someone, and fought hard to look nonchalant, narrowing his eyes against the glint of sun slatting in through the blinds.

'It's not a trick question, mate. Mickey said your ma showed him some pictures you'd took a while back. Said you're good, like.'

'Well, yeah . . . I mean – any fool can take a photo . . .'

She focused hard on him, making sure he was getting the full import of this.

'These need to be good, la. Do you get me?'

He nodded, absolutely not getting her at all. She gestured to him to follow her. They went over to the small office, unlocked the door. She went to the desk, unlocked the bottom drawer and took out a plastic bag. She passed it to Danny, eyes never leaving him. He took out a little black camera. In size and appearance, it wasn't so much different to the Instamatic he and Nicole had had in Paris. This, however, was an Olympus Trip.

'Wow! Nice . . .'

She popped her head round the door, stuck two fingers in her mouth and whistled shrilly.

'Yo! Ruben!'

A tall lad he knew from round and about loped over, chunky dreadlocks piled inside a tea-cosy hat, woven in the red, green and gold of the Ethiopian flag.

'Ruben, this is Danny.'

Ruben nodded, not overly friendly. He stood back, chewing. Marcia placed both hands on Danny's shoulders and looked right into his eyes, making him giddy.

'Right, Dan. I want you to arrange to meet Ruben this evening. What's been going on is the filth have started parking up every night just off Granby, dragging lads in for fuck all. We can't do nothing. Fuck all down for us. Fuck all down for us without *evidence*, by the way . . .'

It started to dawn on Danny. Ruben let out a slow, slightly malicious smile.

'Are you starting to read me?'

Danny nodded dumbly at her.

'No two ways about it, kidder, this is sticking your neck out. They see you, right . . .'

He tried a game grin.

'. . . they see you they will fucking batter you, smash the camera, mark you down for life.'

She winked at him.

'You don't wanna get nabbed.'

'What about the flash and that?'

'This is the thing. What we need to even *try* and bring a case is credible shots of their faces. In a ideal world we'd be looking for before and after. Something that places them at the scene, something that shows them at it . . .'

'Could get both at once, like . . .'

'You could indeed. But the chances of being able to get a clear snap of some twat's face as he's bent over some poor lad kicking fuck out of him . . .'

Ruben stepped forward.

'Lad's got a point though, Marce. If we can stay out the vans and get him a good enough spec, he only needs one good shot. Do you know? He could use his flash, get the shot away and leg it before the cunts know what's gone on. 'Scuse me language and that . . .'

'That's the thing, though. How you gonna control that? How do you keep these fucking animals from dragging you out of sight?'

He shook his head in despair.

'Fuck knows, la. We just got to keep at it. Them gonna make a mistake one time. Them bound to make a big mistake . . .'

Ruben had billeted Danny in a top-floor room of an old house on the corner of Beaconsfield and Granby, overlooking the main drag of Granby Street. Although it was still twilight, the street was eerily quiet and tense. Ruben winked at him.

'Babylon not so fucken stupid as to try nothing in broad daylight. Just you watch, kidder. They gonna park up here or here or here and they gonna get some cunt. You get that camera ready, la. They deffo gonna cane somebody . . .'

Left alone, Danny fiddled with the camera, making sure the focus was right for such a weird night sky. It was blue-black, unbroken by any smoky cloud, but a high summer moon cast silvery light on the streets below. Danny knelt on the window ledge and framed the silent moon behind a silhouette of roofs and chimney pots. He snapped it, just to get a feel for the camera. A sombre crunch of tyres from outside. An unmarked van cruised the length of the street, slow and sinister. There was no siren, no flashing light, but Ruben was right. The police were here – and they were looking to cane somebody.

Somebody came at exactly ten to ten, in the tragic, beaming form of Peter Luala – Danny's friend Peter Lovely. Peter's guilty pastime was chess and, fresh from a marathon session in a side room at the Ibo in which he'd won three pounds, Peter was positively gliding across Princes Avenue when he caught the eye of the police. Cutting up Arundel Street to make the short walk home, he smiled to himself and clicked his fingers to the tune in his head. To the police, Peter was an open-and-shut case. The guy was spanked out his mind on something or other, and they moved in on him with deadly stealth the moment he turned into Granby Street. Danny saw the whole thing unfold, saw the coppers put two and two together. He didn't have time to shout out before the hiding commenced. He looked on, sickened. His first thought was to gallop down the stairs, fling himself out into the street and try and pull them off him, explain how Peter was a church-goer, a teetotaller, a good, good family man. But reality held him back. All the stories he'd been hearing, all Ruben's and Marcia's warnings had made their mark on him. Before he did a thing, Danny was going to make sure he got that picture. Biting his lip, trying to keep his wrist from trembling and his eyes from blazing, he focused down on the dazed, bewildered Peter Luala in his bright white shirt, writhing on the pavement below as four uniformed constables kicked him in the thigh, in the back, in the balls, in the ribs, in the gut. Through-out the kicking, Peter looked up at them, eyes wide and pleading, almost grinning at one point as though holding out hope of them suddenly realising their mistake. Danny focused, framed, snapped. Again. Focus, frame, snap. Somehow he became detached from the brutal detail of the assault, shut out the noise and the venom of the insults and merely clicked away, uncaring whether the police should become alerted by the flash, uncaring if they should batter him, too. He didn't care about any of that. He wanted one indelible, incontrovertible image that could help bring these bastards to book.

He finished the reel and stowed the camera in the narrow crevice under a chest of drawers. He composed himself and took one last look down below before shutting the window. The police had been too busy working poor Peter over to notice anything beyond their wriggling victim. Danny bounded down the stairs four, six at a time. Now he had a decision to make. The moment he opened that front door he'd be right in the thick of it, almost tripping over the prostrate Peter Lovely. He made his mind up, threw the door open and sauntered into Granby Street with as much confidence as he could muster, knowing exactly what was coming next. Three coppers stood off while one knelt on Peter's chest, pretending to search him.

'Hey!' shouted Danny. He ran over but stayed at the corner of Arundel Street, far enough away to be able to run if this didn't go to plan. 'Fuck youse arresting the vicar for?'

One of them started walking towards him. Danny got a look at his face in the glow of the street light. He was young, nasty, inexperienced – and he was shitting it.

'Who are you, son?'

Danny held his hand up in an instinctive 'halt' gesture. The copper actually stopped in the middle of the street, as though Danny might be carrying a hand grenade or a gun.

'Don't matter who I am, mister. You may as well know that

the fella you're kneeling on is a minister at the Pentecostal Church . . .'

The two officers still standing back glanced nervously at each other. The one on Peter's chest stood up. He turned to Danny, drew himself up. He looked like an angry guinea pig, his tiny eyes flashing and his well-packed cheeks starting to turn red.

'Listen, lad, he can be Minister of Funny Walks for all I care. The fella's high as a kite. He's off his head on dope . . .'

'Don't think so, mister. The Reverend don't believe in nothing like that . . .'

'And what exactly do you think we're doing to the good man? What do you think you saw?'

'I didn't see nothing, la. Just this second walked round the corner . . .'

Hamster-face nodded to his colleague to pull Danny in and, reading it, he backed off down Arundel Street.

'Listen,' he shouted over to them, 'just telling youse for your own good and that. I'd get him to hozzy if I was youse. Don't want holy blood on your hands . . .'

He broke into a jog and shook his head sadly as he passed under the statue of Jesus on the cross.

First thing the next morning he was knocking at the safe-house door. Ruben checked him out through the window, solemnly let him in. Danny scoured his face for signs that he'd heard about Peter. Ruben just stared back, blank. Behind him, out in the little yard, lads were dragging in crate after crate of empty milk bottles.

'Bad about Peter, la.'

Ruben just nodded. 'Bad about everyone, man.'

The two stood in silence, a yard apart.

'I left me camera upstairs. Didn't want them twats smashing it up and that.'

Ruben nodded again, slowly, deliberately, his yellow-brown

face lined and aged before his time, but possessed of a calm and calculated intelligence. Danny bounded up the stairs, strangely excited – and immediately guilty for that excitement. He retrieved the camera from under the ancient chest of drawers and skipped back downstairs, eager and pleased with himself. He held up the camera to them.

'If I haven't got something on this . . .'

No one even looked up. They lined up the bottles in rows of six, columns of four. Two more lads appeared at the back door lugging water carriers and paraffin tins. Ruben nodded to one of them, put his arm round Danny's shoulder and walked him to the front door.

'Come 'ead, la. I'll come down with you. See what you got . . .'

They cut down Arundel and hadn't even got to the Avenue when Ruben stopped and turned to Danny, gripping his shoulder hard.

'You still on the other shite then, kidder?'

'What?'

He pinned him back with a menacing stare. 'Don't mess around, softshite. I seen you up and down Windsor Street.'

Danny swallowed hard, looked him in the eye. 'No, kidder. I'm off it.'

Ruben carried on squeezing his shoulder. 'You better fucken had be, la. I need to know who I'm working with here –'

'I swear to you, man. I'm off the bag.'

For the first time he saw Ruben smile.

'Never heard one say he was *on* it, like . . .' He laughed and did a paltry imitation of a strung-out smackhead. 'I'm on the bag, la. Honest and that – it's fucken brilliant!'

They both chuckled, Danny more out of relief than anything. Ruben released his grip and stepped back, his eyes still appraising Danny.

'All right, la. I'm just gonna have to trust you, aren't I? Laygater, kidder.'

He turned to walk away.

'Where you off, man? Thought you was coming to get the photies done?'

Ruben flicked out one manicured hand as though both to silence him and put him in his place. 'Work to do, la. Big work.'

He strolled back towards the house. Danny watched him go, then broke into a gentle jog.

In spite of Danny entrusting him with the details of his mission, old Martin couldn't give him a darkroom there and then. Best he could do was take the film from Danny and, as soon as something came available, develop the pictures himself. He told Danny to go in to town, kill an hour and come back up to City College around midday. If he was going to leave this unexploded bomb with anyone he'd bet his life on world-weary Martin Gough, but it was not without misgivings that Danny loped off down the hill.

Struck by the notion of a trip to T.J. Hughes and a browse around London Road, he cut down Clarence Street and headed on behind Lime Street Station. Coming towards him, struggling with her bag, was a girl whose long legs and blonde-white hair he'd know anywhere.

'Harriet! Fuck you doing, girl?'

He reached to help her with her bag but reflexively, before she could check herself, she snatched it back. She was as tall as him now, and her eyes betrayed all the questions dancing behind. She seemed as shocked to see him looking so well as to see him at all. He stood back, smiled at her.

'Hey! I can't exactly blame you, can I?'

She offered a meek smile, still finding it difficult to look at him. She pulled at her T-shirt, swaying on the spot.

'Where you off, then?'

Contemplating and answering the question seemed to relax her a little, like she was suddenly letting the steam out.

'London, Danny. I mean, like – there's over three million unemployed in this country so what the fuck, hey?'

'London, hey? Nice one . . .'

He was dying to ask, burning up inside, but she prattled on, all nervous energy and fearful excitement.

'I mean, fuck knows what's going to happen, but I've *got* to give it a go. Not even uni guarantees you anything, these days . . .'

She sounded as though she was trying to justify it to herself still. She glanced up at him to make certain he was on her side.

'Like, this scout for a model agency approached me. Nic's checked them out, absolutely genuine . . .'

The mention of her name sent his head spinning. He couldn't hold back a moment longer.

'How is she?'

His eyes must have misted as he spoke of her. Harriet was softer with him now.

'She's fine. She went to Paris –'

'Wow! She *did* it, huh?'

Harriet looked at the floor, unsure how much she should tell him.

'She's back now . . .'

'Well. Least she give it a go, hey?'

She picked up her bag again.

'Look. At least let me carry your bag down to the station, hey? I'm hardly gonna run off with it, am I?'

She looked him in the eye, finally, and laughed.

'Hard to say with you, Danny, isn't it?'

She laughed again, pearly-white teeth glinting in the sun. She'd make it down there. He knew she would. Maybe not as a model – he couldn't think of too many models with such big tits, although her legs were long and slim, and her skin was flawless. Who could say? Who could tell what was going to happen in five minutes' time, let alone tomorrow? What Danny sensed strongly, though, was that young Hattie Watson had what it takes. She was a star. He helped her down to the station and hovered a moment then, feeling awkward, he pecked her on the cheek, wished her all the best.

'Tell Nic you seen me!' he shouted after her.

'I won't!' she smiled.

He watched her go, and felt unbelievably good about the encounter. He turned, thinking he may as well amble on back to City College now.

He couldn't make up his mind whether to slip one of the photos in with the letter. He couldn't make up his mind about anything to do with the letter. He more than likely wouldn't send it at all. He'd written a long, rambling, slightly glamourised account of all he'd been through since their split-up. He tried to make himself sound like the tragic hero of one of those paperbacks she'd given him – Gide or Jean Genet. He smiled at the recollection of her lecturing him, always teaching him something. She'd told him Bowie's 'Jean Genie' was inspired by Genet. He wanted to get that across to her, that he, too, was a slim, wasted, tragic-romantic – but he just sounded pitiful, self-pitying. He screwed that one up and binned it. Then he tried for a more rational, balanced, I'm-not-after-anything tone. He read that one back and it was just too terse. What'd be the point of sending that? Maybe he'd just send the photos. If he knew Nicole at all, he knew she'd be knocked out by those images. They'd come out superbly. In the days he used to sit in the Armadillo flicking through *Actuel, The Economist* and *Time*, they used to run occasional spreads of photojournalistic reportage from war zones, or whole desperate communities devastated by famine. He was no expert, but he couldn't see how his shots of the systematic beating of Peter Luala packed any less punch. The pictures were clear. They were shocking. They were shocking because the story played out so casually, through Danny's pictures. He could have been snapping away at a school's sports day, so detached and yet so precise was his photography. Nicole would recognise the power of the photos, but she'd also see what he was involved in now. She'd approve of his work around Granby. She'd love him for it.

He sifted through the images and sighed and came to his senses. There was no way in the world he and Nicole were getting back together. Why bother? He screwed up his latest effort and got up to put the kettle on the hob. As it was boiling, he caught a familiar chorus and turned up the radio. It was uncanny. 'Ashes to Ashes' was on, and he knew just what to say to her now. He ran back to the table, shuffling through the photos until he found it. Bingo! He wasn't sure if he'd kept the rooftop shot but there it was, the hanging moon bathing Toxteth in silver. He scribbled on the back.

> *'Want an axe to break the ice*
> *Wanna come down right now . . .'*
> Still see our star. Danny, Toxteth 1981

Above the noise of the bubbling kettle, a frantic knocking at the kitchen window. A face pressed against the window. Marcia. The birdie on the kettle shrieked as the seething water boiled and spat all over the hob, damping down but not extinguishing the flame. Danny threw the door open.

'What?'

'Get that fucken camera, kidder. There's fucken murder going on down there.'

'*What?*'

She stood back from the step.

'They've arrested Leroy.' She gave him one long, almost pitying look. 'This is it, la. This is it.'

Even as they stepped out into the warm, bright night, they could hear the commotion. From a few hundred yards down the road in Selborne Street came a thick plume of choking smoke where a car or tyres were burning, and the relentless shout of youths charging into combat. Danny went to turn right into the road but Marcia pulled him back.

'Not that way!'

Even though the night was shattered with the noise of bottles smashing, bricks thudding off car roofs, police squawking into their walkie-talkies for back-up, Marcia whispered urgently at Danny.

'That's where the bizzies are all ranked up. If we start taking photies from behind their lines, it's all coming at us. It looks like our lads are the aggressors . . .'

He nodded and followed. They cut back up along Kingsley Road and through to Granby Street that way, coming up behind a mob of about a hundred mainly teenage lads, but their dads and grandfathers too. Every single one of them had his own story to tell. Every family had tasted a lick of justice from the SPG. They'd had enough. Simple as that. The fightback had commenced. Pushing on towards the first rank of police, the younger element kept up their barrage of stones, bricks, empty bottles.

'Hey! Kidder! Don't lash them, la! Don't waste no bottles! Pass 'em back . . .'

From behind, Ruben and his crew came crab-walking past, crouched low to avoid detection, but weighed down, too, by the milk crates, more cumbersome than heavy to carry. They set up right behind the back line of the mob. Danny checked his lens, checked the focus. Barrie, a big Rastafarian guy and one of Ruben's main men, took control of the things from there. A hard core of six or eight of them went in strict rotation, Barrie ragging, lighting and passing the petrol bombs, giving the boys about fifteen seconds to launch them. Light, pass, launch, whoosh! Pow! One after another, their makeshift bombs skittled through the sky like fireflies. Whoosh! Pow! Danny clicked, reset, clicked. His feet crunched and slipped on the broken glass, he was sweating madly from the sheer heat, but his hand stayed steady. Focus. Frame. Snap!

A big lad he'd seen around came running up with a house-brick and hurled it high into the sky, watching its progress then dancing a jig of joy as it smashed down on to a copper's head. He held his arms aloft like he'd scored the winning goal in extra time of the Cup Final, standing back and waiting for his mates' acclaim. It didn't come. His missile had felled one of the sergeants, creating a gap and momentary panic in their midst. The mob didn't need another invitation. Pouring forward, they broke ranks now and ran into the enemy, striking out with sticks and fists and whatever came to hand. Danny ran with the thick of the first charge, still clicking and reloading as the police reorganised themselves and started to push them back. A huge roar went up as the big lad came charging through from behind, a whole paving slab raised above his head this time. The remaining sergeant looked up at the colossus about to brain him, turned and fled. With that, all remaining order was lost as the jubilant pack gave chase, kicking straggling policemen up the backsides, leaping on their backs, falling over one another to exact revenge on their persecutors. Danny ran alongside, hoping against hope he had a few shots left. This was history in the making! But as the coppers scattered out into Kingsley Road and on towards Parliament Street, there was the screech of tyres as reinforcements poured into the area.

'Come on!'

There was a familiar tug on his sleeve as Marcia pulled him away. Not letting his sleeve go, she led him down a jigger.

'You're too important to get nicked.'

She kissed him, her tongue flickering out for a second, scraping up against the back of his teeth. She pulled away, then touched his forehead with hers as though to tell him that was as far as it went.

He was hard, excited, blown away by everything that was happening. He went to kiss her again but she manoeuvred herself free and carried on down the jigger. He followed her, not sure where the alleyway led to, unsure of anything at all – but excited, impossibly high and wired and ready for whatever might be coming.

She led him through an alley gate and into a tidy backyard, tapping three times at the window pane. A woman, caramel brown with her hair wrapped high in a head scarf, opened up. Marcia held out her hand to Danny, playing it brusque for the benefit of her friend.

'Film.'

Danny unloaded it and handed it over. Marcia smiled at the woman.

'How many more of them you got, girl?'

She shrugged. 'He's not going to like it . . .'

'We'll pay him back, soft twat. Why isn't he out there, anyway?'

She smiled. 'You know Ray-Ray, babe. He'll come out when it's all over and tell youse all how many plod he done in . . .'

The woman padded back inside and returned with two more reels. She and Marcia hugged on the doorstep.

'You be careful now, Marcy girl. You hear me?'

They crept back down the jigger, stumbling into one another in the dark. Danny was desperate to kiss her again. Surely she'd brought him down here to fuck him? She wanted him as much as he wanted her. He knew she did. He could feel it. He pulled her back.

'Marce . . .'

She was breathing heavily. She knew what was coming. He put his hand on her shoulder, then let it fall to her blouse. He undid the top button. She let him. Her breath rising and falling in sharp, staccato gasps, she leaned back against the alley wall again, let him kiss her neck. He pushed his groin against her, wanting her to feel the strength of his dick. She pushed back into him, closed her eyes and rolled her head. He undid another button and felt behind her back for the clasp of her bra. She stopped him. Her hand shot down, caught him by the wrist and held him back. He pushed back on the ball of his toes, putting distance between them again. They stared at each other, neither saying a word. Nearby, the crash and burn of the petrol bombs, the furious shouts and screams and the stampede of feet. Danny took her hand gently.

'I know you think I'm just a kid, like . . .'

Doubt and regret clouded her face. 'I don't, Danny,' she said. 'I don't think that at all . . .'

He put his arms around her and drew her in for a kiss. She seemed to collapse again, sucking him in passionately, driving her tongue into his mouth and biting, nibbling his lips until they were numb. But as quickly as she devoured him she pulled away, with finality this time.

'I don't think you're just a kid, la. But this just ain't –'

'What? Ain't the time?'

She laughed and put her head back to listen. The vicious, persistent barking of wound-up dogs rent the air.

'Hardly.' She smoothed herself down, put a finger under his chin. 'But I don't think there'll be a better time, neither. Sorry, la.'

She started off down the alley again. Crushed, he followed her.

The barking was ferocious and incessant as dog handlers piled out of their vehicles. More and more men filed in, too – officers wearing helmets and padded jackets, perspex shields in their hands. They lined up right across Kingsley Road, one column, then two, then three. Letting the dog handlers walk ahead of them, they started a slow march forward into Selborne Street. Just as slowly, the mob backed off, both sides facing each other as they backed towards Granby. Frozen for a moment, Danny found himself isolated in the middle of the road. The riot police advanced in slow, impenetrable ranks, but instead of any fear or thought of flight, Danny was overcome by that same calm certitude he had at times of utmost creativity or happiness. There were dozens and dozens of police approaching, truncheons drawn, yet he was rooted to the spot, unflappable, loading new film into his camera. A voice cried out, 'Get him!'

Nothing happened. Danny dropped on to one knee and clicked. As the phalanx of coppers bore down on him he snapped again, and kept on snapping until they were almost on top of him.

'Repeat! Get that cunt with the fucking *camera*!'

The ferocity of the command snapped him out of his trance. He took one last look at the invading army and backed away towards Granby Street, where Ruben threw a protective arm around him, drew him back into the secure hub of the horde and offered him a piping hot Cup a Soup.

They slept in shifts, lookouts and scouts reporting back with the latest. There was a huge and ever growing police presence on the peripheries, particularly at the top junction of Upper Parliament Street. They'd evacuated Granby, but this was only Round One. It was looking like the police were setting up a base camp, ready for the long haul. With no hot water in the house, Danny opted to sprint back home while it was still an option. Heading along Selborne Street there was still the thick black smoke of smouldering tyres, the scattered shrapnel of smashed glass and that lingering, caustic veil of gasoline. Yet it was quiet. The streets were more or less deserted. An old Sikh and a younger Muslim couple walked briskly down the road, heads down, desperate not to bring attention on themselves as they scurried off to prayer. The air was still, yet seemed heavy with anticipation. Everyone seemed to be waiting and watching, everything held in abeyance until the next act began. All was perfectly still and quiet. As he walked up Selborne Street in the golden July sun, Danny had seldom seen Toxteth look so serene, so beautiful.

Yet three hours later, back down on Granby, agitation was

rife as rumours spread. Barrie had been told that people were being ambushed by snatch squads, dragged off the streets and hauled in for 'questioning'. Ruben had just come from Lodge Lane where the police were mobilising an army. Worst of all were the hordes of strangers starting to pour into the area, chancers and scallies looking to piggyback the troubles for a quick thrill or an opportunist heist. Most of the impromptu defence committee saw their presence as a potential hindrance, rather than swelling the ranks.

'Can't exactly tell them to fuck off, can we?' said Weekes, a rotund, thoughtful lad whose spectacles belied a savage temper and whose dimpled wrists gave no warning of his quick fists. 'Jus' gonna be one more army to fight if we start kicking every new face outta Granby, la.'

'Is right,' nodded Ruben. 'We just gonna have to ignore them, like, carry on doing our own thing. Start letting any cunt along, know what I mean? Just gonna be chaos, la. Gonna be bad chaos . . .'

Somehow, though, bad chaos sounded fantastic to Danny. He couldn't help himself. As night fell once more he was on edge – scintillatingly, thrillingly nervous. He swallowed hard, trying to keep a lid on his emotions, but there was no fighting it. He was coming down with the Thrills.

The looting started just before dark. News reached them that Duff's electricians on the Lane had gone, and there were sporadic reports of newsagents being stripped of cigarettes, off-licences having entire shelves of spirits cleared into bin bags while their proprietors stood by helpless, broom handles raised in toothless defence. A sense of anger prevailed at first, right-eous ire that these were their shops, their people – *rich* people, OK, people making trade and getting by while so many others were floundering. But the idea of outsiders coming in under cover of the night and the disturbances, using the fightback as a smokescreen for the indiscriminate pillage of *their* neighbourhood – that stung. At first it stung. But while the main crew stood firm and waited for Round Two, individuals started drifting away towards the sound of burglar alarms and plate glass caving in. There were rich pickings up the road.

The rhythmic drumming of their truncheons on their riot shields seemed to give the police, if not courage, then a shape, a marching beat – and as soon as darkness fell they mobilised, ready to break up the first signs of any riotous assembly. Thud-thud-thud! They stretched out right across the road and, step by step, beat out their path into the eye of the storm. Thud-thud-thud! They closed ranks tight, shoulder to shoulder as they raised their shields, sounding out their war dance, stick on shield. Ruben took a sidelong look up the street. He pulled his face scarf up.

'You gorra admit it – that is impressive, la!'

Thud-thud-thud! The tight line of perspex advanced. As far as the eye could see, ranks of armed police were slowly, inevitably descending. Ruben turned back to the troops.

'Let's fuck 'em.'

He didn't shout it. No histrionics or bold oratory. They just covered their faces and walked to meet the invaders head on, only breaking into a run as they sprinted the last few yards to get maximum impetus behind their projectiles. The night lit up as petrol bombs ripped through the sky, hundreds and hundreds of them, more than the previous night, zipping and spinning and smashing into jagged tongues of flame on the road. Danny pulled his sweatshirt up over his head, shield-ing his eyes from the smoke. There were cheers and triumphant dancing as a car went over on its side. Whoosh! It went up in a vermilion inferno, windows exploding as thick black smoke billowed out from beneath the flames. The heat, and the melting tar and rubber, and the gaseous vapours of the petrol burnt his throat, clogged his chest, snagging and chok-ing him – but still he picked out his shots. Youths ran as close as they could get, hammering bricks, slabs, stones into the encroaching wall of coppers, but on they came, relentless, one step at a time. A squalid smog of fumes and flame hung low across the street, and only the shouts and commands of familiar voices guided him back and forth at times. It was a battle zone, and each thrust had to be fast and vicious. They bombarded them but the coppers took it, and continued.

Getting to the junction with Granby, though, the police seemed to stall. On the march they'd seemed awesome, irresistible. As exhilarating as it was to pile into them, it was only stalling the inevitable. There was no way of penetrating that barrier with their meagre cache of street weaponry and, sooner or later, the SPG were going to break out in snatch squads and scatter the mob into the side streets. Yet they stopped, all of a sudden. They stopped their advance and dug in. Shields slatted together into one impregnable shell, they crouched down low, squatted behind their defences and awaited further orders. But in that very act of crouching they seemed submissive, cowardly, hiding from the fray. By hesitating on the front line, it looked like they had no real stomach for the fight – and they handed the initiative right back. Barrie came charging out with a huge metal pole raised high above his head. 'Yaaaaaargh!' he screamed, storming back into the police ranks and smashing the heavy pole down again and again and again. The wall held firm. Weekes ran in with a typewriter and, less than a foot away from them, slammed into the defences as hard as he could. Barrie followed up with his metal bar again and this time there was a murderous shriek of pain as a copper's forearm, as well as the shield it bore, absorbed the splintering shock of the blow. His shield slipped from his grasp as he hopped around, holding his wrist and, for a moment, there was a gap in the barricades. The Granby lads swarmed forward, hitting them with everything they could. Pickaxes, mallets, fire extinguishers – any weapon would do to drive them back. The police tried to shuffle together and close up the breach, but they were under heavy fire. Bricks, bottles, spiked golf balls and tins from the supermarket slammed into them, boom-boom-boom! One after another the makeshift missiles zipped into the wall of riot shields. Panic began to set in, as individual policemen broke rank, standing up and starting to back off. Some of these young coppers had been drafted in from the Lake District and Cheshire. They were stunned by the venom behind these attacks. It was remorseless. Wave after wave of kids ran into them, faces twisted with sheer, naked *hatred*. And it was aimed at them. They were the enemy. But they were just bobbies. Everyone liked them where they came from, more or less – they'd never seen anything like this before.

The marauding mob started to get alongside them as more and more rioters swarmed to the hive from Lodge Lane and the Falkner. Danny found himself staring at a familiar face, set tight in unfamiliar ire as, methodically, he dragged a trolley full of cans. It was Joey Amin – Joey Meanie.

'Dan-Dan.'

'Joey, la. Madness, hey?'

'Pure madness, la.'

Ducking into the trolley, he set about handing out ammunition. Suddenly, the absurdity of it seemed to take him over, and he charged towards the police lines with his trolley as a battering-ram. He crashed into the wall of shields, sending three coppers backwards as tins spun away down Selborne. Shocked and utterly petrified, one rookie stood up wild-eyed and disorientated, turning round and round on the spot. A tin of pineapples crashed into his temple, blood spurting out wildly in thick, spasmodic jets. He dropped his shield, instinctively clamping his hand to his head to stem the flow. Colleagues screamed at him to get back behind them but he was staggering now, deaf to them. Kids ran in, hurling whatever they could. A tin of beans smashed into his chest. A brick and a tin of plum tomatoes flew into his torso before another can burst his nose wide open and dropped him to the floor, white, bleeding and unconscious. Danny caught every beat of the attack.

A roar went up as the mob started wilding now, all sense of strategy and a common enemy suddenly overtaken by a demented charge of adrenalin, a lust for absolute havoc. More and more police were standing up and backing off, more and more were hitting the deck. Anarchy set in as the rioters swarmed all over their defences, hacking, beating and kicking anyone ready to stand their ground. One big, burly, bearded officer stepped out from the fray and, his back to the mob, screamed instructions into a megaphone. Gesticulating violently, he dragged his men back in, physically heaving the wall back together, refusing to let them dissolve. Danny could see it in the copper's eyes as he snapped him. The big guy understood the full gravity of the situation. If they didn't dig in now and claw back the upper hand, people were going to get killed. This was about more than just saving face. Suddenly, it was about saving lives. Slowly, doggedly, he corraled them back into line. Once again, a column of riot police spread out across Selborne Street and, led by their bearded warrior, started a steady march. Step by step. Yard by yard. He snatched a truncheon from a rookie's hand and stood in front of him, whacking out a beat on his shield. Others followed suit, more and more of them picking up the rhythm of bravado.

Some of the new arrivals began to turn and run now, pushing back into the Granby funnel. The hardcore grabbed at them as they fled past.

'Stand!'

'Turn and fight, you shithouses!'

'Babylon's fucked! COME ON! Let's finish the bastards off!'

But no one was listening. A bang, then a sudden explosion behind them. Another. Bang! Then a thick, stinging pall of smoke. People doubled over, coughing, spluttering, shielding their eyes.

'Tear gas! Down!'

The mere words induced panic, hundreds of rioters suddenly pushing and tripping over each other, spilling down the side streets and out on to Princes Avenue. Bang! Boom! More explosions, a permanent veil of choking smoke. Zip! Something hit Danny in the thigh. It was like a bite from a stingray, sharp, vicious and instantly, agonisingly numb. Shit! He hopped back towards the kerb, dragging his right leg painfully. Weekes came over, helped him sit down.

'Fuck happened there, la?'

'Fuck knows! Felt like I got shot.'

'Some of our lads got airguns –'

'Nah, man. This is fucking burning like fuck . . .'

He started unbuttoning his jeans to get a better look. Zip-zip-zip! Regular electric snaps ricocheted past their ears at high velocity. Ping! Ping! Zip! A building crescendo of stampeding feet charged back towards them, accompanied by frenzied shrieking. A tumult of fleeing rioters burst back through the smokescreen, manic and screaming. Leading the evacuation, eyes bright with that electric combination of terror and adrenalin, was a face he'd grown to despise.

'They got the ferrets on us!'

It was Gordon, the sleeves of his Israeli army shirt rolled up for combat. Underneath he wore a Black Panthers T-shirt.

'The pigs are firing ferret rounds!'

He fled past. Danny turned to Weekes. He shook his head.

'It over, man. Plazzy bullets. Can't do nothing 'bout that . . .'

Danny got back to his feet and hobbled to the other side of the road. His whole upper leg ached, as though he'd taken an almighty kick in the thigh. People were running this way, that way, whooping like Apache warriors, running right over car roofs and bonnets, surging through the streets like a seething poltergeist. It was bad chaos. He clicked and clicked as people charged past, pursued by police, truncheons drawn now, ready to exact revenge. He got right up close to a spotty-faced copper, dragging the balaclava off a kid's head and simultaneously cracking at his skull with his stick until the wool of his mask was soaked with blood. For one bizarre second the cop stopped and smiled at Danny, as though surprised himself at the brutality of his attack. Then he stood up, affecting a reasonable front as he walked towards Danny, beckoning him forwards with the cup of his fingertips.

'All right. You. Smart-arse. Camera.'

Danny turned and lost himself in the herd pushing down towards the boulevard. As they fanned out into the Avenue, pouring left and right, he managed a brisk limp across to the central boulevard, putting distance between himself and the main, rampaging pack. There was madness, yet it was far from indiscriminate. Some innate principle of Us and Them seemed to be governing the selection of targets and victims. Anyone or anything representing Business, the System, Success seemed fair game – even the taxi drivers touting the dive bars were deemed a legitimate target. They had money in those cabs. They were part of it – whatever it was. Sussing the danger quickly and tipping each other off by radio, driver after driver U-turned and accelerated away from the baying hordes as more and more buildings went up in flames. The National Westminster Bank got it. The Racquets Club got it. The Rialto got it. Toxteth was burning.

Making the circuit back up Parly towards the Close, Danny stopped and turned to take one last look. The light across the city was unreal. The first purple streaks of dawn licked at the inky sky, but over to his left and beyond was an uncanny extraterrestrial glow, lighting up the sky in brilliant shades of red and violet. A wild fluorescent canopy burned above L8, throbbing and glowing like a huge beacon, telling out the mean streets below. And it was quieter now, the further he made it up Parliament Street. The distant thrum and roar was just a buzz in his head, just white noise, drilling in his ear. He patted the camera, shoved right down the sleeve of his sweatshirt. Fatigued now, utterly drained and dead on his feet, he didn't want to blow it at the last fence. Shadows up the road, coming towards him. Filth, definitely. They'd be mainly looking for black boys, but they'd settle for whatever they could get. He kept his head down low, moving minimally and keeping to the shadows, edging his way to safety.

Next morning it was as though a tornado had struck. Caustic smoke still hung above the burnt-out shells of cars. Wisps and streaks of smoke drifted across a weird sulphuric sky, the cartoon calm after an apocalyptic storm. He headed down towards Granby to see who had survived to tell the tale, but the entire drag of Selborne Street was littered with smouldering detritus. An even greater obstacle lay ahead, however, as news crews laid thick cable across the road, their equipment vans double-parked as they unloaded tripods, cameras, boom microphones. It was hard to fathom. They'd fought back and resisted a bad thing and *now* the world wanted to know?

He cut back on to Parly, past his old stomping grounds – the Caribbean, the Gladray, Jamaica House. He reached Parkway and stopped dead in his tracks. That end of the Avenue was still a smoking mess, but the Rialto was just . . . *spellbinding*. The landmark brass dome, stoked to overheating by the blast of the uprising fires, was now a radiant, ultra-scarlet cupola, blazing out high above the city. He couldn't tear his eyes away. It was beautiful. It was horrible. He felt like crying, but he just could not look away. He went to go closer, but the heat from the backdraft was still fierce. He backed off to the far side of Parly to take in a different perspective of the smouldering old dance hall. He had a sudden vision that next time he walked this way the Rialto would not be there. He wanted to fall to his knees the way the Arab and Kashmiri boys did in front of their golden domes – but the glowing Rialto was somehow above it all, beyond adulation, sneering at the sun as it awaited its final sad demise. He felt for the camera but he knew he'd used up every shot. And that, suddenly, was his mission. He had to get back, get film and shoot this wondrous monstrosity before its light went out. He'd been wrong about that one. The Rialto would never be a happening place again.

He didn't make it. Limping back up Parly, a pale blue Ford Fiesta pulled up beside him. Mickey Mo was driving. Marcia wound the passenger's window down.

'Thank fuck! Get in!'

Dumb and perplexed, he ducked down and got in the back. 'What's up, fellas? What's happening?'

Marcia glanced at Mickey, who spoke up. 'Bizzies are after you, la. Been down the centre, axing after a lad with a camera. *Loads* of description of you, kidder . . .'

Marcia craned round to him. 'But get this, la. They're saying you nearly killed some copper.'

Danny had often heard the expression, and never had it seemed at all real to him – but his eyes almost popped out of his head. 'What!'

'Serious, la. It's what they're saying. Got fucking wanted posters out for the lot of youse. Ruben, Barrie, your good self – you're all cop killers. They want you strung up, la . . .'

Danny hung his head between his knees. 'Fuck! Fuck am I gonna do?'

Once again, Mickey and Marcia exchanged glances.

'Gonna have to do one, kidder. Have to get on your toes, pronto.'

'I'm skint. Fuck can I go?'

Mickey shrugged. 'Can't go home, like. They've got you down as still living on Lodgey, but they'll soon come knocking at your ma's.' He flicked his head towards the boot. 'She's packed you a bag and some butties.'

Jesus! Fuck! What more grief could he bring upon his poor mother? They turned off Catherine Street, headed down towards the Phil, right into Rodney Street, weaving on towards the station. Danny felt as though every passer-by recognised him. He felt lost, wronged, and very, very alone. They pulled up just off Copperas Hill. Marcia turned to him – tough, resolved and unsentimental. She passed him an envelope.

'That's from the fighting fund. More than enough to get you on your feet, la.'

He went to open it, felt cheap, pocketed the money. He bit on his lip, got out of the car and walked round to the boot. Mickey came to open it up for him. He put a hand on his shoulder.

'Hey, Danny. Don't go thinking you got hurt out there. You never. You done fucking great. We don't want to talk about no heroes, but you done fucking brilliant.' He had tears in his eyes. 'And your mam knows it, too. She's proud of you, la.'

He pulled him close, hugged him.

'Leave it a week or two. Phone us at the centre when you get a chance. You take care now, kidder. Hear me?'

Danny got his bag and traipsed off towards Lime Street. He didn't even turn to wave to them. Yet with every step away from them and each new step forward, he felt a slowly rising inspiration. This was not him running away again. This was his big break. He was going to make something of this. He ached to pick up the phone, tell Nicole all his news. He knew he couldn't. Not yet, he couldn't.

The Bicycle Thief

The downbeat atmosphere of the town now the season was over suited his mood. Gone was the brash throng of holidaymakers and, even at the weekend, there was a half-hearted feel about the revelries. Even the punch-ups were low-key. Once the invading hordes had returned to their estates in Birmingham and Stockport and Burnley, small gangs of fun-seekers would come in from the outlying towns to drink the pubs dry. Stout young bucks from Llanrwst and Bangor and Morfa Conwy congregated outside the Winter Gardens to hurl abuse and threats at each other, but the mass brawls of the summer had gone with the sun.

Coachloads of pensioners were arriving at the bigger hotels, giving Danny a regular turnover of work, but their presence only added to that sense of recession. The screech and caw of seagulls was the perfect soundtrack to Llandudno's dull monochrome. The sky was flat and white and, day after day, he'd content himself by walking as long and as far as the daylight would allow. They'd had a good spell – no rain for a while, but no sun either – and now the days were drawing in. He'd have to make the most of the weather while he could, and his only decision was which route to take. Up over the Great Orme again – which only ever filled his heart and lungs with a majestic and quite stirring nostalgia as he looked out to the island and thought back to their time together here – or out along the train track to Conwy and over the back of the hills all the way out to Dwygyfylchi. Although the beginning and end of that journey were humdrum, the mountains were spectacular in autumn – swathed in sump-tuous violet and, from the rocky peaks, affording a view of the ocean that made him shudder.

He'd only been back home the one time, for Ninna's funeral – and even then he didn't stay the night. He'd thought about inviting Nicole. She'd have wanted to come, or at least to learn the sad news, but he had misgivings. Somehow, it felt wrong, even opportunistic to allow the occasion of Ninna's burial to be bent into a reason for their meeting. He asked his ma to send her a card instead. Just let her know. He gathered up his easel and his box, and caught the evening coach back.

He'd been getting along fine out there. He was taking noth-ing for granted, but he was starting to get himself together. He found a small place on the top floor of one of the big houses off Trinity Avenue and, in a small flat in this small seaside town, set about starting a new life. He couldn't put her picture away yet – that gorgeous fleeting memory of Paris, before it all went wrong. Creased, like all the mementos he'd screwed up and tried to throw away, he'd smoothed it out again, put it in a plain frame and stood it there on the table. Tucked away behind the photo, locked up in the frame, was the poem. Tatty and yellowed, smeared with her dried blood, it was barely legible now. On the reverse, her inscription. *Never leave me, baby. Never go away.*

Too painful to contemplate, but he'd kept it. He took his own piece of the verse and, with a trembling hand, joined the two together with tape, imperfectly matched but back in harmony. He slipped it under the hardboard backing of the photo frame. He would keep it there, with her. He looked at her every day, radiant in the Place Dauphine, but other than that he was stoic. He bought things for the flat: a portable TV, a cassette player, some cheap throws and cushions. He ate at regular intervals. And he took himself off on long walks, often taking the camera with him. He got great pictures of the ancient graveyard up at the top of the Orme and his first thought was how delighted – how *over*-impressed – Nicole would be if she could see them. But he couldn't really afford to get film developed unless he'd had a good run with the sketches and, more and more, started leaving the camera behind.

After about a month in the flat – and this coincided with the shortening days and the gradual wind-down of the holiday season – he began to wake up with a vision in his head. And, working patiently, he started sketching it out. He abandoned it three or four times, but he couldn't get the image out of his head. It was agitating him, but it thrilled him, too. For the last few weeks he'd been getting straight out of bed and right into it. He popped a cassette in, put the kettle on and, wearing a thick Aran jumper and boxer shorts, he got to work at his easel. He'd stop only to make tea, wolf down toast and Marmite, slot another cassette in. The Associates, Josef K, the new Bunnymen album were all favourites but the tracks he worked to were the Go-Betweens' 'Cattle and Cane' and 'Grey Day' by Madness. Those were the songs that chimed with his life out there. He felt alone, abandoned, stranded – but he was aloof, too. It was a splendid isolation. He was painting again.

So intense was the emotional input that he could only work in short bursts. From the best of the riot photos, and from his own vivid recollections, he was working on a land-scape of sorts – though it was more Hieronymous Bosch than Constable. He was painting a picture of the Rialto in flames, and it was starting to make him feel faint when he looked at it – not because of the memories it stirred, but because it was so fucking good. It was a masterpiece in the making. He'd never worked in those colours before, reds and purples, and even his walks out on the windy heather-clad mountainsides gave him clarity and impetus. Stroke by stroke, he was creat-ing a work of substance and importance. There were days when his innate ebullience flooded back through his soul, and he thought it a work of genius.

While he kept solemnly and resolutely to himself, he'd forged a living and a life of sorts. With his Liverpool accent and his long hair, he found it easy to meet girls. Sexual encoun-ters came with a health risk, however – at the hands and steel-capped boots of envious local boys. He'd fallen into a routine of working the hotels during the afternoon and early evening, only ever frequenting the handful of pubs and bars he knew were safe. Most nights he'd finish up at the Dolphin. The gay owners were smitten with him, loved the idea of having a resident artist on their premises – and a young one, a pretty one, at that. Toby, the older of the two, was happy to push business and cocktails his way, while Danny was happy with the company. Very occasionally he picked up a woman in there. They were older, married, fuller of figure – but he could take them home to his little place without fear of reprisals.

Instinctively, he felt it was vital he kept up a social life, kept meeting women. Often he felt like an onlooker at his own play, watching himself going through the motions of a too-familiar role. But if he didn't put himself out there, without conversation and company and distraction, he couldn't fully trust himself. Not yet. If the masterpiece was his kick-start and the quick-sketch his middle, a boy like Danny would always need a final act to his day. Even out there – *particularly* out there – he was conscious of the lascivious gap-toothed smile of heroin. Its evidence was all around him. The wasted kids from the estate collecting for Guy Fawkes in September; the lad who came into the pubs, cowed, unable to look anyone in the eye as he flogged his batteries and terry-cotton socks and Mills & Boon books; the older junkies on the benches by the pier, squabbling for first dibs on the next clammy wrap. And there was the pale, thin girl from the ground-floor flat who was always hanging in the doorway when he came downstairs. He didn't even know her name. She just stared at him, half swaying, half smiling. He couldn't say whether she was after his giro, or if she wanted to suck him off for money or she was just plain lonely. What he knew for sure was that she was fresh into gear. She wasn't full-gone yet, but all the signs were there, and that brought it back to Danny how easy, how exhilarating it'd be just to get back on, fuck it all up, fuck himself up, big, for ever. He kept his head down and shuffled out with his pad and his charcoals, taking the next step, then the next.

He never, ever answered the door. He didn't know anyone – no one who'd be calling round in the daytime, anyway – and there was no need, no reason for anyone to knock. The meters were all down in the hall, his rent was all up to date. He'd only just settled into his morning stint at the canvas, and it wasn't coming together at all. He was regretting his work of the past couple of days, seriously considering going back and changing the entire colour tone of the sky. Without the right sky, the picture would be nothing. He'd vacillated, unable to get into his stride at all, allowing any convenient distraction to preoccupy him. He made toast. He promised himself he'd throw himself into painting, non-stop, just as soon as he'd had one more cup of tea. He'd just watch the news while he drank it. Maybe watch five minutes of the Tory Party Conference – see if the inspiration of ire could fire him up. He switched on the portable and, as a concession to the work ethic, positioned himself at the easel again, tea in one hand, brush in the other. And no sooner did he start to work than the knocking started. He ignored it, but the knocker was not going away.

'Dave!'

Girl's voice. More knocking. Tap-tap. Tap-tap-tap.

'Dan!'

Boom! Boom!

He crept to the TV to turn down the sound, but she started kicking at the door.

Bang! Bang! She was throwing herself against the door. He put down his brush and ran to the door, flinging it open. Momentarily, she looked shocked to see him. He glared at her.

'Yeah?'

It was the girl from downstairs – wearing only a white T-shirt and brief pink knickers. She flashed him an apologetic grin.

'Sorry. I don't even know your name . . .'

'*Yorr nirm.*' Blackburn. A rush of sorrow ripped through him, feelings he'd hoped he was finally learning to conquer. Everything reminded him of Nicole, but the greater his progress with the picture, the more he felt able to persuade himself that it was wonderful to have loved like that at all.

'Danny,' he said.

She shrank her head into her shoulders. 'I knew it started with a "D". I'm Tracey.'

'A'right, Tracey.'

He looked her up and down. She put her hand to her mouth.

'Look at me! I heard the post come and I were just checking for me giro and I've gone and locked myself out. I tried the other flats. I heard your radio –'

'Telly.'

He beckoned her inside and closed the door. As he did so, he heard a footfall on the stairs below. He found himself addressing her in that same slightly stern and suspicious tone he'd experienced himself too many times in the recent past – from cashiers at the post office to the bus conductors who'd nudged him awake to see his ticket. She went straight to the canvas.

'Wow! You do this?'

Her enthusiasm seemed hollow, and only made him dislike the painting. When people viewed a work before it was ready to be seen, it didn't seem good any more.

'What can I do to help then?'

Her eyes were everywhere. She picked up the photo. 'Who's this? Girlfriend?'

He forced a smile. 'No.'

'She's pretty.' She looked up at him. 'I'd screw her.'

He took the photo from her, placed it in the kitchen drawer and turned back to her.

'So. Tracey?'

She gave the universal apologetic wince, screwing her face up as though expecting, and deserving, a rejection.

'Wouldn't mind borrowing a pair of jeans, if that's OK. Just so's I can run down and get the spare key from Mr L . . .'

He tried to iron the surliness out of his voice, but still sounded irked.

'Sure, we can fix you up.'

He went through to the bedroom, leaving the door open. He was relieved to see her sit down.

'What you watching?'

'Ah, nothing really. I was half watching the news.'

He came to the door and nodded to the TV. Norman Tebbit was on screen. She stifled a giggle.

'Look at that knobhead! Looks like a pervert.'

'He is.'

He threw her a pair of old cords, ones he used for painting in. He knew he wouldn't be seeing them again. The girl looked so young. She'd been a pretty thing not so long ago herself. With her long hair and slim waist she was still attractive, yet there was a flinty eagerness about her — something beady about her eyes, and a birdlike jerk to her head as she took in her surroundings. She caught the cords and she caught his eye. Very deliberately, she put them down on the sofa next to her and stretched her bare legs out in front of her. Eyes not leaving his now, she parted them, casually and only slightly. His balls tingled. She nodded at his tea mug.

'Wouldn't mind a cup of tea either, if there's one going . . .'

The two of them stared into each other's faces, neither looking away. Danny's stomach was vaulting. A desire he hadn't felt for a long time surged through his groin. He wanted to turn away, but she was right in front of him, bare legs spread. He almost flung himself on her. Kissing her fiercely, he thrust his hand inside her knickers, squeezing her cunt till he felt the juices. She pushed back against him, kissing him in quick, gulping motions. He closed his eyes, tried to slow her down. Her head ducked in and out, her mouth neatly opening and closing, giving Danny the queer sensation he was necking with a fox. He blinked his eyes open and stood up to undo his jeans. Her eyes lapped up his cock, standing hard in front of her face. She licked a finger and ran it along its length. Danny got down beside her, tugging her knickers down.

'You can't screw me . . .'

He ignored her, got her panties down below her knees and started working her fanny again, urgent, desperate to slide his cock in. She turned away on her side.

'No . . .'

He reached over, tried to roll her back towards him. She sat up.

'I've got a fella.'

Rather than embarrassed, she sounded ashamed.

'I'll wank you off.'

She pulled her T-shirt up above her head, pulling her breasts up with it so they sprang back as she wriggled it off. She gave his dick another sly look.

'Come on. Sit here and lick me. We can be nice to each other.'

He laughed and shook his head. 'What's the difference, like?'

She sighed. 'I want to. I think you're gorgeous. But that's for him . . .'

'Weird.'

'He's down there. I can't –'

'I thought you was locked out.'

'Yeah. But I mean – he'll be back soon.'

He nodded to the cords. 'Won't be needing them then, will you?'

'Please?'

Tebbit was reaching the crescendo of his tub-thumping speech. 'I grew up in the thirties with an unemployed father. He didn't riot.' Pause for applause. It arrived, along with cheers of approval. Tebbit drew himself up for the climax. 'He got on his bike and looked for work.'

Thunderous shouts of 'Yes!' and 'Hear! hear!', a mass stamping of feet. Tebbit had to hold up his hand to calm the exultant Tory gathering.

'And he went on looking until he found it!'

The conference was almost in riot itself. This is what they'd come for – tough love from the Chingford Skin. Danny shook his head, switched off the telly and threw her the cords.

'Go 'ead. On your bike.'

The Wasteland

He'd been painting well and could have continued for longer, but the tumultuous sky tempted him outside. It was already dark at four in the afternoon, but great shards of silver shredded the blackness, bathing the cliffs above town in a sinister half-light. Drawn to it like a zombie, he strode up past the pier, past the Grand Hotel and up through the Happy Valley. Only weeks before he'd sketched cartoons of plucky pensioners on the crazy golf course. Now the shutters were down, laughter and scuff-skinned golf balls locked away for a better day. He passed by on the rocky footpath and settled up on the damp and springy moss of the Orme's lower peak. Suffused by a fathomless euphoria, he settled back against a rock and stared out to sea, lighting up a fag with ritual gravitas. He dipped his head right back and looked up at the sky, where drifting slivers of cloud were dragging a smoky veil in front of the swollen moon. This optimism, this general yet giddy sense of hope and possibility, was something he'd left behind him, long ago.

It was only the gradual grip of the cold night sky that brought him round. He'd been sitting there for hours – smoking, thinking, dreaming. He couldn't stop thinking about the Rialto picture. Even if nobody thought it was as good as he did, *he* knew it, absolutely knew it was a marvel. To Danny, just completing it would be a thing of wonder. And he was going to finish it. He lay back and finished his cigarette, staring up at the sky above. Way, way up in the blue-black heavens, the sudden glint of something caught his eye. He narrowed his eyes, unwilling to succumb to hope but it was there. It was the Star of Toxteth. Amazed, enchanted, he bolted upright. The Star of Tocky – he could see it from there! Wherever she was, Nicole could see it too. He squinted and looked again, and he couldn't see it any more. He wasn't sad. He drew his knees to his chest and hooked his arms around them for warmth. He started giggling softly. He sat there and looked out to sea and laughed out loud. He had the Thrills.

Yet, as he cut across Gloddaeth Drive and cut down past the chippy, something started gnawing away at his guts. It grew, the closer he got to the flat. Unlocking the front door, the pallid glow of the ground-floor flat made him falter. Silhouettes flickered behind the meagre screen of the scabby blanket they'd nailed across the window bay, and a sickening premonition dragged him back. He hesitated in the hallway. He could hear the smackheads in their flat, smoke and Genesis seeping out from under their door. He hesitated, put his ear to the door and heard lazy, nihilistic laughter. His heart was in his bowels as he bounded up the stairs, almost tripping over himself, knowing what would greet him before he got there.

His flimsy hardboard door hung off one hinge. He pushed it aside, stepped into the devastated flat. It was wrecked – totally ransacked. Every drawer had been emptied out, every shelf swept on to the floor. Subconsciously it registered with him that the telly, the cassette player, even the kettle was gone. But he wasn't worried about any of that. His easel was splayed out on the floor. Tearful, and with dread gnawing at his soul, he picked it up, placed it to one side. The canvas lay face down on the gnarled cord carpet. The best he could hope for was that the fresh paint might have picked up a bit of dirt, a strand or two, and that he'd be able to paint it out. He lifted the picture, turned it face up.

'Oh, no. Please. No . . .'

They'd stuck a fist, or an implement, through the middle of the canvas. Before doing so, they'd taken his paints and daubed a word across the picture. *Shite.* Shocked, empty inside and too stunned, too bereft even to think, he staggered to the sofa and sat down. Eyes wide open but taking nothing in, he gazed around his flat, his little world in ruins. Something snapped him out of his morbid trance. A yard away, under the table, lay a smashed frame. It was the Paris photo, his memory of Nic ripped to shreds by shattered glass. He jumped to his feet.

Taking the stairs three at a time, he crashed into the hall, stepped back and volleyed their door off its hinges with the flat of his foot. Two lads sat on the couch. Tracey was spread out on the floor. He could see it clearly now. She was calm, self-serving and truly, thoroughly evil. One of the lads jumped up.

'Hey! Who the fuck –'

Danny didn't say a word. He butted the lad in the face, ripped the lead out of the wall socket and dropped the television on his head. He kicked him hard in the side. The lad screamed.

'It weren't *me*!'

Eyes never leaving Tracey's face, Danny backed away, took a run-up and booted him full in the face. Spark out, he didn't make a sound. A bloody trail seeped from the corner of his mouth. Danny walked a few paces to the cutlery drawer and located the biggest, sharpest knife he could find. Testing it, he sliced at the tip of his finger, drawing blood.

'Good.'

He turned to face the cowering Tracey and her boyfriend. She beckoned behind, towards a cheap round table.

'Please, Dan. Your stuff's there. We've not sold much yet. What money we've got is yours . . .'

Most likely anything she'd chosen to say would have detonated his fury, but her wheedling, cunning tone sent him over

the edge. Methodically, he marched towards her, fully intend-
ing to stab her, or slash her face, or butt her, too – anything
to mark her, mess her up, do to her what they'd done to him.
But he pulled up short, grabbed her by the hair and dragged
her down to her knees. Inadvertently, her cowering boyfriend
saved them both from a hiding.

'Suck him off, you soft bitch!'

She threw him a wild and dislocated stare.

'Do it!' he screamed. Danny let go of her hair. He stood
back, head hung low. Neither Tracey nor her beau dared look
up, let alone speak. With a cracked, haunted voice and in
deathly monotone Danny, looking at the floor, broke the
silence.

'Get out.'

They looked at each other. Tracey shrugged, as if to tell
him she couldn't be sure how bad, how final this would
be. Danny went to their cheap teak table and took ten
pounds from a sordid pile of notes. He threw it on the
floor.

'Get right out of town, you pair of no-marks. Be on the
very next fucking coach to Blackburn or Wigan or wherever
the fuck you're from. Don't even look behind you. Keep fucking walking and never, ever come back . . .'

Tracey spoke up, still at work, still unable to cease her
con.

'Can we pack a few things, like?'

'Can you fuck.'

Her boyfriend kicked a foot towards the prone third party.
'What about him?'

Danny looked at him with deadly eyes.

'Get the fuck out before I slam you, you shitbag.'

Tracey tugged him away. Danny walked after them. They
broke into a jerky, sporadic jog. He kept on walking at constant,
menacing pace, eyes never leaving them, catching up closer
as they quickly got out of breath. The lad collapsed on a

bench. Tracey stood behind him, protective but truly afraid now as Danny walked up to them.

'Please, mate – don't hit us. We *are* going . . .'

'You better fucking be . . .'

'Danny . . .'

She circled the bench and came towards him, pleading. What he saw was Tracey, powerless to desist, back on the job again. She thought she could talk him round. She approached him slowly, the makings of a smile tugging at the creases of her narrow mouth. Maddened, his eyes clouded over. He didn't see the thin white smackhead he'd let into his flat, his world. What he saw was a fox's head on her slender shoulders. The sight of her, her proximity, enraged him. She was smiling now, she was confident. She stopped short and held out a hand.

'Danny . . .'

He looked at her hand – then he drove his forehead into her face, smacking her backwards. She collapsed on to her boyfriend's lap, blood running from her cheekbone as he tried to push her off him.

'Give us your gear.'

'We haven't –'

'Give us your fucking bag, now!'

The lad stood up, scowled at Tracey for bringing this latest calamity upon them, dug into his pocket, wiggling two fingers deeper and further down into the tight stretch denim. Downcast, he threw the wrap to Danny.

'That's everything we've got.'

'What's your name, lad?'

He gulped. 'Peter.'

Peetoh. Danny opened up the wrap and flicked the bottom, sprinkling heroin on to the pavement. He continued flicking at the packet, eyes locked on to Peter, long after the last of it had bit the dust. He ground it, every bit of it, into the dirt, screwed up the wrap and tossed it away.

'Peter. Take her and get out of town. Next time I see you, I'll kill you. You get me?'

He didn't wait for a reply, just turned and walked away, head down, going nowhere. He carried on walking, on and on, into the wind and the rain. Finally, utterly fatigued and unable to walk another step, he curled up in a West Shore doorway and passed out.

He awoke with a stiff neck, a headache and intense pain in his throat, his ears and behind his eyeballs. It hurt when he opened his eyes, it hurt when he closed them. He dragged himself up and limped back to the flat, heavy-legged. He was cut adrift, now. He was lost. He had lost. He could plan no further than to get himself back, get up the stairs, step by step, and get to bed.

'Mr Wray? Mr Wray?'

A hazy, hallucinatory image in the doorway. He tried to lift his head, but it fell back like a stone. He was dreaming still. He'd been dreaming for days – grotesque visions stealing up to his bedside, whispering in his ear. He was immune to it all. They could do what they wanted. They could cut him into tiny pieces and feed him to the dogfish. They could take him by the hand and transport him to the gates of hell. He didn't care. None of it could hurt him. Nothing, nothing mattered.

'Mr Wray.'

The voice came from right next to him. With real effort, and with a stab of pain, he screwed his eyes open and tried to focus. Mrs Llewellyn stood over him with a steaming mug.

'Drink this.'

He made an intelligible noise, to show he'd heard. She pushed his neck and shoulders forward, stuffing another pillow behind his head. She placed the mug in his hands.

'Go on. Chicken soup. Better than any of your Panadols or what have you . . .'

Blinking, but with his senses slowly returning, he took a sip of the soup. It seemed to burn right through him. He was propped up on the little couch in his flat. Mrs Llewellyn busied herself, picking up cushions he must have thrown off. She shuffled over to the door and made a show of opening and shutting it as though still assessing the worthiness of the job.

'Mr L's fixed the door for you. And he's put an extra-something lock on – don't ask me! Says you won't be having no trouble from the burglars again, though.'

Danny forced a smile. He could see better now. The flat had been cleaned from top to bottom. They'd put back his TV. The cassette player was there on the table. The only blight was a sorry stack in the far corner – his broken easel, his ruined canvas, bits and pieces they'd salvaged and been too considerate to throw out. His spirits plummeted with the sudden and full recall of his recent horrors.

'How long, like . . .'

She bustled over, tucked him in.

'Don't you be worrying about nothing like that, *bach*. Just get yourself well . . .'

She tilted the cup to his lips, licking her own with each successful gulp Danny managed.

'There now! I'll come and check up on you again. You just rest, Mr Wray . . .'

The door shut behind her. He heard her making slow progress back down the stairs. He craned his head over towards the window. Out there lay – what? What was there for him? What next for Danny May? *Mr Wray!* It seemed queerly apt for his pitiful lot in life that he should even be denied an identity – or could only survive with a bogus one. He felt wretched at the deceit. These were good people – he'd known that immediately, long before her nursing of him, and this evidence of the care she'd taken only confirmed what Danny already knew. The Llewellyns were the very best of folk, and he had come to them with all bad intent. No, he should resist that. He should not let himself think that way. The new identity was expedient. Other than that, he'd done no wrong . . . But try as he would, Danny could only find himself wanting.

He let out a sigh so powerful he almost bellowed it, and flung his legs out from beneath the blanket. He got up, walked to the kitchen and put the kettle on. He was, once again, starting over. How many more times? It was hopeless. It was wrong. He padded over to the table and sat looking sightlessly out of the window. He stared at a blank sky, without sensation – nothing. He got up, flicked listlessly through his cassettes. He hesitated over his most recent purchase – *Heaven Up Here* by the Bunnymen. How long ago that seemed. Only weeks ago seemingly, but an eternity now. He flipped the case open, slotted the cassette in and returned to gazing out of the window. One bold gull soared across the empty sky.

He turned his attention to the pile in the corner. He'd have to tackle it, one day. He got up and prodded gingerly at the paintbox. He was there, picking at his broken belongings, but only just. The corner of the frame was sticking out, barely visible – and the sight of it crushed him. He pulled it out, turning it over and over in his hands, paralysed with grief. Cracked, splintered glass distorted her smiling face, making her eyes seem hard and her smile false, bestowing an eerie deceit upon her. He gazed at the photograph and yearned for her. Somehow, he had to try. How? He couldn't even remember her address. A new song, a slow, heartbroken song started up.

> *My life's the disease*
> *That can always change*
> *With comparative ease*
> *Just given a chance . . .*

He didn't hesitate. If he didn't do this now, he might not ever. He turned the shattered frame over and, dismantling it gently, eased the taped-up verse out, careful not to tear it. Then, scrabbling around for paper, he snatched up the pad he'd got from Woolworths. One sheet remained, a hideous orange. He sat there, pen in hand. What to tell her? There was so much to say. Too much. And, knowing he would never be able to communicate even a sense of what he wanted to, he settled on a sad but savage truth. He had to let her know just how madly wrong his life had gone without her. He had to get her to come. If she didn't come for him, he would die.

Either Or

By the end of the second day she was starting to give up hope. Traipsing back up the stairs of the Ormecliffe, she felt weary and foolish – foolish for thinking that, like some Victorian romance, he'd have been there, waiting for her; in that same bed, or wind-blown on the cliffs where they'd planned their life together. But there'd been no sign of him. The town was deserted – cold, grey and watchful. Few people were out and about, fewer still strode out to the clifftops, but no matter where or when she searched, there was no trace of Danny. Worse, there was no sense of him either. It didn't *feel* like he was out there, just around the next bend. Yet she couldn't bring herself to do the obvious. If she were to enquire at the hospital they could tell her he had died. Ask the police, they could tell her he'd been arrested or jailed. For as long as she kept her lonely mission alive, so she kept her hopes alive, too. She refreshed herself under the dribbling drip of the shower, made herself a cup of tea and slumped down on the bowed bed.

She slept well, rose early and determined to stick with the same formula. If she could stay mobile, just keep walking,

walking, walking – she was sure to stumble across him, sooner or later. It was a brighter day, today, and the glimmer of November sunshine offered her the first real hope that he was out there somewhere. She finished the tough toast, gulped down the last dregs of tea and set out to find her man.

Head down, she battled up the steep lane that winds from the Marine Drive up to St Tudno's Church. A heavy gust pushed against her, bringing tears to her eyes, but, rounding the final and most abrupt of the twists and bends, the wind seemed to drop and reflexively she stood up straight, no longer battling to stay upright. Hands on her hips, she took deep breaths, invigorated and slightly exhausted by the uphill trek. She exhaled hard, looking out across the sea, way out to Danny's island. Could he be there? With him, nothing was impossible. She could well imagine him living the life of a hermit, so long as he had something to draw with – and Prince's salmon paste. She smiled to herself and turned towards the church.

It was small and squat with a low roof, seemingly made of local flint and slate. The graveyard tumbled down one entire slope of the hillside, solemn graves patrolled only by grazing mountain sheep. She stood back and took it all in, suddenly affected by the stillness and serenity of this ancient site. She had no doubts that Danny would have discovered this place. And if she could just pitch a tent, say – stay there a week or a month – she had no doubt that he'd walk back into her life. She eased open the creaky iron gate. Disengaged now, she meandered through the graveyard, dragging her feet through the wet grass. Below her was a stile leading to gently sloping fields. From there she could cut back on to the Marine Drive. But as she trailed towards the furthest dip of the grave-yard, she saw that it hollowed out beneath her, levelling out on to a short plateau. On the grassy ledge was a flat stone bench. Sitting on the bench, his back to her and his eyes out to sea, was Danny.

Trying to suppress the swell of emotions, she stole upon him as softly as she was able. She stopped a yard behind him.

'You know that other graveyard?'

He went to jerk his head round, stopped it, composed himself. He couldn't keep the joy out of his one sharp syllable.

'Yeah?'

'I never told you what that inscription meant, did I?'

He turned to her, radiant.

'You never, no.'

She smiled and went nearer, stopping right in front of him. He swivelled round on the bench, looking up into her face. She took his hands and smiled down at him.

'It means: *he caused his own demons.*'

Danny laughed and turned away for a second, shaking his head. He went to stand up, but she got there before him. They held each other, tight.

The Lake

'Danny, darling – these photographs are just *fantastic!*'

The riot pictures and the photo sequence of Peter Luala's beating were spread on the floor of the flat she was renting in Gambier Terrace. How many times must he have walked past her during those lost days? She looked up at him.

'They're just . . . I mean, what do you want to *do* with them?'

He shrugged. 'Dunno, like. I mean, I think they're *well* powerful, like. But how d'you go about getting pictures printed?'

She clapped her hands together. 'I know! I'll ask Hattie. She's going out with a guy who works on that new mag, what-d'you-call-it?' She screwed her eyes up. '*The Face!*'

'*The Face*? That's all bands and fashion, isn't it?'

'Well, I'm not necessarily saying they'll run the pictures themselves – but chances are he'll know what to do with them. I've only met him the once but he seems like a pretty switched-on sort of bloke . . .'

Danny shrugged again. 'OK.'

Remembering all over again that he was sitting there, with her, his face broke into a childlike grin. When he'd first met her he could hardly crack a smile, now he could hardly stop.

'I'm game for anything, darling. Got to start making a few moves and that, hey?'

She nodded cautiously, careful not to push too hard, too soon. But the moment seemed right.

'And the painting, Dan? What do you think?'

He hung his head. Quickly, she tried to backtrack.

'Baby, I'm sorry! I know how fucking . . . *devastating* that must have been for you.' She took his hand. 'All I meant is – yes, these photos are fucking astounding. Really, they are. But you're a painter. You're an artist. I've seen what you can do, little man – and you're a bloody *genius*!'

He flicked her a sad smile.

'Well, ta for that.'

He made an effort to inject some verve into his voice. Talk of his painting made that hard.

'I'll let you know when the urge comes back.'

They both looked away, ready to change the subject. It was easy circling around anything awkward those first few days – they'd both done so much in their time apart. Nicole, finding few takers for her first-class honours degree in PPE, had started training as a youth worker. She was loving it, though there'd been resistance to her first choice of area – Liverpool 8. She felt she knew the neighbourhood, understood the issues and would be able to bring something extra to the tight-knit team. It was a fight she wasn't going to win, and she found she loved working with the Garston kids, anyway. Through school and university she'd fought shy of ambition.

She'd tell her folks what she wanted to do as soon as she found out – but youth work found her first. She just loved it, and she flung herself into it wholeheartedly. The kids responded. They could weed out a phoney straight away, but they knew the real thing, too. Nicole was pulling up trees for them and, in return, they gave her a chance. Some of them were beyond reach, but the younger ones she could work with. The hours were crazy and she came home bushed, but for Nicole life was good. She was taking part. But as long as Danny was nursing these war wounds, she couldn't look too far ahead. She could only ever hazard at what that must have been like for him, seeing a life's work destroyed and cast aside like trash. She doubted he'd get over that – not easily, and not quickly, at least. But if she could somehow generate some interest in his photographic work it might just build a bridge.

She hated going out to work in the morning and leaving him there, all alone with his thoughts. In that sense, Danny's return was a cause of sadness as she found her mind, time and again, wandering back to the plight of her forlorn, gifted lover. But she had faith in him. If anyone had a higher opinion of Danny's talent than he had himself, she'd have liked to meet them. One thing he had never lacked was self-confidence, almost to a point where it bordered on arrogance. Yet he was never arrogant, Danny. His conviction in his own brilliance was entirely artless. If she could only guide him back towards that natural assuredness, that sense of his own destiny. *That* was going to be difficult. There'd been a variety of remedies she'd seen proposed to combat the ailments of the youths she worked with. For the dopeheads, morphine; for the unwanted pregnancies that sprang from endless afternoons on the dole, abortion; for their venereal diseases, penicillin. But what to prescribe for a death of hope? This was the big change she saw in Danny. He'd never stopped believing he was brilliant – but he'd given up hope anything could come of it. For people like him, it would never be easy.

Their first row came hand in hand with the good news. Less than a week after carefully, meticulously compiling a portfolio of his best shots and sending it off to Harriet, word came back from London. In spite of fierce advocacy in Danny's favour from the art director, *The Face* felt unable to use the photographs. However, he'd shown them to a friend at London Records who was knocked out by them. He wanted to work with Danny May. Nicole hugged Danny tight.

'He wants you to shoot this new band they've signed from Glasgow. Oh, baby! I'm so *proud* of you!'

He tried to sparkle back at her, but he felt wretched — wretched for being such a martyr, wretched for being so ungrateful, wretched that his surly reaction to this ray of light was going to drag her down low, too.

'Nice one,' he managed. He might as well have flung himself to the floor, weeping. Frightened, and concerned for him all over again, she held his face in her hands.

'Aren't you pleased?' She tried to transmit her pleasure to him, through her eyes, through her voice. 'Aren't you *excited*? You could be . . .'

She dropped her hands and crossed to the window, looking out on to the cathedral, spieling out loud.

'I don't know! You could be working for *NME* or *Blitz* before long. You could be taking fashion shots of Hattie . . .'

Danny just looked at her. Could she not see the pain in his eyes?

'Yeah.' He took a deep breath and let it out slowly, as though relinquishing all hope with it. 'Yeah, that'd be good, hey?'

She turned to face him and she couldn't help herself.

'For fuck's sake, Danny! It's not a fucking playground out there! Some of us have to just . . . *work*, you know!'

He wasn't angry with her. She was right. Most people did have to do things they'd rather not.

'I know.'

She tried to soften her voice.

'It's, like . . . how long are you prepared to wait? How long will you hold out for, I don't know . . . *truth*?' She hung her head, sure she was killing him. 'And what happens in the meantime?'

Something came over him. He forced another grin and lifted her chin with his finger.

'Hey! It's sound. I'll be a photographer then . . .'

She checked her watch, saw she'd be late for work, pecked him on the cheek and let herself out. Danny followed her to the door. He was still trying to smile.

'It'll be sound, you know. It all makes sense.'

He pulled her back for a kiss, tried to hold her.

'Sometimes you need a little push, don't you? Need a little shock or something to help you see . . .'

He hugged her close, but she looked at his face – beaming, traumatised – and she knew he wouldn't be there when she got back that evening. She trudged down the stairs. By the time she got outside she was full of remorse. How could she have been so, so . . . *selfish*? That's what had happened, back there. She *knew* he wasn't ready, yet she pushed, pushed, pushed. She convinced herself she was saving his soul, but this latest thing had nothing to do with Danny. It was her. It was her all over. Not only was she intent on nursing Danny back to life, she wanted something to show for her efforts. She wanted people to see she'd been right to put her trust in Danny May. And now she'd driven him away again. She felt conflicting emotions as she waited at the bus stop – anger at Danny for his refusal to get better, contempt at herself for thinking it.

By lunch she'd devoured herself with worry. Jumping on the first bus back to town, she promised herself that, if he was still there, she would never, ever try to change him. He could sit around forever dreaming his dreams and she would never get cross with him. She just wanted him back. She wanted to tell him it was him and her, for ever.

The flat was empty. How could she have allowed herself to hope otherwise? She'd shown herself in her true light and he'd taken flight. Who could blame him? She was a pushy, ambitious bully. She hated herself, and she deserved every shred of her punishment. She closed her eyes and tried to remember what he'd said to her, just as she was leaving. He was smiling, but she'd felt the sinister edge to it. Something about needing to be shocked into action. Well, she'd done that, all right. She picked up the phone and was about to call in sick when she saw it, pinned to the back of the door. A page, torn from one of the books she'd given him, one of the many she assumed he'd never read. Carefully, but with heart pumping now, she removed the page from the door. She knew the line straight away.

'*Dreams are like shooting stars. They shine their hardest at the moment they burn out.*'

And she knew where he would be. She put her hand across her mouth, like a damsel in a silent movie. It was shock, yes – but she was choking back a surge of joyous relief. She felt the giggles rising up from her bowels. She reached for her bubble jacket and almost fell down the stairs in her rush.

He was sitting by the lake, staring up at the sky. He heard her coming.

'Bit early, yet –'

'Sorry, I – I came home from work early –'

'No, no! I mean the star. Perfect weather for it, like. It'll come. But it needs to get darker, yet.'

She knelt beside him, took his spare hand. She watched him work, eyes agleam, patiently laying down his backdrop, a daunting, cavernous sky. She snatched a look at his face, intent, engrossed. He was back. Her poet ruffian was back, painting again. She rested her head gently on his arm, then stood up. He tore his eyes away from the canvas.

'Where you going?'

She crouched down, kissed him on each eyelid.

'I'm going for a walk.'

'Stay?'

She stood up, wanting to, not wanting to. Danny pulled her towards him.

'Please? Just stay for a bit?'

She took out her cigarettes, lit one. He smiled up at her, love in his eyes.

'Stay, Nic. I can't do this without you.'

She ruffled his hair and passed him the cigarette. She laid down her jacket and sat down beside him, and waited for the stars to come out.